THE BOY WHO KILLED DEMONS

A NOVEL

Dave Zeltserman

Duckworth Overlook

First published in the UK in 2015 by
Duckworth Overlook

LONDON
30 Calvin Street, London E1 6NW
T: 020 7490 7300
E: info@duckworth-publishers.co.uk
www.ducknet.co.uk
For bulk and special sales, please contact
sales@duckworth-publishers.co.uk
or write to us at the address above

NEW YORK
141 Wooster Street, New York, NY 10012
www.overlookpress.com

A catalogue record for this book is available
from the British Library

Book design and type formatting by Bernard Schleifer

ISBN: 978-0-7156-4989-3

Printed and bound in the UK

THE BOY
WHO KILLED
DEMONS

To Benjamin Del Cid

THE BOY
WHO KILLED
DEMONS

MY NAME'S HENRY DUDLOW. I'M FIFTEEN AND A HALF, AND I'M cursed. Or damned. Take your pick.

The reason? I see demons.

Now don't get me wrong—it's not like I see demons lurking in the shadows or hiding under my bed or in my closet or anything like that. But I still see them. There are people out there who—well, you might see them and think they're normal, just everyday people; but when *I* see them I see them for what they really are: demons. And I don't mean this in the figurative sense (I sometimes get *literal* and *figurative* mixed up, so I made sure to look up the definitions), so it's not like I see certain people as innately evil and think of them as demons. The ones I see as demons are evil alright, but they're also honest-to-God demons (or I guess honest-to-Satan): flaming red skin, yellow eyes, horns, grotesque faces with twisted misshapen noses, pit bull-like jaws filled with glistening jagged teeth, thick talon-like claws where there ought to be hands, the whole nine yards. They might be

9

wearing suits, or a pair of Bermuda shorts and a T-shirt, or if they're masquerading as a girl or a woman, a dress or possibly a skirt and blouse. I've even seen one once in a two-piece bikini. But underneath all that they're demons. It's just that most people can't see them as they really are. Maybe nobody can, other than me. I hope that's not true, though—I really hope there are others out there who also see them the way I do.

You're probably thinking I'm mentally ill, that all this is nothing but the ravings of a crazy mind. I thought so, too—at first. I was two months past my thirteenth birthday when I saw my first demon—Mr. Hanley from three doors down the street—and I was convinced that something had to be seriously wrong with me. Mr. Hanley has lived on our street my whole life, and before that day I saw him the same way everyone else did: a middle-aged man with fat legs and arms, heavy jowls, a huge bald spot, and a beer belly that would always be peeking out from the bottom of an undershirt on hot summer days. He was just this guy in the neighborhood who would always nod and smile pleasantly and go about his business. I had no reason to think about him as anything unnatural—I had no reason to think about him at all. But a little less than two and a half years ago I saw him for the first time as . . . well, as an inhuman creature. Ever since, that's the only way I've ever seen him. And others too. Twenty-three others, to be precise.

In case you're thinking drugs or alcohol played a part— I can tell you that they didn't. I've never touched any of that stuff, other than a few sips of my mom's wine at dinner when she'd let me. And I'm not crazy, either. I know I'm not, even though I tried hard to convince myself that I was after my first demon sighting. Would a crazy person even think they're crazy? I don't know, but I did think something was seriously wrong with me that day and for months afterward.

If I'd suffered some sort of head injury or had experienced a recent traumatic episode, it would've made things so much easier. That could've explained why I was seeing demons, and at least I would've been satisfied that I was off in the head and that I wasn't cursed. But nothing like that had ever happened. That day was like any other day. I was riding my bike to school and was approaching Mr. Hanley's house when he walked out his side door to pick up his newspaper, wearing his usual morning outfit—a bathrobe and slippers. He started to nod to me in his pleasant way, but froze when he saw my reaction. I don't know if he knew for sure what I'd seen, but he was suspicious about it. For just a fraction of a second, his expression was transformed into something both malicious and ferocious—whatever it was, it wasn't anything human. He must've caught himself, though, because just as quickly he was back to his mask of smiling amiability. What I did next was pedal as fast as I could to get away from him.

That flash of rage and monstrousness that came over his demon face should've been enough to convince me that what I saw was real, but instead I continued on to school thinking I must've gone crazy. In class I tortured myself with thoughts like that. No one else at school looked like demons—not that day and not since—so I tried to convince myself that I only imagined what I saw, but the word *schizophrenia* kept pushing its way into my head. I was only thirteen and I didn't know what schizophrenia really was, but I couldn't pay any attention to what my teachers were saying—I wanted to get back on my bike, get onto the computer, and find out if I was suffering some sort of textbook case of schizophrenia. If not, I'd have to figure out what mental illness I *did* have.

Later that day I read enough about schizophrenia on the Internet to convince me that that wasn't what I had. According to what I read schizophrenia developed slowly, over months, sometimes even years, and the people that had it had trouble sleeping and concentrating, were withdrawn and isolated. None of that described what my life had been like before I saw Mr.

Hanley as a demon. Before seeing demons (BSD), I was like any other normal kid. I had friends, played little league baseball, kicked ass in Guitar Hero, and never had trouble sleeping. I still have a few friends—or at least I go through the pretense of having a few of them to keep my parents off my back—but I'm way more anxious and withdrawn than I was in my old, idyllic life. In those early days I didn't completely dismiss the idea that I was suffering from schizophrenia, but I didn't think it likely.

After reading every blog post and article about schizophrenia, I started to research delusions, trying to learn whatever I could about the disorder, which was when I came across the phenomenon of malperceptions. That's where some people see faces transform into a monster. Even back then, my gut instinct was telling me that this wasn't what I'd experienced, but I still had to consider it as a possibility.

I heard my dad come home a half hour ago, and my mom less than five minutes ago, and from the smell of it she brought home Indian takeout, though it could be Thai. Sometimes I get the smell of their curry dishes mixed up. If I get a chance, I'll write another journal entry later tonight—I want to explain how exactly I know that these are really demons I'm seeing. I'll also write about Clifton Gibson. How that would've cinched the deal for me by itself even if it wasn't for the dogs.

I haven't told anyone about the demons. I can't afford to—not my parents, not anyone. If I told my parents, they'd either have me institutionalized, or they'd drug me up with so many antipsychotics that I wouldn't be able to do what I had to. And if I told anyone else, word might get back to my parents—or worse, to the demons themselves. It's bad enough that Mr. Hanley is already suspicious. I know I have to be careful, which is why I'm writing this journal old school using a notebook and pen. If I wrote this on the computer, a demon might be able to hack into my Mac, and I can't take that risk. All of this might sound para-noid, and maybe it is, but who can blame me?

If something happens to me, I have to hope that this jour-nal finds its way into the hands of someone open-minded enough to believe that what I'm writing here is true, or at least plausible enough to take seriously. And maybe if what happens to me is bizarre enough, whoever finds this will decide to investigate. If I'm dead, someone out there has to be looking into these demons.

My mom's yelling again for me to get downstairs for din-ner. I better do it before she comes up here. More later.

Wednesday, August 24th 2:05 AM

A S I SUSPECTED, MY MOM BROUGHT HOME INDIAN TAKEOUT. ASD (After Seeing Demons) I became a vegetarian—to the great annoyance of my parents—so tonight my mom brought me a vegetable korma dish. It wasn't so much the sight of Mr. Hanley as a demon that turned me off meat, although I'm sure that was part of it, but more that when I was researching the different mental illnesses and brain diseases I thought I might be suffering, I read about Creutzfeldt-Jacob disease, which is the human form of mad cow disease. In my mind I knew then that I didn't have enough of the symptoms, but it still turned me off to eating meat and I haven't touched it to this day.

I should explain more about myself and my parents. We live in Newton, Massachusetts, a suburb of Boston. Newton's a wealthy area, although not as wealthy as most people around here think. There are towns near Boston that are wealthier, but that's beside the point. Not only do we live in Newton, but we live in a village of Newton called *Waban* which actually is every

15

bit as wealthy as people think. Very exclusive, very snobby, and yes, the people here do act as if they're special and entitled simply because they have a Waban address, but again, that's besides the point. BSD I probably acted the exact same way even if I was only a pampered and somewhat spoiled kid who didn't know any better, but ASD my perspective on things changed dramatically. I now see the bigger picture. Wealth and material possessions don't mean spit in the larger scheme of things, and they haven't held any importance to me since that first demon sighting. Wherever I live or whatever possessions I own no longer matter to me. My only concern now are the demons living among us and what to do about them. The only reason I care about money ASD is so I can buy what I need to in order to deal with them.

Getting back to my parents, I don't know whether they're rich, but they're certainly well-off. They're both these high-powered, driven types—my dad's an attorney for a high-powered law firm that helps companies find legal ways to get around environmental laws, and my mom's a high-powered marketing executive for a consumer products company that makes mostly worthless junk—cheap medical equipment, toys that no one wants, that kind of thing. I suspect that my mom and dad make very good salaries, although probably not nearly as much as they wished.

They also care a lot about appearances—especially their own. Every morning they each spend a minimum of forty-five minutes in their individual bathrooms. They're in there tweezing and snipping and doing whatever else they have to do to get themselves perfect, so when they leave the house each day their hair is immaculate—not just on top of their heads but their eyebrows also. My mom's lipstick is applied with the precision of a neurosurgeon, and my dad's face is expertly shaved with just the right dash of cologne splashed on and not a single nose hair visible. Genetically, they both lucked out. Both of them are well-proportioned and got long legs and narrow waists and thick heads of hair, with my dad a few inches over six feet tall, and my mom also on the tall side, around five foot nine. Being purely objective, they're both superficially good-looking—or at least my dad is. My mom used to be, but she's been losing the battle with middle age of late, and her Botox treatments and her near manic hysteria to work out each day in a futile attempt to keep herself toned and slender has left her looking mostly freakish and bony. It's sad when I look at pictures of her from just five or six years ago and see what her desperation to stay young has driven her to.

I'm an only child. My mom took time off from her career when she was thirty-four to have me, and I guess she didn't want to take off any additional time to have other kids. Or maybe she was afraid of what it would do to her body—that she'd get permanently fat if she had more than one kid. Or maybe she didn't want to have to convert her yoga room back into a bedroom if they gave me a sister or brother, or give up the bedroom that they'd made into a home theater, or lose their guest room, even though I don't remember them ever having a guest stay overnight. But none of this really matters. I'm fine being an only child, and BSD, they were pretty happy with me. ASD, though, is a different story. Things changed quickly after my first sighting.

As you can probably guess, my schoolwork slipped pretty badly once I started seeing demons. It's hard to concentrate on school when you're worried that (A) you might be mentally ill or suffering some rare brain disorder, or that (B) the demons are real and there's a reason why you were the one chosen to see them when nobody else can, and if it's (B), then there's something far greater than yourself at stake. Given how high-achieving my parents are, it did not sit well with them that my school work slipped badly, and even worse, that I went from being a well-adjusted extroverted kid who was socially active and fit in nicely with the rest of the neighborhood (and generally didn't make a fuss) to an unhappy, sullen loner.

No, my parents were not happy. It didn't help either that my personal hygiene and grooming suffered ASD and that I quickly went from wholesome to grungy-looking and more than a little distasteful in their eyes in the span of a few weeks. Nor did it help that I transformed quickly from a cute thirteen year-old to a gangly-looking teenager. Physically I take after both my parents, although maybe my mom more than my dad. After a six-inch growth spurt I'm now as tall as my mom, at least when she's not wearing high heels. I've got that same lean body type they both have, except on me it looks gawky and awkward, at least for now. Both my parents have these long faces with dimples (although my mom mostly lost her dimples thanks to her Botox treatments) and well-chiseled features and straight, classic Greek noses. Like them, my face is on the longish side, but I don't have any dimples. My lips look too big, my chin too weak, and my nose too large. It's more of an aquiline type (I suspect my mom must've had a nose job when she was younger, but if she did she would never admit it to me).

So given my plunging grades, my anti-social behavior, my lack of attention to my grooming and cleaning habits, and my generally more awkward appearance, my parents were not at all happy, and they came close to sending me to a therapist, or possibly even a psychiatrist, but fortunately I caught on to that and was able to make the necessary changes to keep that from happening.

My parents don't know what to make of me anymore. I went from perfect suburban child to bitter disappointment to now a mixed bag. It took me six months ASD to fully research all the mental illnesses and brain disorders and convince myself that I wasn't suffering from any of them, and that Mr. Hanley and the others I saw are actual demons. By the time that happened, my parents had completely cut me off as far as giving me an allowance or any money at all, probably because they were convinced I was buying drugs. I needed money to investigate these demons, but I didn't want to be beholden to my parents, so I started shoveling snow that first winter, and I used the money I earned to buy a secondhand lawnmower, so I could mow lawns that next summer.

All this left my parents even more confused. When you live in a rich, pampered neighborhood like Waban you don't find too many kids shoveling snow or mowing lawns to earn money, and my parents were embarrassed by my doing this, though I could tell that they were somewhat proud of my industriousness. Then, in the middle of ninth grade, I started digging into math as if I were a demon myself. Mostly probability and topology theory, but I had a lot of ground to cover before I could understand the concepts in those books. The end result was that I went from a D+ to a solid A in math, with my teacher telling my parents how remarkable my turnaround was, and how I had a real aptitude for the subject. And then, at the beginning of this summer I started studying German on my own, which really confused my parents. My dad is overall happy that I'm learning a new language—though he has no idea why I picked German—while my mom is suspicious. She hasn't voiced these suspicions directly, but she's dropped hints about them while trying to ferret out my sudden interest in that language. I have a sneaking suspicion that she's afraid I might be on my way to becoming a neo-Nazi, or something similarly bizarre.

Why did I suddenly become so interested in probability theory and topology? Because I realized that I needed to better understand how many of these demons there are out there, and where more of them might be showing up. I had to try to predict these numbers from different sample sizes, and to do that, I needed to understand things like Poisson distributions, and other such esoteric concepts I'd never heard of previously. My interest in German was also based on need. At the beginning of the summer, I'd gotten my hands on a copy of *Daemonologie*, by the eighteenth century German occultist Claus Schweikert. At first I thought I'd use one of the online translation services, but they turned out to be too expensive—and anyway, I'd lose important nuances. Next, I had the bright idea of finding someone who knew German at a local nursing home and convince this total stranger to read me the book in English. I did find an eighty-seven year-old who seemed to have his mental faculties and also seemed interested, but when I showed him the book he waved his liver-spotted hand in a gesture of disgust and asked why a nice boy like me would like something like that read to him. After that I decided it would be best if I just taught myself German, so that's what I've been doing. I'm about a third of the way through translating *Daemonologie*—so far the book is proving to be a disappointment. I suspect Schweikert was either a quack or mentally unbalanced, but I'll give it some more time.

Between bites of Lamb Vindaloo, my dad tried to give me a pep talk.

"Henry," he said, his eyebrows severely knotted to impress on me how serious he was, "your mom and I are very pleased with some of the initiatives you've been taking of late. The way you bounced back in math last year was impressive, as is the continued interest that you've been showing in it. We're also very impressed with how you decided on your own to learn a foreign language."

"Thank you for these kind words, Sir."

He was annoyed by that, I could tell, since he wasn't completely sure if I was being sarcastic or genuine, but it didn't deter him. I wasn't being flippant, at least not entirely. Over the last year and a half I'd gotten into the habit of addressing him as *Sir* and my mom as *Ma'am*. I'm not sure exactly why I started doing it, but it's become a way to distance myself from them. Maybe it's my way of making it easier for them to deal with what happens if the demons ever discover me.

My dad's eyes narrowed as he stared at me, which made his carefully groomed eyebrows bunch up even more. It looked to me that they could use some additional trimming, but I kept that to myself. He took another bite of his dinner and chewed it slowly before continuing with his pep talk.

"You're going to be starting tenth grade in a couple of weeks," he said, as he pointed his fork at me for emphasis. "I know you hit a, um, rough patch, a couple of years ago, but this new interest in math is good, as well taking the initiative to teach yourself German, which has really paid off in more ways than simply learning another language. I've noticed over the last few months the improvement in your overall vocabulary, and your mom has also. We'd like to see this recovery of yours continue. This is important, Henry. Tenth grade is when things really start mattering, and you can make up for the last two years by making a real effort this year. You need to do this so that you can get into the right college, and you need to show this same interest in all of your subjects. And your social skills also. Sports, too. You showed a lot of promise when you played little league. Your coach agreed with me. I think it would be a good idea if you tried out for the junior varsity team. What do you say?"

I nodded subserviently. I wouldn't have time to play baseball, or for any other high school activity. Not with having to focus my energies on demons. But baseball was a Spring sport and a long way off. It wasn't worth disappointing him now. That could wait.

His eyes stayed narrowed as he tried to read my expression for my true intentions, but in the end he decided to give me the benefit of the doubt. "Good," he said, nodding slowly. "We really are happy with the improvements you've made. I'd still like to know the reason for your earlier setback, and maybe someday you'll be willing to tell us what triggered it, but we want you to focus on the future, so we've decided to pay you a weekly allowance again. Fifty dollars, which should be enough for you to stop your snow shoveling and lawn maintenance business, which was certainly admirable in its own right. But this is an important time in your life and you need to concentrate your efforts on your school work and other social activities."

I nodded affirmatively, though I knew I wasn't about to quit my businesses. I couldn't allow myself to be reliant on my parents and their money. What I was doing was too important.

A look of relief softened my dad's chiseled features, and he smiled in a relaxed sort of way. "So Henry, why the sudden interest in German?"

"I'm thinking of majoring in psychology in college, and thought it would be good to be able to read Freud in his original writings."

Of course this was an outright lie, but I wasn't about to tell him that I was studying German because I needed to be able to translate an eighteenth-century book on demonology. Nor was I going to inform him that I had no plans to go to college. How could I, with what I was going to have to do? Fortunately, he mostly accepted my lie, though out of the corner of my eye I could see my mom making a sour face, at least as much as the Botox injections allowed her to. But she wasn't about to accuse me right then of having other motives for teaching myself German, and she caught herself before my dad could look at her.

"Sir," I said, "given all of my improvements *of late*, can we reconsider having a dog?"

From my peripheral vision I could see my mom preparing herself to complain about what a dog would do to her carpeting, but she closed her mouth and let my dad handle the dirty business. He frowned in an apologetic sort of way, saying, "Henry, it just wouldn't make sense for us to get a dog right now. Not with you going off to college in three years. Your mom and I would be stuck with it."

"I could take the dog to college with me."

He started to dismiss the idea, but instead left it open, telling me that we could revisit the subject during Christmas break, which was kind of a dirty trick to get more leverage on

22

me. I guess I've always wanted a dog, and they've always had their excuses for why we couldn't get one, but now I had new reasons.

I had promised in my last entry to talk about dogs and demons, and also about Clifton Gibson, but it's late now and I'm tired. After dinner I put another four hours into my translating of *Daemonologie,* which convinced me even further that the book was worthless, although I haven't quite reached the point where I'm willing to toss it. Close, but not quite there. After I quit for the night I felt like I needed to watch *Spider-Man,* which is what I always watch when I'm feeling like my situation is hopeless. I think I've watched it over 100 times ASD. I know it's corny, but I can relate to the whole thing about how 'with great power comes great responsibility.' Watching that movie helps keep me going.

It's almost three o'clock. I'm yawning and having trouble keeping my eyes open, and I have a busy day ahead tomorrow. When I write my next entry, I'll talk about dogs and Clifton Gibson. Promise.

MY PARENTS MUST'VE LEFT FOR WORK AT LEAST THREE HOURS AGO, and thank God they didn't feel the need to give me a parting lecture about staying up late to watch movies, probably because they knew I'd spent a good part of last night with my German self-studies. Right now I'm writing this journal entry sitting in my bathrobe at the table in their top-of-the-line stainless steel chef's kitchen while drinking a triple espresso made with their eight hundred dollar Italian espresso machine. One of the perks of living in a McMansion in the middle of Waban, Massachusetts. Eight-hundred-dollar espresso machines. It doesn't quite make up for my lot in life being fated to deal with demons but at least it's something.

Even after seven hours of sleep and a triple espresso, my head's still too wonky to think straight, kind of like my brain's wrapped in a wool sock. I shouldn't have gone to bed so late, not with all the stuff I have to do today. Hopefully a couple of chocolate crullers from Dunkin' Donuts will help knock some of the fuzziness off. I should have time to ride my bike there later.

I promised last night to write about dogs and demons. The short answer: dogs don't like demons very much or at least they don't like Mr. Hanley. And when I say they don't like him, I mean they're terrified of him. I haven't been able to witness him crossing paths with a dog, though one day I will. But I *have* seen the way they act when they get near his house. They're too terrified to growl or snarl or even show their teeth instead they just want to get as far away from his house as fast as they can. I have my theories on why this is. A big part of it has to be that they must sense something about him, or they can pick up an odor that freaks them out. If I had a dog I could perform some tests on him, like blindfolding him or overloading his olfactory senses with another odor to see if he still behaved the same. But I have other reasons.

I didn't make the dog-demon connection right away. It really didn't happen until six months ASD. Before then I was a wreck. I avoided any further Mr. Hanley sightings, afraid of what I might see, and was well along the way to convincing myself that something was seriously wrong with me, and the only thing that kept me from doing that was I couldn't find any disorder that looked like a good enough match. What helped me finally accept that Mr. Hanley was an actual demon was when I saw his picture in the local paper. I doubt he even knew his picture had been taken. He was in the background carrying an odd-looking package wrapped in white paper, like he had gotten it from the butcher's shop, except it looked too big and cumbersome to be steaks, more like it would have to be a small side of beef. When I saw him in the photo it was as a heavyset square-faced balding man and not as a demon. That made me want to see him again, badly, so I camped out and hid in some bushes across the street where he wouldn't be able to see me. I couldn't camp out like that all the time, only an hour here and there so my parents and nobody else would know what I was up to, and because of that it took me three days before I saw him again. When I did he was still a demon, but this time I brought my iPhone with me, and guess what? Through the viewfinder he was the same chunky and balding Mr. Hanley that I used to see BSD. Somehow this didn't surprise me. I took several pictures and they all showed him as a human and not as a demon.

So where do dogs and demons come into all this? While I was camped out, I saw how every time a dog approached Mr. Hanley's house, they acted the same. They'd start shaking like crazy, their tails going straight between their hind legs, and they'd dig in and fight against the leash with everything they had to keep from being led past that house. Some owners would give in and turn around and their dogs would make these awful wheezing strangled noises as they fought against their leashes trying to race away in a blind panic. Others, especially those owners with smaller dogs, would just about pull their dogs past the house, but once they were beyond Hanley's property they'd also struggle to put some serious distance between themselves and that house. In none of these cases was Hanley actually out-side, so I knew that these dogs weren't reacting to the sight of him, but rather to a smell or something else that they sensed. Whatever it was, it left them terrified.

I only saw seven different owners try to walk their dogs past that house, which wasn't a lot, given that I was camped out for over eight hours during my three-day surveillance mission. None of these people were from the neighborhood—I'm guess-ing that anyone living nearby with a dog must've learned long ago to avoid Hanley's house. Watching this play out also made me think about the dogs that have gone missing in our neigh-borhood over the years. The Goldsteins' black lab that disap-peared from their fenced-in backyard. The Michelsons' old Saint Bernard that used to lay like a lump on their front doorstep. The Andersons' overstuffed English Bulldog. And there were others too. There was talk for a while how there must be coyotes living on a nearby wooded golf course, but nobody ever saw or heard any coyotes, and if it was coyotes then the neighborhood cats would've been disappearing also. The other thing is that all the dogs that disappeared were big dogs. None of the yapping little terriers in the neighborhood ever went missing. When I thought of that, I immediately thought of the large package wrapped in white paper that Mr. Hanley was carrying in that photo.

So yeah, I want a dog. Worrying about how to protect the world from demons is a lonely life, and it would be nice to have some companionship. More than that, I want to be able to do the experiments I mentioned earlier, but also I want to see how a dog would react when brought face to face with Mr. Hanley and other demons. It couldn't be just any dog, it would have to be a special one. Maybe a bull terrier. I've read about them, and I think that breed would be perfect. Strong, fearless, probably even able to hold its own against a demon. Somehow I don't think that breed would act the same way as these other dogs did. I think a bull terrier would be able to look a demon in the eye, and instead of wanting to run away would want to rip its ugly flaming red throat out. At least I hope so.

So that's the scoop between dogs and demons. I need to do more experiments and tests, but I've seen enough to be convinced that dogs aren't fooled by these demons. They either sense or smell what they are, and one of these days I'll know whether they also *see* them for what they are.

I also promised to write about Clifton Gibson, and yeah, he's the same Clifton Gibson you've been reading about the last two years. The one who was found in a warehouse in Brooklyn with dozens of cages filled with little kids, none of them older than four. The papers didn't give much in the way of detail, but the charges were lengthy, with kidnapping, illegal imprisonment, torture, mutilations, performing depraved acts on children: the list goes on and on. The pictures they showed of Gibson in the papers and on TV had him as this creepy-looking guy. Tall, bald, with these dead eyes. Kind of like a human snake. The story broke seven months ASD and when I first saw his photo on TV I felt this certainty about him that I couldn't explain. After that I became obsessed with reading everything I could about him, and I searched every website and message board that mentioned him. There were a lot of rumors about nearby missing children and what he must've done to them, and there were other rumors about the children they found.

Nobody in the police or DA's office would talk about what was done to the children they rescued. It was a privacy issue. But you had the charges filed against Gibson, and you had all the rumors, and you knew the reality had to be bad. The one rumor I couldn't shake was that he had sewn their eyelids and lips closed.

When the trial started I took a train to New York so I could get into the courtroom. My parents had no idea. I just left the house early that morning and left them a note about how I had a heavy day of mowing lawns ahead of me, and that I'd be eating dinner at Wesley Neuberger's house and would be home late. Wesley is one of the handful of friends I still stay in contact with to keep my parents off my back, and I'd worked it out with him ahead of time to cover for me. After I was out of the house, I rode my bike to a neighboring town, Needham, took the train to South Station, and from there got on the Acela train to New York and made it to Penn Station by eleven o'clock. It took me another hour to get to the Kings County Courthouse in Brooklyn where the trial was being held, and as you know if you caught any of the news clips a year ago, it was a complete circus with the media and mobs of angry local residents fighting to get in and lines of police keeping all of us at bay.

I squeezed my way through this mob and one of the police officers gave me a stony stare and told me to beat it. I lied to him and told him that a four-year-old cousin of mine was one of Gibson's victims. ASD I'd gotten very good at lying—I had to in order to keep my parents in the dark as to what I was doing, and I must've lied convincingly enough to this police officer, because instead of dismissing me for being full of shit, like he probably wanted to, his eyes wavered a bit, and although he now had a hard smirk on his face, he asked me the name of my cousin.

This is where I got lucky. Most of the stuff I read online about Gibson seemed like total BS, but there was one blog that felt more reliable, and I threw out one of the names I'd seen listed there.

"I need to see him," I said. "After what he did to my cousin, I don't think I'll ever be able to sleep again at night if I don't."

That did it. Again, I'd learned with a lot of practice with my parents how to be a convincing liar, but I hit the jackpot with the name I gave him. I could see it in that police officer's eyes after he checked the name against a list he had.

"You'll behave yourself?" he asked.

"Yeah, I promise. I just need to see him. Even if it's just for one minute."

He studied me carefully for a long ten-count, then nodded. "You wait here," he said. "I'll see what I can do."

He left, another cop took his place, and the crowd pushed hard behind me making it difficult to breathe. The world started to grow red on me, and I had a moment where I thought I was going to pass out, but eventually the cop came back and led me through the police line.

"One minute," he told me.

I nodded, still dizzy from the crowd nearly suffocating me moments earlier, my heart racing too much for me to say anything. He escorted me into the courthouse, and there a court officer took over. He gave me a stern lecture about what would happen if I made any noise inside the courtroom, and I nodded my acquiescence. Once he was satisfied he led me inside, and you can guess the rest. Yep, Clifton Gibson's a demon. He was taller and thinner than Mr. Hanley, but he had that same flaming red skin and horns and claws and all the rest of those demon features. Even though I was expecting it, the whole thing still took my breath away. And the really crazy part was that he wasn't the only demon in the courtroom—there were two others, both spectators. One of them turned my way, his expression puzzled as he looked at me. At that point I figured I'd better get out of there, and I indicated to the court officer that I'd seen enough. He walked me out of the court, and after that I was moving fast down the hallway and out of the building. I had a funny feeling as I was squeezing my way through the crowd, and sure enough, after I had gotten out of that scene I turned to see that the demon from the courtroom was trying to push his way through the crowd also, but not having much luck given his larger bulk. He had followed me and was after me. I ran then.

I made a mental note to myself after that that I had to be more careful when looking at demons. I wasn't expecting other demons in that courtroom, but it was still no excuse to let down my guard. They're sly and clever and have an innate sense of when they've been recognized. If I make a mistake like that again, it could be the end for me.

It's a quarter to eleven, and I have to get going if I want to get those Dunkin' Donut crullers. I have a busy day planned. First up: I have to mow Mr. Hanley's yard. I'll explain in my next journal entry how that came about.

Auf wiedersehen for now.

I WASN'T PLANNING ON WRITING ANOTHER JOURNAL ENTRY until later tonight, but I'm still shaking from what went down minutes ago at that demon's house. I need to get this on paper now while the details are fresh in my mind. If I save this for later I might leave out important details, or worse, add in some exaggerations, and what happened was bizarre enough without doing that.

Let me explain first why I've been mowing Hanley's yard, although you probably can guess. After he found out I was mowing other lawns in the neighborhood, Hanley made a point of watching for me so he could barrel out of his house and wave me over to offer me the job. I think he wanted to test me, see how I'd react, but he probably also wanted to keep an eye on me so that he could decide whether I suspected anything. What was I going to do? Turn him down? That would be the same as telling him to his face that I knew what he was. Instead I quoted him a rate, adding in a fifteen dollar demon surcharge. He gave me a little demon snarl, as if he suspected that I had inflated my price for him, but he accepted my price, and for the last year I've mowed his lawn every week during the summer.

Today, like every day that I've mowed his lawn, he watched me through his kitchen window while I tried to act as if I wasn't noticing, only allowing myself to catch *accidental* glimpses of him. During the forty minutes I was there I don't think he moved once, probably not even to blink (do demons blink? I don't think so), but that wasn't anything unusual. He always just sat watching me through the window like some sort of demon Buddha with his demon muzzle set in a scowl. The deal we have is for him to mail me my payment each month, but today as I was finishing up he came out his side door and tried waving me over. I pretended I was too wrapped up in what I was doing to notice.

"Henry, boy, come over here. Let me pay you."

I looked up then and tried to act surprised that he was there. "I didn't know you were home," I lied, probably pretty badly. "Just mail me a check like you always do."

"You can save me a stamp," he said in his flat demon growl. Just as I could now see them as demons, I could also hear them as such, and they don't sound anything like humans. Their voices have a deep, unnatural sound with far too much bass echoing in it, like they're inside an echo chamber with all these hisses and snarls mixed in.

I tried to smile sympathetically and act as if he wasn't a demon. "I have another job after this one," I explained. "If I take a check from you now I'll probably lose it before I get home. Or it'll get too soaked through with my sweat for my bank to take it. I'll tell you what, why don't you deduct the cost of the stamp from your payment?"

From the way his jaw twisted I could guess he would've been smiling pleasantly if I could've seen him as a human, but all I could see was malevolence in his demon face and dead yellow eyes.

"You're sweating right now, Henry," he growled. "You could use something to drink. Come on in. I'll get you something."

I felt the hair on the back of my neck tingling. My voice caught in my throat as I told him thanks, but no thanks. Maybe this was a test, or maybe he still had his doubts about me and finally decided he wasn't going to risk me knowing what he was. I had a bad feeling about his intentions and what would happen to me if I went inside his house. I wondered then for the first time how fast a demon could move. I had no idea. We had only thirty or so feet separating us, and he was edging closer. If I had to, I'd leave my lawn mower behind and make a run for it to escape him.

"Come on over here," he said, still waving his claw at me. The thing was so red in the sunlight it looked like it had been dipped in blood. He kept edging closer to me. The distance had shrunk to only twenty feet. I took a few steps further away.

"There's money in it," he said.

I didn't respond to that. This wasn't a test. He wanted me inside his home for ill reasons. He would probably take his time in killing me. God knows what he'd do to my body afterward.

"Five hundred dollars," he said.

I forced myself to play along. My voice was little more than a whisper as I told him I wasn't gay.

"Really? Are you sure?"

"Yeah, I'm sure. Why would you think I was gay?"

He shrugged. His jaw contorted—he must have been smiling more broadly in human form. "Boy, the way you look and the way you carry yourself, and also the vibe I'm picking up from you. You may not know it yet, but you're gay. A thousand dollars. Trust me Henry, you'll enjoy the experience."

He was having fun, both in testing me and playing his mind games, trying to wound me by questioning my sexuality. As I've been discovering, demons can be an especially nasty breed. Or maybe he thought he'd piss me off enough to take a swing at him, and then he'd be able to grab hold of me. In either case, it didn't work. I backed further away from him, dragging my mower with me as I did so. I had only ten feet or so to go before I'd be out of his fenced-in backyard, and after that any passerby would be able to see me and he'd be taking too big a chance if he tried charging me. I had a good idea then that if he could've moved fast enough to grab me he would've.

"What's to stop me from telling my parents or the police about you trying to solicit me?"

He laughed then. Or at least I'm assuming he laughed. The noise that came out of him was something awful.

"Who'd believe you, Henry?" he asked. "You're the street flake. Everyone knows it. If I have to, I'll tell the police you're lying. That you're a disturbed child who tried extorting money from me by threatening to make up a ridiculous lie. They'll believe me over you."

"They'd at least search your house. And they'd find something."

He tensed then. I could tell that he was judging the distance more carefully, trying to decide if he could make up the distance fast enough to grab me.

"What would they find, Henry?"

I bit my tongue. I wanted to say a freezer full of dog meat, maybe dog carcasses also, and worse. But I knew that that would be a dumb thing to say. Instead I told him they'd find child porn all over his house and on his computer.

A change came over his demon face then. It was a subtle change, but it was there. The violence that was so imminent seconds ago was gone. Like a valve had been opened releasing it. He was sure then that I only suspected him of being a perv, not a demon. I was safe. At least for now.

"You're going to have to find a new lawn person," I yelled out as I pulled my mower out from his backyard and from behind his fence. "I quit."

He laughed his demon laugh at that, and I'm still shaking.

It's twenty to one. I wish I was going into Boston alone, but I promised Wesley Neuberger he could go with me. He's been bugging me for days about us doing something together, and as much as I'd like to cancel, I better not.

I'm feeling almost too shaky to eat, but it will be a while before I have another chance, and I need the energy since Wesley and I will be riding our bikes into the city. At least eight miles and through a lot of traffic. I'll make a couple of lettuce, tomato, and cheese sandwiches and bring them with me.

Fucking Hanley.

Fucking demons.

Have I mentioned before how much I hate demons?

Wednesday, August 24th 9:37 PM

I DIDN'T TELL MY PARENTS ABOUT THE DEMON HANLEY TRYING
to solicit me—for one thing, they'd never believe me. I'm
sure they would've believed Hanley's lie over whatever I told
them. I mentioned earlier how ASD I cut off most of my social
activities. You can't be worrying about sports and girls and dating when you have to spend all your energy figuring out how
to protect the world from demons. I know my parents are wondering why I'm not dating and seemingly showing no interest
in doing so, and I know they have their suspicions about me.
Nothing they voice to me directly, but they drop hints and make
innuendos as they try to ferret out of me whether I'm gay. I
think they're also convinced that the two supposed friends I
hang out with, Wesley Neuberger and Curt Tucker, are also gay.
I don't think either of them are, although I don't know for sure.
They're both social misfits for reasons having nothing to do
with demons and that's why I hang out with them, or at least
enough to keep my parents off my back. It would take too much

effort and time to hang out with any of the cool kids, time that I don't have.

So about Curt and Wesley. Curt is deep into everything goth, and that alone has probably convinced my parents about his sexual identity, but my parents are clueless in such matters. Wesley, well, he might have some effeminate mannerisms, but I don't think that means he's gay, not that it would matter. Both he and Curt seem to show real interest in girls, at least from the type of stuff they're always saying to me.

So if my parents wouldn't believe me, it would be foolish to think that the police would. And it's probably better this way. Hanley thinks he has me fooled. That I believe he's only a perv and not a demon. Maybe now he won't be so careful, and he'll screw up and make a mistake—something that I can use against him and the other demons.

At least I hope so.

I had another demon sighting today. This was in Boston. Before I write about it, let me give some background on Wesley and me, since he was with me at the time.

The two of us go back a long way together, all the way to the second grade. That was when we were moved into the same class and became friends. Wesley lives only two blocks away, has my whole life. Back when we were second graders we played the dumb games second graders play and read comic books and watched cartoons on TV. Wesley was always into comic books, especially superhero ones. Most little kids are, I guess. I used to be also, but in his case his dad is really into it, too, and has this rare comic book collection. Some cool stuff, including the first hundred Spider-Man comics, all wrapped up in plastic bags.

Even in second grade Wesley was a thin, gawky-looking kid with curly hair and thick glasses. I'm gawky-looking now too, but it took me until I was almost fifteen to get that way—

Wesley was that way from the start. For whatever reason he was just one of those kids who came out of the womb uncool, but as I've been learning with this demon business cool and uncool mean squat in the larger scheme of things.

So from second to fifth grade Wesley and I were best friends, but in fifth grade we started going in different directions. We both played T-ball early on, with Wesley showing little co-ordination even then, and in fifth grade we were both assigned to the same little league team. I pitched and played centerfield, while Wesley mostly sat on the bench. That was when our friend-ship started drifting. I was good at all the positions the coach put me in, and ended up being our best pitcher and outfielder. Wesley just wasn't cut out for sports, so he didn't sign up for lit-tle league the next year, and by then we'd become more like un-comfortable acquaintances than friends, where we'd nod *hey* to each other but little more than that. It stayed that way until ASD.

As I already mentioned, Wesley has been bugging me for days about us doing something. What he had in mind was us hanging around reading comic books, but I didn't give him a choice; it was either ride our bikes into Boston and hang around there, or nothing, and after some whining on his part he tagged along.

Wesley hasn't moved to wearing contacts yet and still wears these goofy-looking glasses with thick brown plastic frames that cover a good third of his face, and has mop-like curly brown hair. He's still what most kids at my school would call a skinny runt. While I've had my growth spurt, he hasn't and maybe never will.

Wesley's bike has to be some sort of old-fashioned an-tique, unless it's a retro number. I'm guessing his dad had it when he was Wesley's age and saved it all these years so he could em-barrass his own child with it someday. It's not even a ten-speed—I think it only has three gears, and even on moderate inclines Wesley's huffing and puffing when he's pedaling it. Whenever we're riding bikes, I have to keep slowing down—otherwise I'd lose him. It doesn't help that he's such a timid rider if there's any traffic. Once we hit Brookline I had to stop every couple of blocks and wait for him to catch up. By the time we reached Kenmore Square he looked winded and needed to rest. That was okay with me. I take these trips into Boston so I can be on the lookout for demons, sometimes also so I can visit Cornwall's Used Books, this dusty and cluttered used bookstore in this rat hole area of Boston that has a surprisingly strong occult book section, sometimes with rare books that other stores have never heard of. Cornwall's is where I picked up my copy of *Daemonologie*, and other books on demonology from the eighteenth and nineteenth centuries. I wasn't planning on going there today—not with Wesley tagging along—but that was okay. Today was reserved for spotting demons.

Once we reached Kenmore Square, Wesley went into Store 24 to pick up bottles of Vitamin Water for both of us, and after that he went into UBurger to get himself a potential dose of Creutzfeldt-Jacob disease on a sesame bun with pickles and ketchup and a bag of French Fries. While he did this I ate one of my tomato, cheese, and lettuce sandwiches and counted the number of pedestrians walking by. This was good. Kenmore Square is a busy area and I hadn't done a count there in weeks. What I've been trying to do is perform counts at strategic locations throughout Boston and Cambridge and see if I can spot any trends with these demons. Once I was done eating I sat and continued my count until Wesley came out of UBurger. After he sat on the steps and joined me, he distracted me by telling me how he saw Sally Freeman two days ago.

Some of my sandwich almost came up on me. I struggled to keep it down and took another swig of my heavily sugared Vitamin Water. My heart was racing like crazy, and my voice didn't sound right as I shrugged and said, "Yeah?" It came out more as a squeak. Wesley was nice about it and pretended he didn't notice my reaction, and instead told me how he saw Sally at the Chestnut Hill mall when his mom took him there to get him new back-to-school clothing. It didn't seem like the best time to tell him that I hadn't gone clothes shopping with my mom in over two years.

"She asked about you," he added.

Well, that just shot my count to hell. Let me explain about Sally Freeman. We went to grade school together, and I had a crush on her the first moment I saw her in my kindergarten class. Back then I used to watch reruns of the old Dick Van Dyke show with my dad. I was too little to get much out of it other than the silly clowning around that Dick Van Dyke used to do, but my dad got a kick out of the show, so I liked sitting there with him. I also thought that Mary Tyler Moore was the most beautiful woman imaginable, at least until I saw Sally. Sally had that same cute button nose, brown hair, big brown eyes, and probably looked the same as Mary Tyler Moore did at age six. I didn't let her know it, and instead teased her the way little kids always do, yet I had that crush on her all through grade school. But Sally lived on the opposite side of Waban, closer to the Charles River, and I was assigned to Bigelow for middle school while Sally went to Brown. I hadn't seen her since we were assigned to different schools, and ASD I've tried not to think of her.

"What did she ask about?" I said as I tried really hard to sound nonchalant while doing a lousy job of it.

"About how you're doing. Stuff like that. I told her you said hi."

"Yeah. Whatever," I said, but felt a hotness burning in my cheeks, and was pleased that Wesley did that. Say what you want about him. He might be an uncool gawky kid who spends too much time with his comic books and graphic novels, but you could always count on him.

"She's transferring to Newton North this year. So she'll be slumming it with the rest of us."

That stunned me. I didn't expect to see Sally again, and the thought of her going to the same high school as me started me getting an erection, which was embarrassing. I forced myself to think of demons until the erection went away, hoping that Wesley didn't notice.

Let me explain:

Last year when I started high school, I'd heard through the grapevine that Sally was going to one of the elite local private schools we have in the area. That was why I assumed I wouldn't have to think of her again.

Let me explain further:

BSD me and a few other friends would go to Chuckie Horan's house. His parents were clueless as far as computers and the Internet went, and had no idea how to put up parental controls to limit the sites Chuckie went on, or to figure out after the fact which sites he visited. So being curious twelve- and thirteen-year-olds we'd find free porn sites. It wasn't hard. We did this maybe a half dozen times before the novelty wore off, and I think also while what we found excited us it also sickened us. I hadn't hit puberty yet, and that was as far as it went. Before puberty came so did demons. If it wasn't for the demons, once that event happened I probably would've been like a lot of other boys my age finding porn any way I could. But because of the demons, it was like I had become sort of a monk who had taken a vow of celibacy. Or maybe more like I was being given chemicals; at least the effect was similar to chemical castration. All my focus became demons and what I needed to do about them. I had no energy left to think about girls or wanting to masturbate or anything like that. So at fifteen, not only am I a virgin, but I guess I'm pure in the sense that I haven't even masturbated, and ASD, this was the first erection I experienced. Which is part of why it was so embarrassing.

That's enough on this topic. If anyone finds this journal it's because I'm dead, and all I'm trying to do is explain things the way they were so you can decide for yourself what's true and what isn't. I'm sure if the demons are responsible for my death they've put together a convincing string of stories and lies to cover what happened to me, but that's all they'll be. Stories and lies.

Getting back to Wesley and me. After he finished his charbroiled, artery-clogging, and cancer-inducing meal, I noted the time we'd been in Kenmore Square and I texted myself a message with what then was only a very rough guestimate of the number of pedestrians who passed by. No demons. Wesley gave me a funny look as I did this but didn't say anything. After that we got on our bikes and continued with our trip.

We ended up riding our bikes a couple of miles down Beacon Street, then down Tremont, taking a left on Boylston to lower Washington Street, which ended up maybe being four miles in total from Kenmore Square. We got off our bikes across the street from two strip clubs. This was where I had planned to do my demon watching and counting. I was curious about whether demons would be attracted to places like these strip clubs. Maybe not so much by the naked women but by how gross and unseemly these places are. I was thinking they might come here to soak in the desperation and unhappiness that must permeate clubs like these. It was a new theory I was working on, and I was also planning to do counts outside of divey, skeevy bars, the types that attract lowlifes and down-and-out alcoholics. Wesley started complaining right away.

"This is weird," he said. "Why are we here?"

I didn't bother answering him, and instead concentrated on counting the people who walked by. These were mostly men going into and out of the strip clubs, but others walked by, as well: some businessmen who were cutting through the area, a few other stragglers, and one woman who I thought at first was a stripper with the way she was dressed, especially her huge high heels. She tottered over to us, looking unsteady on her high heels as she crossed the street. Up close she didn't look too good. Without her shoes, she would've been shorter than Wesley, probably no more than five foot two inches. She was also on the chunky side, and her body was stuffed into a halter top that exposed her belly and a pair of ultra-short mini-pants. Her thighs had a flabby look to them and her exposed belly made me think of a dead fish I once saw washed up on the beach. Her complexion was a mess, and she had so much makeup on that she looked sort of ghoulish. I don't think she was more than twenty, but she looked so much older than that to me. She gave me a smile, then Wesley, and asked what we were doing there. That was when I noticed a sore on her upper lip. Wesley was too scared to say anything. I looked away from her and returned to my count.

Out of the corner of my eye I could see her licking her lips, her tongue caressing her sore.

"If you boys have twenty dollars, I'll take you two behind that alley and make it worth your while."

Wesley might have peed a little in his pants right then. At least I thought I detected a whiff of urine.

"Not interested," I told her as I tried to keep my focus on my count.

She moved so that she was right in front of me. The expression on her face had tightened and her mouth was squeezed into an ugly little oval that made her sore look even more gross. I tried looking past her, but she was blocking me.

"You think you're too good for me?" she spat out in a tight, angry voice. "Both of you with your half-inch lily white dicks? I oughta cut them off. And cut your lily white faces—"

This was getting annoying. More than annoying. Not only was she scaring the crap out of Wesley, but she was interfering with my count. And as she was spewing her threats I saw a demon exit one of the strip clubs! This one was wearing a business suit but was still as grotesque as all the other demons I'd seen. I took out my iPhone so I could snap a photo of it but she slapped my hand away.

"Get away from me," I demanded, my voice barely above a whisper. "What I'm doing here is important and you're interfering with me."

I took a step toward her and she nearly fell over backing away from me. A look of fear flashed across her face and she hurried across the street to get further away from me. It wasn't until then that she started shouting more threats at us and how she could suck us off better than any little rich white girl we'll ever find, but I'd mostly tuned her out and she became not much more than background noise, like if someone a block away had been honking their horn. I needed to get a picture of that demon, but he was already too far away for that and had his back turned to us. I told Wesley to wait where he was, and I got on my bike and raced after this demon. As I pulled up in front of him I took his photo trying to be as inconspicuous as I could. I don't think he noticed. At least I hope he didn't. I kept riding straight ahead and used my iPhone as kind of a rear view mirror. When I saw the demon turn down Nassau Street, I circled back so I could pick up Wesley.

Wesley's face was as white as milk by the time I got back to him. The chunky prostitute who had offered to suck us off was still right across the street, but she wasn't yelling anything anymore. Wesley gazed at me with an expression both livid and dazed.

"You just left me," he said. "How could you do that?"

"Get on your bike now and follow me," I ordered.

"No, you tell me what's going on!"

"I don't have time for this." I gave him a disgusted look. Here I was trying to identify another demon, and he's giving me this type of aggravation? "You can find your own way home," I told him. I then got on my bike and pedaled hard toward Nassau Street. I didn't bother looking over my shoulder, but I could hear Wesley struggling to keep up with me. When I got to Nassau Street I kept going and waited until I got to Oak Street to take a left, then pedaled furiously until I approached Harrison Avenue. I pulled my bike over so that I was against a brick building at the corner there and edged forward to look down Harrison Avenue, but kept close to the building so I wouldn't be seen. Wesley was coming up behind me, and I signaled for him to follow my lead. He was huffing pretty badly as he pulled up.

"Henry, what are you doing?"

"Be quiet," I ordered. As I expected, the demon had gotten onto Harrison Avenue from Nassau Street and was now walking in the opposite direction. I couldn't afford to let him see me again. If he did, he would know I was following him, so I stood where I was hiding and watched him. When I saw him enter one of the buildings on Harrison, I let out my breath and realized for the first time I'd been feeling dizzy. I'd probably been holding my breath ever since I snuck up behind that building. I collapsed forward with my hands on my knees and the dizziness passed. I put a hand to my forehead and felt a sticky wetness. I was sweating badly and hadn't even realized it.

"You look like you're sick," Wesley said.

"Yeah? You looked like you were going to pee in your pants when that prostitute came over to us."

He closed his mouth and gave me a hard stare. Then he shook his head.

"We shouldn't have come here," he said. "My parents would be pissed if they knew I came here."

"No one twisted your arm," I said.

Wesley closed his mouth again and gave me another long look. This time it was one of pity.

"Why is that man so important?" he said.

"What are you talking about?"

"That man who came out of the strip club. The one wearing the dark gray suit. The one you had to take a picture of and follow here. Why was it so important for you to do that?"

I wanted to kick myself for bringing Wesley along. He had come with me on other trips to Boston so I could do my counts, but this was the first he'd been with me when I had spotted a demon. This was a mistake. I knew it in the pit of my stomach.

"I don't know what you're talking about," I said. "I was just fooling around, that's all. Let's head back home. We've got a long ride back."

"You're not planning on doing something stupid, are you Henry? Like trying to blackmail that man because you caught him leaving a strip club?"

I felt my cheeks reddening as Wesley questioned my motives. Here I was, doing what I had to because of these demons, and I had to listen to Wesley insinuating that I was a blackmailer?

"Don't be an asshole," I said.

Wesley didn't want to let it drop. I guess he was still angry at me for leaving him on Washington Street before.

"Something's up with you," he said. "All your spying and note taking." He paused for a moment before adding, "Who do you think these people are that you're spying on? Terrorists? Enemies of the state?"

"Stop it now. If you want to stay friends, stop it."

It was a mistake taking Wesley on one of my missions, and I wasn't about to make that mistake again. From now on I was going to take these trips alone. I got on my bike and headed down Harrison, so I could pass the building the demon had gone into. I wish I could've investigated more at that time, but it would've been impossible with Wesley alongside me. I noted the building's address, then kept going straight until I turned down Boylston Street so that Wesley and I could head back to Waban.

I'VE BEEN SICK IN BED THE LAST TWO DAYS. WEDNESDAY NIGHT around one in the morning I woke up shivering like crazy with my teeth chattering, and was soon throwing up the rest of the night. I must've overexerted myself riding into Boston and chasing down that demon. Or maybe when that chunk of a prostitute had gotten in my face and yelled at me some of her diseased spittle got in my mouth. Whatever caused it, I haven't been this sick in years. For part of the last two days I've been delirious with all these hallucinations involving demons, at times believing that demons were hiding in my room. It was as if I was seeing them trying to hide by the foot of my bed, or catching their unblinking yellow eyes spying on me from inside my closet. At times I was imagining them sitting on my bed next to me, at other times my hallucinations had me other places with them. I hope I didn't say anything while I was having these hallucinations, or at least nothing that my parents could've made sense of.

My fever broke three hours ago, which is why I'm now

51

at my desk writing. I'm weak and I'm damp with sweat, but at least I'm out of bed. My mom came home early from work today. She wanted me to have chicken soup, and I had to remind her once again that I'm a vegetarian. She actually went out after that to get me vegetable broth, and also bought me a quart of fresh-squeezed orange juice and a bag of Milano cookies, which are my favorite. For the first time in a long time ASD she's been acting as if she actually cares about me.

I lost precious time the last two days, especially with school starting soon. There's so much I need to do. Even if I'm still weak tomorrow, as long as I can get out of bed I'm going to Boston. I need to identify the demon from the other day, and I want to go back to Washington Street and do a longer count outside those strip clubs. I need to see whether that one demon was an anomaly or if other demons are attracted to those clubs. Also, I've been wanting to stop by Cornwall's for days now to see if they have any new books.

After my fever broke and my thinking became clearer, I picked up my copy of *Daemonologie* and a German-English dictionary to continue my translation. I hadn't totally given up on the book yet, and this time I found something that excited me and made me think that the book wasn't completely worthless. According to Schweikert dogs and demons are natural enemies. He hypothesizes that the reason for this is because dogs can detect the scent of a demon. He further goes on to say that for this reason demons will hunt dogs to create a dog-free area where they live. He doesn't say anything about demons eating dogs. Maybe centuries of hunting dogs has caused them to acquire a taste for them. This passage lines up so closely with what I've observed that it's causing me to reconsider previous passages in Schweikert's book that I had earlier discounted. In any case, I'm now determined to finish my translation.

I hear my mom in the hallway–she must be coming back to check on me, so I better hide this journal. *Ciao* for now.

S OMEONE ANSWERED MY AD. I DIDN'T THINK THAT WOULD happen. I put the ad out there as a million to one shot, but now I'm both excited and nervous. Maybe even scared. Let me explain.

From the moment I accepted that I was really seeing demons, I've been obsessed with the thought that someone else must see them also. *Genuinely* see them like I do, not someone suffering from a brain injury or mental disorder. What I finally decided to do was put an ad in the *Avalerian*. The *Avalerian* is this alternative newspaper we have in Boston where people place personal ads for everything imaginable. Every possible sexual orientation there is has pages of ads. Things outside of sex, too. Lonely hearts ads. Tracking down old boyfriends and girlfriends. The great thing about putting ads in the *Avalerian* is you can do it anonymously. I was able to mail the ad in without a return address and simply included the cash payment. My ad read 'Do you see demons also?' and included a codename and a password to a private message board to leave a message.

My ad ran a month ago, and that first week I checked the message board compulsively. Nothing. Now I was only checking it every couple of days with no real hope of finding anything.

But this morning I found something. Waiting for me on the message board was this message: *I see them too. Blood-skin ugly bastards. How do we meet?*

I'd created my message board user account so it couldn't be tracked back to me. The person who had responded used the name *Virgil*, and had done the same. I hadn't thought far enough ahead to know what I'd do if someone answered my ad. As I tried thinking about what my next step would be, I realized I was stumped. It was possible Virgil was legit. It was possible he or she was a flake, or someone just goofing around. But it was also possible Virgil was a demon trying to discover who it was that could see demons. If I arranged for us to meet somewhere, I could be walking into a trap. And if Virgil was legit, he'd have the same issues with me. If I gave him a location so I could spy on him from a distance in order to make sure it wasn't a demon showing up, Virgil would have to worry about giving himself away, too. It exhausted me trying to think of all the possible different scenarios of how we could safely meet, and it depressed me to realize that none of them would work. It was possible I'd found someone who'd been cursed the same as I was, someone I could team up with, someone who could help me lessen the burden that had been placed on me. But how? Since I couldn't think of anything better, I sent him (if Virgil was a he) a test and asked him to send me a photo of one of the demons he had spotted.

I'm still not close to a hundred percent. My legs are rubbery, and when I stood earlier I felt lightheaded. But time is running out before school starts. Once that happens the amount of hours I'm going to be able to dedicate to this is going to drop off dramatically. I'll be heading off to Boston soon to do the things I have to get done, but as a compromise I'll take the subway instead of riding my bike.

MY PARENTS—ESPECIALLY MY MOM—WERE NOT HAPPY THAT I snuck out of the house without telling them, and even more that I didn't answer my phone. They made sure to give me an earful about it when I got home later, which I found incredibly hypocritical. I've been coming and going without their caring for almost two years, and all of a sudden they're going to start acting like uberparents? Please. Give me a break! I'm surprised they even knew my cell phone number.

Since I wasn't up for a lecture I fed them a line about how I'd forgotten to charge my phone before I left the house, and that was why I'd turned it off. I also forced a puzzled look as I told them that I thought I'd left them a note, and that I left it because I didn't want to disturb their Saturday morning private time. Most weekends they're both heading off to work on Saturday mornings. Occasionally, they don't, though, and when they don't, it's because they're spending the morning going down on each other. Whenever I hear a CD playing from their bedroom, especially on a weekend morning, I know it's to drown out the noise they're making. That morning I heard one of those old mellow rockers they like, the guy who does *Moondance*. His music was seeping from their bedroom, and that made it easy for me to sneak out without them hassling me.

Since I wasn't up to riding my bike into the city, I walked to the Waban T stop and took the subway into Boston. No demon sightings or anything else unusual during the ride. I took out my phone and studied the photo I'd snapped of the demon who'd left the strip club. His human appearance was that of a square-jawed type; someone who could've been a fullback or linebacker in high school. A little cleft in his chin, his blond hair cut short into a bristle cut. The type that women probably fawn over. If only they knew the truth. I wondered if demons ever took women back to their places to fuck. They probably did. I couldn't help feeling queasy thinking about how that would work. Women probably looked at these demon dicks and thought they were normal human ones, but in reality they must be grotesque appendages—like everything else about these demons. *Daemonologie* claimed a demon's dick was razor sharp. If that was true, they'd be slicing the hell out of the poor women that they were bedding. And even if that wasn't true, what type of diseases would they be passing on? Thinking about that made me shudder. It also made me realize that if they were bringing women back to their dwellings to fuck, these women wouldn't be leaving alive. I wondered more about this—about whether these demons trafficked in missing women, women whose bodies would never be discovered. The possibilities were awful.

I've been able to identify and discover addresses for eighteen of the twenty-three demons I've spotted, not counting this latest one. So far, all of them live alone. That's another argument in favor of the fact that I'm not mentally ill—that these are real demons. Statistically, it would've been impossible to pick eighteen people out at random and have them all living alone. But with these demons, there's not even a pretense of marriage or family. Maybe they led a celibate life, but somehow I doubted it. Seeing that demon leave the strip club made me doubt it even more.

It was making me sick thinking of this, so I forced myself to stop. I started thinking instead about how to make contact with this Virgil, who claimed to see demons, but that was also too frustrating to think about. A woman sitting nearby was staring at me, and when I caught her eye she asked me if I was okay. I gave a bleak nod. I guess I was about as okay as any fifteen-year-old who saw demons could be.

It was easy identifying the demon from Wednesday. A piece of cake, really. And all it cost me was ten dollars.

I went to the building on Harrison Avenue where I'd tracked him to and found it open, and showed the security guard manning the front desk the photo I had snapped of the cleft-chinned demon. I told him I'd seen the guy drop ten dollars outside on the sidewalk, and that I wanted to return it. The security guard gave me a suspicious look, which all but told me that the demon hadn't come in that day, so how could I have seen him drop ten dollars?

"When was this?" he asked.

"Yesterday." I gave the guard a guilty smile. "It fell out of his pocket when he pulled his wallet out. It happened right after he left this building. I should've told him then, but I guess I was going to keep it. I don't know. All night I've been feeling bad about it and I guess I need to return it. Do you know who he is?"

The guard made a face. He didn't want to tell me, but he did. The demon's name was Scott Weston. I then gave the guard my most innocent look and asked if he had an envelope.

"I'm thinking I could seal the ten dollars in it and you could give it to him," I added.

That got the guy moving fast, and when he handed me an envelope he tried hard to keep the larcenous glint out of his eyes. I put a ten-dollar bill inside the envelope and then acted as if I had a change of heart.

"Maybe you could give me his address," I said. "I probably should mail it to him."

"Why would you want to do that?" he asked. "It'd be easier if I gave it to him."

"Forget it." I put the envelope in my pocket and headed for the door. "I'll find it out myself."

"Hold on, hold on." He made a disgusted face as he pulled out a directory and started searching through it. "Here it is," he said. He pointed out the address for Scott Weston. I wrote it slowly on the envelope while at the same time memorizing it. While I did this he was watching on with kind of a hopeless expression. "Kid," he said without much enthusiasm. "If you leave it with me, he'll get it faster. Why risk it in the mail? Someone in the post office opens it up and Mr. Weston never gets his ten dollars back."

Of course, I was planning to leave the ten dollars with him the whole time. That would guarantee he'd never mention anything about me coming to the building to the demon Weston. So I pretended to give the matter some thought, then handed the envelope to the security guard. He had to fight hard to keep the smirk off his face as he took it.

"You'll be sure Mr. Weston gets this?"

"Don't worry about it, kid."

I hesitated for a moment. "What does Mr. Weston do?"

"He's a lawyer."

Why didn't that surprise me? Other demons I'd discovered were lawyers also. I turned and left without looking back, and I was sure that within three seconds of my exiting the building the envelope was ripped open and the ten dollar bill shoved deep into the security guard's pocket. Regardless, it was money well spent. In the past I had paid far more than ten dollars to identify and locate the address for a demon. As far as I was concerned, I got off cheap.

Cornwall's Used Books is not a store you're going to stumble on by accident. Unless you know exactly where you're going it's doubtful you'll find it. It wasn't far from that office building on Harrison Avenue where the demon Weston worked. Walk up Harrison, take a left on Kneeland, then turn down Knapp Street. From there it's a maze of narrow unmarked alleyways before you reach Cornwall's. Even if you get the maze right it would be easy to miss the store, since it's tucked away in the basement of this old dilapidated-looking red brick building, something that must've been at least a couple of hundred years old. If you're not careful you'd walk right past Cornwall's without ever noticing the little sign they have below street-level tucked in a window. As far as I know they don't advertise, and the only reason I found out about the store was that another used bookstore recommended them to me for any books I might be looking for on the arcane arts and the occult, and gave me their phone number. After I called Cornwall's and talked to the owner about the types of books I wanted, he gave me careful directions to the store. I wondered how they stayed in business. I doubted that they got any foot traffic. They must have a very loyal clientele.

The owner is the only person I've ever seen inside the shop, and he isn't what you'd expect for this type of eclectic and odd bookstore. From what I'd been told about Cornwall's, I had my preconceived notions already built up and imagined the owner being a thin bookish man, maybe with long thinning red hair and an aloof look about him. Someone who'd wear a tweed jacket and have trouble looking at you directly. That's not this guy. His last name is Dorthop, and I have no idea about his first name. He's maybe ten years older than my dad. Not that tall, about my height, but with this thick wide body and Popeye-like thick forearms. His face is shaped like a jack-o-lantern, complete with missing teeth. Once when he was staring open-mouthed at me, I was able to count four yellowed and rotting teeth, and that was it. While he's mostly bald, he's far from hairless, with his thick caterpillar eyebrows (and not just any caterpillar, but like the Woolly Bear variety—I know that's an odd association, but I was really into caterpillars when I was ten) and black matted hair that covers his arms and pushes past his shirt collar. He reminds me more of a butcher than a bookstore owner, and his disposition is also more like a butcher's. But he knows his books—if I press him, he talks to me about them, so I've learned a lot from him, including the histories of certain books that most people—really, most bookstore owners —have never heard of.

When I walked into the store, it had the same dank, musty smell it always has. Dorthop was sitting behind the cash register with his face buried in a book. He was wearing what looked like the same T-shirt and khaki pants that he has on every time I go there. Maybe he just has a lot of the same T-shirts and khaki pants, or maybe he never changes them. From the stale muskiness that came off him, it was probably the latter. He looked up briefly to give me a disinterested stare, and then was back to his book.

"Nothing new's been added to the collection since last time you were here," he grunted at me in a thick Boston accent.

"You haven't found a copy of *L'Occulto Illuminato* yet?"

That brought a grim, closed-mouthed smile to his lips. Dorthop never smiled with his mouth open. Probably because of all his missing teeth. *L'Occulto Illuminato*, written in the seventeenth century by Lazzarro Galeotti, is supposedly the most reliable text on the arcane arts, although few know about it. I doubted whether any used bookstore owner in Boston other than Dorthop even had a clue about the book. I'd certainly never heard of it until Dorthop mentioned it to me. After that I was able to find a half-dozen obscure references to it on the Internet. Supposedly the book provides explicit details on the dark beings that have crept into our world, and explains their purpose for doing so. Some of these references claim the book is a myth, others claim that a few dozen copies survived through the centuries. It has basically become my holy grail, and Dorthop knows how badly I want a copy.

"Why don't you leave your phone number and I'll call you if I ever track it down?"

I wasn't about to do that. Call me paranoid, but Dorthop didn't know my name or how to contact me, and I was going to keep it that way. One of these days these demons were going to get smart and start thinking that people like me might try learning more about them through bookstores like Cornwall's. I ignored Dorthop's question the way kids my age are so good at doing, and asked him if it was okay if I checked out the books anyway.

"Knock yourself out."

And then he was back to his book as if I wasn't there.

The interior of Cornwall's was even more of a maze inside than the jumble of alleys you had to walk through to get there. Shelves and stacks of books were everywhere—all of them either history or philosophy, though there was a lot more history. And a good chunk of that was made up of books about wars.

I went through the maze until I came to the wall of books about ancient Egypt. If you pushed on the right side of this wall, it went in and the left side swung out, and inside was a small alcove where Dorthop kept his occult book collection. I don't know exactly why he kept his collection hidden like this, but I had the feeling it was so a demon wouldn't be able to stumble on it.

I pushed on the wall to open it, then once I was inside the alcove, pushed it closed again. It was a small space, but Dorthop kept the area lit, and it probably had more ventilation than the rest of his shop.

All the books were at least fifty years old, and many of them were from the nineteenth century or older. A few were cloth bound, many others leather bound. With some of them, I had my questions about what type of animal was used to provide the leather. Some were in English, but others, like *Daemonologie*, were in foreign languages. These types of books tended not to be translated, and were usually only found in their native languages. Through my research I was always learning about different books that might be of interest, and I carefully went through all the titles that Dorthop had. There were a few that I wanted, but they were too expensive and in languages that I would have to learn, so I decided they could wait until I was through with my translation of *Daemonologie*. I did pick up a couple of the English language books and thumbed through them for a while until I decided I'd had enough. After that I pushed the wall open so I could get out, then closed it after me. I navigated back to the front door and still found no one else in the shop besides Dorthop. He didn't bother looking up from his book, instead murmured out of the side of his mouth to me that he knew I was wasting my time.

"I told you I had nothing new," he grumbled.

"I still would've picked up *Mystere Des Esprits Noirs* if it wasn't so expensive. How about giving me fifty percent off for all the business I've given you?"

"Jean-Francois Berjon. 1857," Dorthop said without any hesitation. He had all of it memorized. Probably every book in that alcove, maybe the whole store. He looked up from his book to give me a quizzical look. "You know French?" he asked.

"One year of high school French. If I buy the book, I'll learn what I need to, just like I'm doing with German now so I can translate *Daemonologie*. No big deal."

His look turned sour as his eyes sort of glazed over. "What's your interest in these books?" he asked.

"I figure I'll become an expert in something no one else knows," I said. Over the last two years I'd learned how to lie very convincingly. I had to, given the work I was doing. "This way after college I can write books, appear on talk shows, and find a nice cushy job in some university."

"You have it all figured out, huh?" His mouth closed into a tight line, and for a moment I thought he was going to add something, maybe warn me about the dangers of what I've been delving into. That my interest in the black arts could be putting me in mortal danger, or that at the very least, I was contaminating my soul with such readings. But whatever interest he might've had in doing this faded, and instead he stuck his face back in the book he was reading. As far as he was concerned I wasn't even there. I left his shop and headed back to lower Washington Street.

Later I was back across the street from those two strip clubs to do another count, standing in the same spot I was at a few days ago. It was quieter than it was when I was there with Wesley— a lot less foot traffic. After only forty minutes of standing there and minding my own business, a police officer approached me. Up to that point I'd had no demon sightings and only counted eighty-seven people. Six men had entered the strips clubs, four men and one woman had exited them. The rest of my count were people walking by the area. The police officer asked me for my name.

"Why?" I said. "I'm not doing anything."

"Yeah? What are you doing here for over an hour?"

"I haven't been here an hour. I've only been here forty minutes."

He gave me this fed up look like he was just itching to hit me. His piggish eyes narrowed to slits and he moved a step closer to me. He was a big blubbery-looking man with a thick red neck and light reddish hair that was shaved close to his scalp.

"What are you doing here?" he demanded, his voice meaner now. He was close enough to me that I could smell his sour breath. Kind of like cat food that had gone bad.

"I'm waiting for someone. Why? Is there a law against that?"

He didn't like my questioning him. A nasty glint sparked in his eyes. "If you're hanging out here looking for trouble then yeah, it's against *my* law. Boy, you better give me your name now."

His hand moved toward his nightstick, and I didn't wait. I took off running, and fuck, he ran after me. I didn't expect that. For some reason I thought he'd let me go, that all he wanted was for me to leave. He looked too fat to want to chase after me, so I didn't think he would, but there he was only a few yards behind me yelling at me, the sound of his footsteps loud and heavy as they pounded the pavement. I risked a glance behind me and saw that he had his nightstick out so he could hit me if given the chance. I was both scared and furious as I ran down Washington Street. I started crying because of how furious I was. Here I was sacrificing my life to do what I had to to protect us from these demons, and this fascist cop had to interfere with me and terrorize me.

With how weak I still was from being sick and my legs so rubbery, I didn't think there was any chance I'd escape him, and I knew deep in the pit of my stomach that he was going to do more than arrest me, probably work me over with that nightstick for making him chase after me.

I could barely breathe I was crying so hard. I was

scared, but my crying was only out of fury. By the time I reached Stuart Street I was so exhausted that I was going to give up when I noticed I was no longer hearing footsteps pounding out behind me. I turned to see that the cop had given up and was standing hunched over with hands on his knees, red-faced and breathing hard. I turned down Stuart Street and forced myself to keep running.

I was near choking with rage that that cop would treat me the way he had. I had moments where I thought of just saying *fuck it* and living my life without worrying about these demons. It just didn't seem fair for a fifteen-year-old to have to worry about something like that, and on top of it having to be chased by some asshole cop?

I continued up Stuart Street to Tremont and cut through three different alleys until I reached Boylston. At times I'd stumble to a stop, too tired and choking in rage to continue, tears and snot streaming down my face. Then I'd force myself to keep going, afraid that that cop might be close behind, or if not him, someone he radioed. The people on the sidewalk that I passed gave me a wide berth. Not one person tried stopping me to see what was wrong—not that I would've let anyone stop me.

It wasn't until I reached Copley Square, which was a good mile and a half from where the cop accosted me, that I was able to stop crying. Instead of getting on the subway, I kept going until I reached the Prudential Center mall. I wanted a chance to use a bathroom so I could clean up, and I was wiped out by the time I got there.

I was a mess. My eyes were red and puffy, my face drawn and pale. I stood frozen for at least a good minute staring at my reflection in the bathroom mirror before bending by the sink and splashing cold water onto my face. I did that for several minutes until I felt calmer, and then moved away from the sink and dried off my face. I had to use toilet paper since the bathroom only had air dryers instead of paper towels. I was still angry, but now it was more at myself than that cop. I guess all the emotional stress of what I've been dealing with ASD must've been building up, because the way I reacted to that cop hassling me was pathetic. I'd actually considered tossing my responsibilities because of one idiotic incident? Pathetic! I must've been on edge for a while, and I'm sure my recent encounter with the demon Hanley didn't help matters. I realized then that I needed to be more aware of the stress I was feeling, and that I needed to manage it better. Maybe start doing some meditation or yoga or something.

I gave one more look in the mirror and didn't much care for what I saw staring back at me, but there wasn't much I'd be able to do about my puffy, red-rimmed eyes. My shirt, though, was stained with tears and dirt, and there was something I could do about that. I stopped off at one of the stores in the mall, bought a cheap T-shirt, and wore it out of the store, tossing my grimy used shirt away. I didn't want to have to deal with my parents catching me sneaking the shirt into the house and questioning me about it.

I took the subway home after that. I caught a few people staring at me, but they all looked away once I caught them. I guess I must've been looking pretty troubled during the ride. After the third time I caught someone looking my way, I got up and moved to the back of the train. At some point I took out my iPhone. I knew my parents had left messages, but I didn't care about that. I wanted to look more at the demon Weston's photo. As I mentioned earlier, demons have claws instead of hands, kind of like what you might see on a hawk, except their claws are much thicker and more grotesque, and their nails long and deadly looking. I wondered how they dressed themselves without shredding their clothing, and in Weston's case how it was that he could tie a Windsor knot with those things. They must just be extremely dexterous.

• • •

You can probably guess that when I got home I wasn't in any mood to get lectured to by my parents, but I was feeling too wasted to do anything other than sit there and take it.

It's past midnight now. I'm tired and am calling it a night. But no worries, I'm not about to shirk my responsibilities regarding these demons. I know what I have to do.

T ODAY JUST PLAIN SUCKED.

I have only a little over a week before school starts and had mapped out where I wanted to do more countings during this little time I had left, but my parents just threw a monkey wrench into the works.

I'd gotten up at seven, put some clothes on, and was going to make myself an espresso before slipping out of the house and heading to Cambridge and Somerville to do more demon watching and counting. Usually on Sunday mornings my parents stay holed up in their bedroom until ten with their CD playing to drown out the noise they're making, but I guess since they had gotten off on each other yesterday morning, I found my parents instead in the kitchen lying in wait for me. My dad wanted to have a heart-to-heart. He and my mom decided that we needed to act more like a family, that the old days of me running off by myself had to end, and that the three of us were going to go to Crane Beach. I didn't worry about this being a long-term problem—I knew they'd lose interest quickly enough—but I couldn't afford to let them mess up my remaining time. I told my dad that it was a good plan, and on principle I could see the value in what he was proposing, but that I already had plans today. He told me tough, and the look he gave me made it clear that I had no choice in the matter. It was a similar look I'd seen on him when he and my mom were considering shipping me out to a military academy.

"This isn't fair," I argued. I could feel my cheeks heating up with anger, and I knew that was wrong. I've been getting angry too easily. Yesterday, right now. If I was going to be any use in dealing with these demons I needed to stay cool and detached. So even as I was confronting my dad, I knew I was making a mistake, and that I needed to get control of my anger. This is something I need to work on. I can't afford to let my emotions get the better of me or I'll be useless against these demons.

"Too bad," my dad said.

"I have commitments for today. Mowing and otherwise. You can't just spring this on me without any warning!"

"Too bad," my mom threw in, her mouth tightening into a harsh line, "because that's exactly what we're doing."

At least I had the presence of mind to realize how badly I almost screwed things up. I had opened the door for them to question me more thoroughly about my plans, and that would've most likely led to me being caught in a web of lies. I realized my tactical error, and was thankful for my mom's spitefulness—otherwise I'm sure my dad would've questioned me, and being a lawyer he would've caught me in some sort of inconsistency. Realizing all of that also made me realize I'd better let this drop, especially given the steely look my dad was giving me.

"Fine," I said. "You want to play family today, we'll play family."

My dad glared at me to let me know I'd better watch it. So we ate a family breakfast of bagels, cream cheese, and espresso and headed off to Ipswich and Crane Beach. I spent most of the time there walking along the shore alone. No demons in bathing suits or bikinis. A complete waste of a day. I couldn't even bring my copy of *Daemonologie* along to do any translating. It's pretty brittle as it is, and if I brought it to the beach it probably would've disintegrated on me. And even if I didn't have to worry about it getting ruined, I certainly didn't want my parents seeing it and questioning me about what *Daemonologie* meant in English or what the book was about. So I had an utterly wasted day, and we didn't get home until twenty minutes ago, because my parents wanted to have dinner at Woodman's in Essex, where the only thing that didn't contain fried clams, fish, or meat was a house salad, onion rings, and corn on the cob. My mom tried to argue that if I ate lobster or fish I wouldn't be breaking my vegetarian vows, but fortunately my dad made her stop. At least I caught on quickly to the situation and didn't complain or act sullenly that day. Things would've only been worse if I had. All I can hope for is that this family unity stuff ends very soon. I know it's only a phase with them, and they'll get tired of it once they get caught up in their high-powered careers, but it sucks when they go on these kicks.

FIFTEEN MINUTES AGO I FOUND THE FOLLOWING MESSAGE FROM Virgil:

> *If you knew about demons you'd know that they look like normal people when you take photos of them. So who are you and what's your game?*

So most likely Virgil isn't a fraud. There's still a chance, though. The thing about demons and photos could've been a wild guess on his part so he wouldn't have to send me a photo, but I don't think it's likely. Which means Virgil is either legit, or he's a demon trying to uncover me. It's a coin flip which one it is, with the slight possibility the coin could end up balanced on its edge.

I sat and tried to think of what to send Virgil next, and what I came up with was the following:

That's true. I wanted to make sure you didn't try photoshopping some monster and trying to pass it off as a demon. But you can still send me a photo you've taken of one of them and the demon's identity and address, as I'm doing here. This way you can verify for yourself that he's a demon, as I'll be able to do with the demon you send me. Tell me about dogs?

I included in the message a photo I had taken a year ago, as well as the demon's name and an address in Revere. I'd checked recently and he was still living there. If Virgil's a demon there's no way he'd be able to track me down from that photo or the information I sent him. If he's like me, maybe it will lead to us figuring out how we can meet and team up.

Virgil's message has left me excited and nervous again. But enough of that.

After my wasted day at the beach I just couldn't get myself psyched enough to tackle *Daemonologie* and instead decided to find something on cable to veg on. I ended up turning on this old John Carpenter movie called *They Live*. I had no idea what the movie was about and it ended up blowing me away. It turns out that these ugly-ass aliens (although they're downright beautiful compared to demons) are living among us and look like everyone else, unless you're wearing these special glasses. If you put these glasses on you can see them for the ugly-ass aliens that they are. Their goal isn't just to live among us but to enslave mankind for their own ends. The star of the movie was some ex-wrestler, and once he found these glasses he felt the responsibility to expose these aliens for what they were to save his fellow man. I found myself caught up in this movie, and at times in tears because I could relate so well to the burden that had been placed on this man, and to the ultimate self-sacrifice he had to make. I also couldn't help thinking whether glasses could be made so that others could see these demons just as I could see them. If I was able to see through their camouflage, maybe others could, too, with the right equipment. The idea of that left me buzzing as I wondered how I could get glasses like that made. There had to be something unique about my eyes, maybe the shape of my corneas, and I was going to have to go to an ophthalmologist and see what they came up with.

I know I'm not going to be able to get any sleep, not with all these ideas from *They Live* buzzing through my head and with how psyched Virgil's last message has left me, so it looks like I'll be cuddling up to *Daemonologie* tonight after all.

I ENDED UP FALLING ASLEEP LAST NIGHT. AROUND FOUR THIRTY I must've conked out, and next thing I knew my parents were waking me up at seven so they could toss another grenade into my plans. More about that soon. Let me tell you first about Ginny Cataldo. She's a little three-and-a-half-year-old girl who was reported missing this morning. According to the TV reports I've been watching she either wandered off or was taken from her preschool in Everett. They have a small fenced-in playground outside the preschool and one minute preschool workers remembered Ginny sitting in a sandbox, the next minute she was gone. This might have nothing to do with demons. The odds are it probably doesn't. Still, I keep thinking of Clifton Gibson and those cages of children they found in that abandoned warehouse in Brooklyn, and all the rumors surrounding what was done to those children. The photo they showed on TV of Ginny Cataldo was of a tiny little girl with big dark eyes and a mess of dark black hair. The thought that she might've been taken by a demon makes me sick. I keep trying to tell myself that's probably not what happened, but I might have to go down to that preschool and check the area to see if I can spot any demons. If I do, I'll track them down and make an anonymous call sending the police to the demon's address, and maybe they'll find Ginny there. I have no idea how to get to Everett, but I'll figure it out.

Now for the grenade my parents tossed. As I mentioned, they woke me up at seven this morning and dragged me out of bed even though I was complaining that I was feeling lousy and needed to sleep more. They ignored my complaints and told me that they wanted us to have breakfast as a *family* and they wanted to talk. It turns out they're still on this big family kick of theirs, that our trip to the beach yesterday didn't quite fill their quota for the year for quality family time, and that they made plans for us to go away to Quebec City from this Wednesday until Labor day. I almost blew my espresso out my nose when they laid that bit of news on me. As it was I singed my nostrils. So there you have it. The precious time I have before school starts is being taken away from me. It wasn't going to do any good arguing with them, but I tried anyway, telling them that I had jobs lined up for the week. My dad gave me this haughty look that he's so damn good at—probably something they taught him in law school—and he told me how it was already decided that since they were reinstating my allowance I would stop my mowing and snow shoveling enterprises. Of course I never agreed to anything like that, but I wouldn't have gotten anywhere trying to argue that with him. So I tried a different tack.

"I can't just leave my customers high and dry like this," I said. "I gave them my word."

My dad rubbed his upper lip as he considered this. He nodded to himself and took a sip of the cappuccino he had made for himself, leaving a line of froth on his upper lip. He carefully wiped it off before telling me that we wouldn't be leaving until Wednesday. "That gives you two days to mow whatever lawns you need to," he added. "But this is the last year you're doing this."

This wasn't a battle I would win now, so I didn't bother trying. Once he got busy at work again he'd drop his uberparent act and ignore me like he'd been doing the last two years, so I nodded my acquiescence, then remembered the movie I watched the other night—the one with the ugly-ass aliens that could only be seen with special glasses—and thought again how I wanted to have my eyes checked out so I could figure out the abnormality I had that allowed me to see demons. If I knew what that abnormality was, I might be able to have glasses made to replicate the same defect so others could see demons, too. I told my mom how I needed to see an eye doctor, using the excuse that I was getting headaches whenever I read for any length of time. I wasn't getting headaches, but it seemed like a good excuse to give her.

"If you weren't staying up so late, you wouldn't be getting these headaches," she told me in response. I just stared at her open-mouthed, not quite believing what I'd just heard. She recovered quickly from that, realizing how bad that would sound if I ever repeated it to anyone, like a teacher. "Fine," she sighed in her well-practiced put-upon manner. "I'll make an appointment for you to have your eyes checked out. Anything else I should know about?"

I didn't think it would do any good to tell her about how her only child also sees demons, so I just shook my head.

So there you have it. My parents ruined my plans for the week. Plans that I can't afford to have ruined, not with what's at stake. This morning I've been mowing lawns, as well as weeding (one of my customers, Lorna Field, has me weed her garden), and I'll be spending the rest of the afternoon doing the same. Tomorrow morning, too. I can't afford to lose my customers, especially since most of them also hire me to shovel their driveways and sidewalks during the winter. Hunting demons isn't cheap. Hopefully I'll be able to finish my jobs by late tomorrow morning, so I can have the afternoon free to check out that Everett neighborhood for demons.

TOMORROW MORNING WE'RE LEAVING BRIGHT AND EARLY FOR Quebec City. I know we're leaving bright and early because I've been reminded three times already in the last forty-five minutes by my mom. Just fucking awesome, huh? And awfully thoughtful of her to keep drumming it in. I can't tell you how excited I am. Yeah, sure. The only thing that doesn't completely suck about this trip is that my parents booked a suite at the Fairmont Le Chateau Frontenac. At least I'll have a separate room so I can continue my translation of *Daemonologie*. I'm not taking my journal, though. I can't afford to have my parents find out about it. So it will stay hidden in my bedroom. Carrying around Schweikert's book is risky enough as it is.

My mom's yelling through the door at me that I'd better turn off my lights and go to bed, that if I'm not up and ready tomorrow morning they'll be dragging me into the car in my pajamas if they have to. I take a deep breath and count silently backwards from five before yelling back that I'll be going to bed soon and for her not to have a cow. I imagine her mouth tightening from that, and can picture the wrinkled lines around her lips that would be showing if it wasn't for her Botox injections, but she doesn't yell anything back.

Let me mention again how much I'm looking forward to spending all this extra quality time with them. What a joke. They'd be happier going off by themselves, and I'd sure be happier being able to stay back here alone so I could do the things I need to do.

I spent the entire day yesterday and this morning taking care of all the lawn work that I would otherwise have spread out through the week. I finished today around noon, and after I had something to eat, I took the subway to Haymarket and then a bus to Everett, which took over two hours. When I found the preschool where Ginny Cataldo was taken from, I saw what must've been several plainclothes police hanging around the area. One of them gave me the stink eye big time, as if I had to be the one who had taken Ginny and for whatever reason had decided to come back to the scene of the crime. I pretended I didn't notice the look he was giving me, but it was pretty clear that if I tried hanging around to look for demons, the police would arrest me. Instead I spent two hours walking around different neighborhoods nearby. No demon sightings. If there are demons living in Everett, I didn't see them. I left at ten minutes past five and didn't get home until seven-thirty. No demon sightings during my travels. All in all, a wasted day. But that's the nature of demon hunting. Most days are wasted days.

And nothing new from Virgil, either. He's probably trying to verify that the demon I sent him is in fact a demon. That's assuming Virgil isn't a demon himself.

I turned on the eleven o'clock local news earlier. Still nothing new about Ginny Cataldo.

A thought has hit me. Hanley might not be fully convinced yet about me, and he might try breaking in during our absence. My parents have a state-of-the-art alarm system for the house, so I don't think he'd be successful if he tried, but still, the thought of Hanley somehow getting into my room and searching through my possessions makes me sick. And if he does and finds my journal, I'm dead. Yeah, I know, I'm being paranoid, but I can't help it. When you're dealing with demons twenty-four seven you tend to get paranoid easily. I have an idea where I can hide the journal so that the demon Hanley would never find it.

SOMEONE—OR I SHOULD SAY *SOMETHING*—SEARCHED MY room while I was gone! I don't how they did it without setting off the house's alarm system, but they did. My heart's pounding so hard in my chest right now that I can feel it in my temples!

I need to take some deep breaths and try to calm down before my heart explodes.

Okay, I've taken some deep breaths. Enough, anyway, for me to slow down and describe as much about the break-in as I can piece together. Before we left for Quebec City, I took precautions and put up safeguards so I'd know if anyone searched my room while I was gone. I placed a small strip of paper between my closet door and the door frame and laid out some hairs across the opening of dresser drawers—stuff like that. At the time I thought I was being overly paranoid, but I put up those safeguards anyway, and every one of them has been disturbed. The small strip of paper is now lying on the floor near my closet, showing that someone had opened the door. Same with my dresser drawers—they've all been opened! Even without these safeguards, I would've known from the smell I picked up when I first walked into my room that my room had been violated. It was faint, but definitely the same sickeningly sweet mix of onion and sulfur that I've caught whiffs of from Hanley and other demons.

How in the world did they get in here without setting off the security system? How? What is it, do these demons possess some sort of supernatural powers where they're not picked up by electronic sensors? The thought of that has me trembling right now. I can't believe this. This is too much. Oh God.

I'm better now. I had to stop again to take more slow, deep breaths, and I've been doing that for the last several minutes, and it's helped. I'm not freaking out that much anymore, and I've calmed down enough so that I can at least think straight. Demons can't just slip in through walls and wander houses undetected by a security system. I know they can't. If they could, Hanley or one of the other demons would've visited my room months ago.

Yes, they got inside our house, there's no denying that, but they didn't do it through supernatural means. It's not like we're the Pentagon. Somehow they figured out how to bypass the security system we use—which probably isn't all that hard if you know what you're doing. I'll do some research later, but not tonight.

Still, no matter how they got into our house—demon power or sheer ingenuity—it's not good news. But it's not worth freaking out over, at least not yet. At least not until I know whether they found my journal. They didn't get into my Mac— I know that. I had the screen password protected, and I can see the most recent login, which was before I left for Quebec City. So at least they didn't get onto my computer. If they had, they might've found the message board where I met Virgil.

I'll get up early enough tomorrow and check the windows and outside door locks and see if they were tampered with, although I'm not quite sure what to check for. Maybe I can find a website that will give me some ideas.

I'm kicking myself for not thinking ahead and buying spy cameras for my room. If only I had, I'd have Hanley dead to rights—or whatever demon he sent in his place. First chance I get I'm buying some spy cameras. I would order some over the Internet right now, but I can't afford for my parents to somehow beat me to opening the package. If that happened, they'd be questioning me relentlessly on why I need spy cameras, and as I've mentioned before, my dad's a lawyer. When he gets his hooks into you, he doesn't give up until he's satisfied that he has squeezed every drop of truth out of you.

Anyone reading this can clearly see that I'm writing this entry on loose sheets of paper. That's because I haven't retrieved my journal yet from where I hid it in the basement. Three thirty in the morning before we left for Quebec City, I snuck down into the basement. I had set my alarm for then, so I'd be sure my parents were asleep before I attempted to smuggle my journal out of my room. All I can do now is hope that that precaution paid off. God help me if the demons found it down there.

I can hear the showers running, so my parents must be in their respective bathrooms. We got back from our trip only twenty minutes ago. We would've been home earlier, but after flying into Logan Airport, my parents wanted to stop in the North End for dinner. I didn't fight them on it. I was hungry, and any Italian restaurant would give me plenty of vegetarian options. Besides, the North End was one of the places I'd like to do more demon counts. In the past I've spotted two demons there. This time none.

While I probably could've gone down to the basement already and retrieved my journal, I don't want to risk running into my parents and having them see how shaky I am. Even now I'm way too shaky to risk it. If they saw me in my current state, they'd question me every bit as relentlessly as if they'd caught me buying spy cameras. Even though I'm not freaking out as much as before, I'm still scared to death, and I'm not going to give them a chance to see me like this. It doesn't much matter if I wait. If the demons found my journal, I'm dead regardless. There's no way around it. I accept it. For the record, I'll be attaching these sheets in the proper place in the journal so anyone finding it can be assured I didn't write any of my journal out of order, nor did I at any time go back and rewrite or change anything. I'm determined to maintain the integrity of my journal, and it will remain an accurate accounting of my struggles with these demons. No fudging, no rewriting.

Okay. I'm taking another deep breath.

If you're wondering about my family's trip to Quebec City, not much of interest to report there. No demon sightings. Not much of anything other than a lot of forced quality time with mom and dad. A lot of walking around. A lot of museums. A lot of eating out. A lot of old buildings, which we have plenty of in Boston. I can't believe I wasted valuable time with this stupid trip when I could've been doing more of what I needed to regarding these demons. I didn't even have that much time alone at night because of all the running around my parents made me do. But I was able to finish my translation of *Daemonologie*. More about that later.

I HAVE MY JOURNAL BACK NOW. I WAITED HALF AN HOUR AFTER the lights went out in my parents' room before sneaking down into the basement, and I found my journal where I had hid it—inside a box of old books, the ones I had as a little kid, well BSD. I can barely remember what it was like to be the carefree kid who read Dr. Seuss and *Curious George* and *Make Way For Ducklings*. The box also has books I read later, like *The Black Cauldron*; *The Lion, the Witch and the Wardrobe*; my Harry Potter books; and the Freddy the Pig books that had originally belonged to my dad and were his favorites—maybe mine, too. My journal was exactly where I'd left it, buried among them, and the safeguards I'd set showed that neither the box nor my journal had been tampered with. All the tension and anxiousness that had been building up inside of me bled out in a rush when I realized my journal was safe. I just sat on the floor and started crying—I couldn't help it. I was so terrified that the demons had found my journal, and I was equally relieved when I discovered they hadn't.

That was a half hour ago. Now I'm back in my room writing this entry. So why did I hide the journal in a box of children's books? My parents have a service clean the house weekly, and they go over it top to bottom dusting everything, so I didn't have to worry about a lack of dust on the box giving me away, since there isn't any dust buildup anywhere—not in the basement or elsewhere in the house. I knew my parents wouldn't be opening up that box unless I was dead—so if something happened to me in Quebec City, they'd find my journal and maybe do something with it. As far as any demon looking inside that box of children's books, I had a gut feeling that the wholesomeness of those books would repel them. Maybe that had nothing to do with it. Maybe whatever demon broke into the house didn't have the time to search the basement. Maybe it was just dumb luck that my journal wasn't found. But I can't shake the feeling that it was the wholesomeness that kept the demon away from that box and my journal.

So about *Daemonologie*. Now that I've finished my translation, my verdict is mixed. There were a lot of places in Schweikert's book where he was clearly passing on superstitions and old wives' tales as fact; or, as my dad likes to say, where he was talking out of his ass. But there were other places where he genuinely seemed to know what he was talking about—like the way dogs and demons are mortal enemies and the strange odor that demons give off—he described that odor exactly as I've smelled it. Schweikert also writes about *L'Occulto Illuminato* as the one true source about demons. He doesn't mention the book—or even the author—by name, but he describes how this *mythological book* that was given birth to in Florence (where Galeotti was born and lived his entire life) does in fact exist and says that he procured a translated copy of it. He writes that after reading several passages, Schweikert recognized it instantly as the truth. According to him, this unholy gospel from Florence was stolen from him before he could read more. The last fifty pages of Schweikert's book chilled me. In these pages Schweikert theorized that after the new millennium, demons disguised as human beings would start to appear in major population areas in the New World for the sole purpose of opening the gates of hell. He didn't know exactly how they would accomplish this, but suggested that Galeotti described their plan in great detail in his *L'Occulto Illuminato*. Or as Schweikert says in his book:

> *The dark Oracle, from the same birthplace as the*
> *Medici and Leonardo Da Vinci, foretells in his*
> *secret book how Satan's minions will bring about*
> *the apocalypses.*

When I read this I had no idea who the Medici were, nor where Leonardo Da Vinci was born, but I guessed it was Florence, and a couple of quick Internet searches showed I was right. There's no doubt about which book Schweikert was referencing. I found it both interesting and disheartening that even in the eighteenth century, *L'Occulto Illuminato* was only rumored to exist (even if Schweikert claimed to have once seen a translated copy). If the book was that rare and hard to find then, how would I get a copy now?

It's almost one o'clock in the morning. In five and a half hours I'll be getting up for my first day as a sophomore in high school. The way I'm feeling right now, I can't imagine sleeping for even one second, and it has nothing at all to do with being nervous about starting tenth grade.

I should also report that I haven't received any new private messages from Virgil, which makes me think he's either a fraud or a demon. He should've been able by now to verify the demon I gave him in Revere. There also haven't been any new developments in the Ginny Cataldo case.

Tuesday, September 6th 10:15 PM

T ONIGHT'S ENTRY ISN'T GOING TO HAVE MUCH TO DO WITH demons, but somehow my first day of tenth grade seems significant enough for me to write about it, if for no other reason than to give anyone finding this journal a better picture of my state of mind. First, let me get the formalities out of the way: no demons sighted at school (you could argue that some of the upper-class dudes were almost big, ugly, and hairy enough to qualify, but none of them came close to approaching the sheer repulsiveness of the average demon, except perhaps Ralph Malphi). No news on Virgil or Ginny Cataldo. *From* this point on I'll only mention when something does happen—if I don't mention any demons, it will be because I didn't spot any. Same will be true about Virgil, and as for Ginny Cataldo, I'm pretty much convinced at this point that demons had nothing to do with her. There just doesn't seem to be any evidence to the contrary.

But first things first. I got out of bed this morning at four thirty. As I expected, I couldn't sleep. My mind was racing, and

I was too much on edge after finding out that a demon had searched my room while we were gone, so instead of tossing in bed for another two hours, I got a flashlight and checked the outside door locks and windows, and if Hanley or one of the other demons had tampered with them I couldn't tell. After I gave up on that, I came back inside and watched *Spider-Man* for about the thousandth time. It helped calm me down. At six-thirty I washed up and dressed and was going to grab a granola bar and an apple on my way out, but my mom surprised me by having breakfast ready for me. Oatmeal with blueberries and maple syrup. I can't complain, though it was the first time in over two years that she'd had breakfast ready for me on a school day. I can't imagine that this new kick of hers will last long—soon enough, I'll be back to being an afterthought as far as she's concerned.

Newton North is about three miles from my house. An easy bike ride, but instead of riding my bike I took the school bus, which meant taking a detour through several yards so I wouldn't walk past the demon Hanley's house. I just wasn't up to seeing him this morning—not that I'm up to it any morning, but especially not these days. Not only do I have to pretend that I think he's only a perv, and not a demon, but I can't let him know that I think that he (or one of his minions) broke into my house.

Usually I always ride my bike to school—at least when it's not raining or sleeting out. I like the freedom of it, and it saves time when I'm going into Boston or Cambridge after school for demon hunting. I didn't realize at the time why I had decided to take the school bus this morning—or if I did realize my true reason I lied to myself about it. But I guess I did it hoping I'd run into Sally Freeman. Thinking about seeing her again was part of the reason I didn't sleep last night. It was all for nothing, though. I didn't see her waiting at the stop or on the bus. Her parents or someone else must've given her a ride.

Wesley and Curt were both at the bus stop. Wesley still must've been mad at me over our last bike ride because he gave me this cold, aloof nod while mumbling *hey*, just like he used to do during those years when our friendship had drifted apart, and otherwise he kept his distance while we waited for the bus. I was too anxious about both demons and Sally Freeman to worry about him being upset with me, and also too busy listening to Curt tell me how he had officially converted to worshipping Yog-Sothoth. Of course, Curt was just being his usual suburban Goth self. Yog-Sothoth isn't an actual religion, but instead an ominous deity that H.P. Lovecraft created in *The Dunwich Horror*. It had been over three weeks since I had last seen Curt, and he looked pretty much the same as he has every time I've seen him over the last two years; as heavy and shapeless-looking as always. As usual he wore his rich-kid suburban Goth uniform, which consisted of a black T-shirt and black pants—which didn't help matters as far as his general blob-like shapelessness went. Part of the reason I hadn't seen him in three weeks was that it would've been pointless to have invited him along for one of my demon spottings, since he would never have been willing to ride a bike any distance, or even walk around Boston or Cambridge if we were to take the subway. Curt was allergic to any physical activity, especially the voluntary kind. Not that strenuous exercise would necessarily send him into anaphylactic shock, but it would come pretty close. Every week for the last two years, he's found a way to conjure up a note excusing him from gym class.

Curt's naturally yellow hair was dyed ink black, and he was wearing black eye-liner and black lipstick. He'd drawn some strange little symbols on his knuckles, which he said were related to the *Cthulhu* mythos, which was also created by Lovecraft. While I never read Lovecraft, or really any Goth or demonology fiction (I'm too involved as it is to want to spend any additional time immersing myself in any fiction on the subject), I tried to pay attention to Curt as he told me about Yog-Sothoth. Some of what he was talking about reminded me of Schweikert's book—Yog-Sothoth's connection with the old ones, his being the guardian of the gate that lets them back into our world. This was similar to Schweikert's warnings about the demons trying to open the gate to hell. I'd been working on a theory that many of the mythologies that work their way into fantasy and supernatural literature—like from H.P. Lovecraft and Robert E. Howard—originate from a universal consciousness and have a greater level of truth to them than anyone realizes. That's why I like listening to Curt when he tells me about these weird-ass books he reads; it keeps me from having to spend my time reading these same books.

When the bus came, Wesley got on quickly without waiting for me and Curt. Wesley and Curt were more friends through me than any sort of organic friendship that might've formed between the two of them, and when Curt saw Wesley getting on the bus without us, he assumed Wesley was doing it to avoid him and his Goth appearance—not me. Maybe he thought Wesley was trying to make a clean break from him in an attempt to become more popular in high school. Whatever he was thinking, his mouth squeezed into a hurt, tiny oval, but otherwise he didn't comment. Wesley took a seat in the middle of the bus, and Curt and I sat together four rows back.

The bus had only driven two blocks when Ralph Malphi got out of his seat to put Wesley in a headlock, all the while taunting him, saying stuff about how faggots like Wesley weren't allowed to take seats on the bus without his permission. Malphi was two years older than us. It was a pleasure not having to see him while we were in middle school, and last year when we started high school, Malphi would pick on Wesley, and occasionally on Curt, but would leave me alone. Even when I was in third grade and he was in fifth, he was this big, ape-like kid, much bigger than the rest of us, and now it was worse. He was enormous, much hairier and uglier, with a wide face that had al-

most no forehead. Instead of two eyebrows, he had a thick connecting unibrow, and there was a cruelty shining in his eyes as
he leered at the rest of us and played up the torment that he
heaped on poor Wesley. This must've been exceptionally galling
for Wesley, especially since there were now younger kids on the
bus that Malphi could've targeted, and I felt sorry for him as he
begged and pleaded for Malphi to let go of him, his voice near
tears, which only made Malphi tighten his headlock on him. At
that moment I spoke up, telling Malphi to let go of him. Malphi
opened his eyes wide to give me this exaggerated look of surprise, as if he couldn't believe anyone on the bus would dare to
speak up to him.

"Fuck, you're ugly," I said. "Maybe not the ugliest thing
I've ever seen, but you're damn close."

He let go of Wesley and stared at me with this angry, puzzled look as if he were trying to remember who I was. I noticed
then that his hands were thick and massive, almost the size of
baseball gloves, his knuckles every bit as hairy as his unibrow.
The fake puzzled look in his eyes faded as he played up his act
of remembering who I was, since I couldn't possibly be important enough for him to bother knowing. What was left in his
piggish eyes was something cruel and malicious.

"You're asking for the same treatment, huh, scrub?" he
asked. He took a step towards me, and then turned to leer at the
rest of the bus over what he was going to do to me.

"I sure hope not," I said. "Your armpit stink would
probably kill me."

That got some of the other students laughing. Not Curt,
though. He was too close in proximity, and he sat terrified that
he might end up a recipient of some spillover violence from Malphi. My crack certainly enraged Malphi. His face reddened and
his eyes narrowed to knife slashes. He started moving towards
me while I braced myself, ready to attack one of his vulnerable
areas. Part of my demon routine was studying self-defense on

my own, and if Malphi got close enough, I was going to strike him in either the throat, groin, or go for his eyes. Of course he didn't have much of a target with his throat since he had almost no neck, but I'd take advantage of whatever I could. Before I had a chance, though, the bus came to an abrupt stop.

The bus driver had pulled the bus over and now stood in the aisle. The driver was a beefy middle-aged woman, probably my mom's age. She pointed a thick, stubby index finger at Malphi.

"You," she ordered in a gravelly voice that must've been ruined by an untold number of cartons of cigarettes. "Off my bus now!"

Malphi's mouth dropped open as he stared incredulously at her. For one stunned moment he said nothing, then he sputtered, "But we're not at the school yet. What am I supposed to do?"

"Walk!"

He didn't like that. He started to shake his head, but when the bus driver took a menacing step towards him, his expression turned pinched as he resigned himself to the situation. He turned to point at me and petulantly complained that I was the one who started everything.

"I was minding my own business when this jerkoff had to snap at me, calling me names. Totally unprovoked!"

"That's not true. I have a rearview mirror. Get off my bus. Now!"

The way the bus driver stood with her hands on her hips, I could see how big her forearms were. They were massive, maybe even bigger than Dorthop's, the owner of Cornwall's Bookstore. I was sure Malphi noticed the same, and probably the last thing he wanted was to be manhandled by a woman bus driver in front of an audience of other students. Reluctantly, he trudged forward, but not without first telling me I was dead. I shrugged and told him he was still ugly. That drew some laughter from some of the other students, but it was a nervous kind. Malphi shot me one more death stare, and then he was off the bus.

As the bus drove off, I looked back to watch Malphi trudge along after us, a dark fury muddling his face.

"I don't think that was a smart thing to do," Curt said, a queasy, scared look still on his face.

"Eh, I deal with more dangerous cretins every day," I said. "Besides, if Malphi causes us anymore problems, you could always summon *Cthulhu* to our rescue."

Curt gave me a look as if I was crazy. He repeated again how I shouldn't have pissed off Malphi like that, and after that he stayed quiet the rest of the ride, which was fine with me. I didn't feel like listening to any more talk about Yog-Sothoth.

After the bus pulled up to the school and we all departed, Wesley hung around by the front of the bus waiting for Curt and me to catch up with him. His face was still mottled purple from the headlock Malphi had put on him, and there were imprints from Malphi's arm left on his cheek. In a voice that sounded like he was still fighting to keep from crying, he thanked me for helping him with Malphi. I nodded as if of course I would do that. Wesley then walked with us into the school. Once inside Curt left us to find his homeroom while Wesley and I continued walking together.

"That was so uncool of you ditching me like that in Boston," Wesley said once Curt was out of earshot.

"Yeah, well, I'm sorry and all that, but I couldn't help it."

"Why couldn't you help it?"

I hesitated. I wasn't going to tell him anything, but I relented and said, "One of these days maybe I'll be able to tell you."

Wesley gave me a sad look, as if something was wrong with me. I bit my tongue so I wouldn't say anything else, and we walked in silence for another minute or so with all the other students jostling past us in the hallway before Wesley asked me again about the picture I took of the demon Weston.

"What did you do with that picture?" he asked in a hushed voice so no one could overhear him. "If you did something illegal with it, you need to tell me. I could be an accomplice."

He had such a worried look on his face that I had to tell him not to worry about that picture—that it was taken for the good of mankind, not for evil purposes. I shouldn't have included that last part. It was stupid of me to say that, but I was operating on no sleep and the recent viewing of *Spider-Man*, and that movie always has its effect on me.

Wesley gave me another sad, worried look. Shaking his head, he said, "Henry, you need to stop living in this fantasy universe you're stuck in. You're not out there saving the world from evil forces like you think you are."

I laughed at—partly out of nervousness that he somehow had an idea of what I was up to (even if he thought it was only insane nonsense on my part), and partly that someone who lived as much of his life in comic books as Wesley did would lecture me about living in a fantasy world.

"Don't worry about me," I told him. "I know what's reality and what isn't."

His eyes dulled enough to show that he didn't fully believe me, but he didn't say anything else and we soon separated to go to our respective homerooms. It wasn't hard to find them since they had the building color-coded. When I walked into mine, my heart nearly stopped. Sally Freeman was sitting in the front row. God, she was beautiful. She still had those large brown eyes and dimples and long brown hair, and she had that same little overbite that Mary Tyler Moore used to have on that old show. Even though she was sitting down and wearing a bulky sweater jacket, I could tell she had a slender, athletic body. Our eyes met and she also recognized me instantly. She gave me a smile that turned my knees to water. I wanted to smile back and sit next to her, but instead I kept my face a blank and nodded *hey* to her and took a seat a couple of rows behind her.

My head was pounding as I sat there, and all my old foolish feelings of longing for Sally came rushing back. I tried telling myself that I didn't sit next to her because I couldn't afford to have a girlfriend. That my responsibilities with the demons were too great to allow myself to have a girlfriend. That's what I tried telling myself, but I knew the real reason: I was a coward. How's that for irony? I'm chosen to see these demons as they really are and have to come face to face with them and have all the responsibilities associated with that heaped on my shoulders, and here I was too much of a coward to sit next to a fifteen year-old girl. I wanted to get up and take one of the seats next to her—wanted it so badly—but I couldn't force myself to do it, and soon it was too late because a plump frizzy-haired redheaded girl and an ultra-preppy-looking boy took the open seats and sandwiched her in. I hated myself right then. God, I was pathetic.

The rest of the homeroom period was pure misery for me as we went through orientation for the year. We already had our schedules for our core classes, but as tenth graders we now had the option of electing out of Spanish or French and picking a different foreign language. I glanced around the room. Six of the twenty-some-odd kids in the homeroom had been friends of mine BSD; one had been on my seventh grade Little League team. Now the ones who looked my way did so as if I was a freak. None of them bothered saying anything to me or even nodding to me. Just dull, empty stares. A few of them whispered stuff to the other kids sitting next to them. Fine, I didn't care. It was all part of the sacrifice I had to make, same with why I couldn't be near Sally. Still, though, it made the orientation miserable, knowing that she was in the same room as me and all I could do was stare at the back of her head. If we were sitting together, we'd be able to compare our class schedules and sign up for the same foreign language study. It was pure torture, and it became even worse when I saw the preppy kid buddying up with her and telling her about his class schedule, just as I should've been doing.

Finally the hour-long orientation ended. I knew I had to switch homerooms. It would be difficult enough knowing Sally was in the same high school as me, but it would be impossible for me if I had to see her every day, especially if she got together with the preppy kid. I was steeling myself to that realization when I felt a hand touch me lightly on my shoulder. I looked up to see Sally grinning at me. My insides just turned to slush. I hadn't noticed her walking over to me. For the last five minutes I'd been staring intently at my desk as if I were trying to burn a hole through it, terrified I'd catch Sally and preppy boy walking out of the room holding hands. I could live if I never saw Sally again, but seeing something like that would kill me.

"Henry, I can't believe it's you! I haven't seen you since sixth grade! And we're in the same homeroom!"

I forced myself to give her this look as if I was trying to place her. "Oh yeah. Sally . . . Sally Freeman. Hey, that's right. I think Wesley might've said something to me about seeing you. How are you doing?" I stumbled out trying to sound nonchalant, but my voice cracked at the end, showing what a liar I was. Sally almost broke out laughing, but she kept it contained in her eyes. They were dazzling eyes, which turned my knees and legs into the same helpless jelly that my insides had become.

"It's such a shame you didn't recognize me," she said, her lips pursing in an amused way. "If you had, you could've sat next to me and saved me from being bored to death by Lucas Anderson. Uggh!" She took the seat next to me, and even though my heart had already turned to slush it still pounded like crazy. I didn't know if she was wearing any perfume—she probably wasn't—but she smelled every bit as wonderful as she looked. Kind of like lilacs mixed with sea breezes. I was *definitely* going to have to change homerooms. There's just no way I could focus on demons if I was constantly thinking about Sally. Which I would be.

"If we'd sat together, we could've compared our class schedules," Sally continued, her lips forming a slight frown. She handed me her class schedule for her core curriculum, and I did the same. Her brow furrowed when she saw we weren't in any of the same classes. I felt a pang of regret, but also some relief. "That's too bad," Sally said with genuine disappointment in her voice, "we're not in any of the same classes. What foreign language did you pick?"

I mumbled out that I had signed up for Italian, my voice barely working enough for me to do that.

"Me too! That's amazing that we both picked Italian. I've always wanted to travel to Florence and Venice. It just sounds so cool and romantic. I'm hoping to be able to go Junior year. This is so great that you're taking it, too. We'll have to study together!"

The way she looked, the way she smelled, and the fact that she was inches away from me made me so dizzy that I thought I might pass out. I lied and told her sure, we could study together, and that I signed up for Italian for the same reasons she did, hoping also to go there my Junior year. My real reason was in case I ever got my hands on a copy of *L'Occulto Illuminato*. I knew that was a crazy reason to take Italian, since the odds were so small that I'd ever find a copy. Even if I did, it was possible the book was written in Latin, despite the Italian title. I almost continued on with French instead so that I could translate Berjon's *Mystere Des Esprits Noirs*, which I knew I could get a copy of, but I switched to Italian on impulse. Since there was only one first-year Italian class, I was going to have to switch back to French, *and* change homerooms.

A throat-clearing sound from up front interrupted us. It was the homeroom teacher not-so discreetly getting our attention to let us know we were alone in the room with her; that all the other students had already gone to their first class since the bell had rung several minutes earlier. From the heat burning up my cheeks, I knew I was blushing as Sally and I walked out of the room together and our fingers accidentally brushed for a moment. Or at least accidentally on my part. She didn't show any indication that we had had that physical contact. Instead, she just looked happy and excited, and stayed close by my side until it was time for us to split up to go to our different classrooms.

Not much else to report about my first day of tenth grade. I tried concentrating on my classes, but my thoughts kept drifting back to Sally. That wasn't good. I knew I was going to have to avoid future contact with her, or I'd be lost.

If Ralph Malphi was looking for me, he didn't find me. But that was understandable. Newton North is a large high school, with over three thousand students. I wasn't in the mood to deal with him after school ended, so instead of taking the bus, I walked home, and afterwards rode my bike to Watertown so I could buy some spy cameras. When the school bus passed by I heard Malphi yell out the window that I was dead. I didn't care. I was too busy thinking of Sally. I knew I couldn't afford to do that, that I had more important things to think about. But I couldn't help myself.

MY EYES ARE NORMAL. THE OPHTHALMOLOGIST USED A VIDEO-keratography computer to create a complete corneal imaging of my eyes. No defects, nothing oddly shaped, nothing to explain why I see demons that other people don't.

Of course, for my mom, not any ophthalmologist would do. She wanted only the best, so she wouldn't be embarrassed in front of her friends. Which was why she arranged for me to see a leading specialist in downtown Boston. She didn't go with me, obviously, but she put on a show last night of acting the concerned mom, probably for my dad's sake.

"Henry," she told me, "while you don't need me to, if you'll feel more comfortable, I'll come with you, you know I will. The doctor's office is only a several minute walk from the Government Center subway stop."

A flash of anxiousness showed in her eyes while she sat hoping I wouldn't double-cross her, but she probably knew I wanted her to accompany me even less than she did herself. I let her off the hook and told her I'd be fine going myself.

My appointment was at ten thirty, which meant I would be missing school, but my mom needed to have the right *chichi* doctor for me, and Dr. Robert Gelman fit the bill and was a busy man and hard to schedule appointments with, and she wasn't about to face the social stigma of having me see a lesser ophthalmologist just so I wouldn't have to miss school. When I got to Dr. Gelman's office, a technician performed half a dozen tests, including a corneal topography. After that I waited forty-five minutes before I was brought in to see Gelman. He was in his late fifties. Tall, broad shouldered, full head of silver hair, and looked a lot like Tom Selleck without a mustache, except that he didn't dye his silver hair black. He smiled patiently as he looked over the test results and then peered into my eyes as he shined a penlight into them, and finally tested my vision. I was crestfallen when he told me my eyes were perfect. If I was seeing demons because of a physical deformity, then that would've been only a random event, something that could've happened to anyone. Maybe I would've been able to replicate the deformity with a pair of special glasses like they did in *They Live*, maybe not, but at least the fact that I saw demons when others didn't wouldn't have meant anything. But if it wasn't physical, then it was something else—like I had been chosen by a higher power and for a higher purpose. The responsibility I'd been feeling ever since I accepted that Hanley and the others were truly demons was real.

"Are you sure there's nothing wrong with my eyes? Nothing out of the ordinary? Nothing oddly shaped?"

"No, nothing at all wrong with them, Henry. You have perfect eyesight and perfectly shaped corneas." He gave me an inquisitive, yet patient smile. "You seem disappointed?" His smile shifted from patient to patronizing as he considered me. "You may need to get more sleep at night," he said. "Or possibly take more breaks from your reading. Try to remember to simply close your eyes every ten minutes for a few seconds of rest. But your eyes are fine."

So that was it. It was noon when I left his office. Lower Washington Street where the strip clubs were was only a fifteen minute walk away, and I made my way over there thinking I'd do another demon count, although this time with a more heightened awareness of any cops in the area. After a half hour of counting the number of suited guys and lowlifes walking into and past the clubs (but trying hard to look like I wasn't loitering) I lost my enthusiasm for doing a demon count and I left the area. Cornwall's was close by, and it had been two weeks since I'd been there, but I didn't even have the enthusiasm for that. Instead I bought some pizza for lunch, then picked up a couple of Dark Knight comic books and read them on the subway back to Waban, which was one of the few pure kid things I'd let myself indulge in since seeing demons.

I KNOW. IT'S BEEN A WHILE SINCE I'VE WRITTEN. I'LL EXPLAIN the reason for that soon.

How to begin? This is difficult, much more so than I ever imagined, but it's important that I give a full accounting. Even though this entry won't have any additional information regarding demons, it's still significant—maybe my most significant entry yet.

I didn't change homerooms. I didn't switch out of my Italian class. Everyday I've been walking to school—not just to avoid Malphi (whom I still haven't seen, although Curt tells me he's looking for me), but because Sally's mom drives her to school each morning, and Sally's been getting her to stop and pick me up. That's why I haven't been riding my bike. If I did, I'd be missing out on time with Sally, and I can't get myself to do that. We walk home together, too. And sit together in homeroom. And have lunch together every day in the cafeteria. We'd be sitting together in our Italian class, too, if the teacher didn't

make us sit in assigned seats. You're probably thinking this is
pathetic on my part. Maybe it is, but I can't help it.

Each day after school I walk with Sally until I'm a couple
of blocks from my house, then we separate so I can cut through
yards, which allows me to get home without passing by the
demon Hanley's house, and Sally continues on to her home.
Today she asked me if I'd come over to her house with her so
we could study Italian together, and I told her I would. It got
quiet after that as we continued walking. Not an uncomfortable
quiet, but an intense quiet. I didn't quite understand the reason
for it, but I felt a hotness throughout my body. When I looked
at Sally, I could see an intensity burning in her eyes, her face pale
and very serious. She looked younger then. Without realizing it
her hand found mine and the rest of the way we held hands, hers
small and almost feverish in mine.

Sally lives off of Waban Avenue, which is on the south
side of Beacon Street, past Waban Square and Angier School. The
houses on her street were far more modest than the McMansions
my parents and most of our neighbors owned. They seemed more
real—like what houses should be. Her parents' house was a ranch
style, which Sally told me was built in the fifties. It was much
smaller than my parents', but I liked it better—it felt more solid
and substantial. Sally took me to her room. It had such a girly,
feminine feel to it, the bed covered with this big, fluffy quilt,
everything surrounded by stuffed animals and pillows and other
frilly things. It just felt so perfect for Sally, and it smelled wonderful too, just like she did. I couldn't believe I was there alone
with her. No one else was in the house. I tried not to think of
that. Instead I sat on the beanbag chair opposite her bed, and
took out my Italian course book while Sally sat cross-legged on
her bed, also with her course book out. And we spent the next
twenty minutes reading our assigned lesson and talking about it.

I found myself feeling better than I've ever felt in my life
being in that room with her. More than that, it felt so right. But

I also felt as if my skin was burning up even hotter than before. And when I looked at Sally, at how beautiful and natural and relaxed she looked sitting on her bed, I got an erection. I couldn't help it. It was embarrassing, and I tried hiding it with how I sat and with how I held my textbook. I tried making myself think of something else—demons, anything—but it didn't help. In my mind's eye all I could see was Sally sitting cross-legged on her bed, her long brown hair hanging over her left eye.

There was a tug on my textbook. Sally had left her bed and was on the floor next to me and was taking my text book out of my hands. I let her. I didn't say anything as she smiled wickedly at me and started to unzip my pants. It was only when she reached inside them that I squirmed and told her we shouldn't be doing this.

"It's no big deal," she said, her smile growing. "I want to do this. And you'll like it."

"We're too young."

"I'm not." Her fingers grazed my penis and felt how hard it had become, and her smile turned impish. "And Henry, you're clearly not either. *Siediti. Godetevi.*"

She was telling me in Italian to sit back and relax. We hadn't gone over those verbs yet in class, so she must've been planning this ahead of time. I knew those words only because I'd been studying extra in case Cornwall's found a copy of *L'Occulto Illuminato*, and I was six chapters ahead. I did as she asked, and found myself terrified but also filled with this intense longing for her. What I was most terrified about was that I would disappoint and disgust Sally, that she'd want nothing to do with me after this. That this was some sort of test of character and I was failing it miserably. But I couldn't push her away, and soon she had my penis out and her tongue and then lips on it, while her large brown eyes remained fixed on mine.

It was the look in her eyes that did the trick more than anything else, and it was over almost before it started. Sally was finishing up when we heard the front door being opened and Mrs. Freeman calling out to see if Sally was home. Sally had left the door to her room wide open and her face flushed with excitement over the prospect of us getting caught. She giggled and flashed me this smile as if we were co-conspirators in some great crime. Whatever was left of my erection disappeared instantly. By the time Sally's mom stuck her head in the door, I was zipped up with the Italian course book in my hands, and Sally was back sitting cross-legged on her bed. Sally smiled innocently and told her mom that we were studying together.

Mrs. Freeman gave Sally and then me this icy stare, as if she were trying to penetrate our minds. Somehow I held it together, but when she inhaled deeply, I thought I might pass out. I was sure she'd be able to smell what had just happened seconds earlier. Coldly, she told me that I needed to head home, that she wanted to talk to her daughter alone. I tried to act as innocently as Sally looked as I put my book back into my backpack and pushed myself off the beanbag chair. Mrs. Freeman had to step aside so I could go past her. When I got to the door I nodded so long to Sally, who did the same, looking as innocent as if all we'd been doing was studying. My heart was pounding so hard in my chest that I could barely hear above it.

I felt sick to my stomach as I walked home. Sally's mom must've known what had happened. If she hadn't smelled the aftereffects of sex, she'd probably find signs of it on the beanbag chair. I didn't care about what trouble I might get into, but I was terrified that I'd be banned from seeing Sally again. The thought of that made me nauseous.

Sally called me fifteen minutes ago on her cell phone. We're in the clear. Her mom doesn't want us alone together in her bedroom again, but if she suspects anything she kept it to herself. I almost burst out crying I was so relieved, but somehow I managed to play it cool. Sally ended the call by telling me how she couldn't wait to see me again.

So you can see why this is significant. There's no hope for me. I can't do this demon stuff anymore. Not after what happened today. I can't give Sally up. It's just not fair to ask me to.

It wasn't fair to give this responsibility to a thirteen-year-old boy in the first place. I tried over the last two and a half years. I really did, but I just can't do this anymore. At this point I'll try to find Virgil and figure out if he's legitimate or not. If he is, I'll give him this journal and hope it helps him. If he's not, then that's that. When I see Hanley and other demons, I'll just pretend they're like everyone else. There's nothing else I can do.

I'll keep this journal going until I'm able to figure out what's up with Virgil, and then I'm out.

VIRGIL MIGHT BE DEAD. FORGET *MIGHT*. I'M CONVINCED HE is—well, at least ninety-nine point nine percent convinced. That's not all. Another nearly four-year-old kid was taken. This time a boy. I'll explain about Virgil first.

Late last Thursday night I sent Virgil another message. I was getting antsy thinking about him. I don't want this demon stuff hanging over my head, so if Virgil was on the level and also saw demons, I wanted to give him my journal—after first expunging all references to my identity, which would have to include all mention of the demon Hanley. If Virgil gave me a name and address that checked out, I'd hide my journal somewhere in Boston, send him a message letting him know where he could find it, and at that point I'd be done. If Virgil ended up being a demon, that would be unfortunate. But at least I would've tried.

That was my plan. I don't want months to go by only to have Virgil contact me out of the blue and drag me back into this demon business. To use an expression my dad likes to re-peat, I want to wash my hands of it once and for all.

I know what you're thinking. I could've just gotten rid of my message board account, and I would've been done with it. But I couldn't do that. Not with the possibility of giving my jour-nal to someone who sees demons the way I do. So I sent Virgil a second message, and then checked Friday morning and late Fri-day night to see if he had sent anything back. Nothing. Same with Saturday, Sunday, and this morning. Again nothing. Then today when I got home after spending the afternoon with Sally I saw on the Internet the story of a nearly four-year-old boy taken from his mother during a carjacking in Chelsea. Chelsea and Revere are close enough to each other that that made me start thinking more about Virgil, about whether something might've happened to him. And that led me to an article buried in the back pages of the *Boston Globe* from two and a half weeks ago.

> *September 2nd. Revere. Revere Police and the US Coast Guard found a body late last night off of Revere Beach. Police received a call just after 8 p.m. about a possible sighting of a body in the water. The State Police working in conjunction with the Revere Police had dispatched a marine unit, a dive team, and a helicopter for the search. The Coast Guard said in a statement that a 47-foot utility boat and a 25-foot rescue boat were to assist at the scene.*
>
> *The victim was not identified. A Revere Police spokesman, Walter Jenson, warned how this tragedy underscores the dangers of drinking and boating.*

The article gave no clue whether the victim was a male or female, the age, or anything else, but I didn't know anything about Virgil either, so none of that mattered. After more searches I found another article that ran in the September 5th edition of the *Globe*. The police had ruled the death an accidental drowning, with the victim a thirty-four-year-old male, with a blood alcohol level of point two percent. The body was found less than a mile from the address of the demon that I had given Virgil. I had no concrete evidence, but I knew instantly that this person's death was no accident. It had to be Virgil. Somehow the demon had discovered Virgil spying on him and had known that he'd been seen for what he was. That's what had to have happened. After that the demon must've subdued Virgil and made him drink that alcohol before drowning him in the ocean. I suspected this immediately, but once I saw that the police had identified the victim and what his name was, I knew it was my Virgil. *Vincent Robert Gilman*. Get it? He used his name to form his message board identity. *VI* from Vincent, *R* from his middle name, and *GIL* from his last name. When I read more about him, there was no doubt. The article stated that Vincent Gilman was a loner with no wife or girlfriend. According to his parents, he had been an outgoing boy until the age of thirteen, when he suddenly became withdrawn and aloof. Later as an adult, he worked odd jobs and had the reputation of being an eccentric; someone who kept to himself and always carried a camera with him as he walked the streets. There were hints in the article that he probably suffered from schizophrenia, although the writer begrudgingly admitted he had never been diagnosed as having any mental illness. Real nice of them to make those innuendos, huh?

Nobody they talked to knew why he would've been at Revere Beach that night. According to his parents, he had never demonstrated any interest in boating or the ocean, and nobody knew of any friends there or anywhere else. But I knew the reason. Vincent Gilman had dedicated his life to trying to do something about these demons, and because of that he was now dead, dismissed as an unbalanced loner who had most likely been mentally ill. Of course, I couldn't prove that this was the same man who had contacted me on the message board as Virgil, but I knew it was, just as I knew that his fate was the very same one in store for me if I kept trying to battle these demons. There was just no way of winning that battle. No way for any one person to do that, especially a fifteen-year-old boy.

Even though I had decided to give up this demon business, understanding that Virgil had not only been legit but was now dead left me in a cold, dark despair. I had never felt so alone as I did right then. To think that there had been someone else like me, and now that person was dead and gone and that I was in a way responsible for his death . . . I wanted to burn this journal and bury its ashes. I wanted to get rid of any trace that I'd ever admitted to seeing demons. But I couldn't. As much as I wanted to be done with this I couldn't force myself. I was happy being with Sally, with being normal again. But then I thought about the abducted boy. The boy might not have anything to do with Ginny Cataldo. And both of these abductions might be isolated incidents without any connection to these demons. But how could I just ignore this after the demon who masqueraded as Clifton Gibson and the evil that happened in Brooklyn? This could be the same thing all over again, except now happening in the Boston area.

There's not much to say about the abduction of the boy, Trey Wilkerson. The news reports so far have been sketchy. Trey's two months short of his fourth birthday. His mother had him strapped into the child seat in the back of a beat-up 1998 Chevy Malibu. She had the car parked in a strip mall parking lot in Chelsea, and as she opened the driver's side door, she was rushed from behind and thrown down, and the car was then driven off. Whoever did this didn't bother with her pocketbook, and I checked the Blue Book value of the car, and it's under three thousand dollars. It's possible all the carjacker wanted was the car, but he must've seen her strapping Trey into the back child seat. Who'd risk a kidnapping charge on a beat-up Chevy Malibu? The car wasn't the target. It was the boy. And I can't help thinking that his abduction was connected with Ginny Cataldo—especially with the ages of both of them so close to the demon Clifton Gibson's victims. I can't shake this sickening feeling that demons are responsible for this. That they're trying to finish whatever they were interrupted with in Brooklyn.

So that's why I can't just burn this journal. I have to try to find someone else like me. Someone who sees them. I don't know what good it will do, but I have to at least try. Maybe I can run another ad, and then I'll be *really* finished.

Unrelated to this demon business. I've been riding my bike every day to school now. I've been doing this so I won't get picked up by Sally's mom when she drives Sally each morning. Sally thinks I'm being ridiculous, but I just can't imagine sitting there in the car with her mom, not after what she almost caught Sally and me doing that afternoon, and especially not after what Sally and I have been doing after school every day in the woods behind a private golf course. I can't shake the thought that if I got in the car, her mom would start questioning me and I'd crack.

So now I ride my bike each morning, and Sally waves to me when she and her mom drive past, an impish grin etched on her face. After school each day, she squeezes onto the bike seat with me and holds on tight as I pedal her first to the golf course and then later to her house, although I let her off a block away so her mom doesn't catch us.

I also know Ralph Malphi is still looking for me. Curt brings it up almost every day, and Wesley's been talking about it, too. I know they're both jealous of me and Sally, but when I see them in the hallway they try to act as if nothing's going on, and I don't tell them anything.

But they tell me about the threats Malphi's been making. I've seen Malphi a couple of times in school hallways, but I'm always able to see him before he sees me and have been able to avoid him so far. It's not because I'm afraid of that knuckle-dragging Neanderthal. Part of me wants to confront him and be done with him—but I also don't want the consequences of what would happen if I stood up to him, because I certainly wouldn't just stand there acting defenseless. If I confronted him I'd probably end up being suspended from school, and I'm not going to let that happen. Not now that I've decided to ignore the demons and act as if I'm normal again. Also, if I were suspended, I'd see Sally a lot less. So I'm choosing to avoid him. This morning he was hanging around the bike racks waiting for me, but he didn't see me. I made sure of that. It was almost funny watching him glare angrily at each bike in turn, trying to figure out which one was mine. He was probably contemplating vandalizing all of them, but then a teacher stopped by to ask him what he was doing, and Malphi ended up trudging back into the school, his large wide face muddled with petulant rage. I waited for a few minutes before riding up to the bike rack and locking my bike up.

Maybe at some point Malphi will forget about me. Maybe not. We'll see.

MY WORLD TURNED UPSIDE DOWN TODAY. COMPLETELY AND utterly upside down. I know what you must be thinking. That I'm only fifteen and that kids my age like to exaggerate, and that's what I'm doing now. Well, no, not even close. This isn't some sort of teenage hormone-induced drama play.

A new student was brought into our homeroom. Supposedly his name is Connor Devin, and the story we were told is that he had just moved to the area. They didn't tell us where he lived before, and Devin didn't volunteer the information, but I knew where he really came from. Hell. Because Connor Devin is a demon. And I know it's no accident that he was put in my homeroom—not with the way he took a desk one row directly behind me, and not with the way I could feel his demon eyes burning into the back of my neck. And for the *pièce de résistance*. He's in every single class I'm in. Every single damn one!

The demon Devin is thin with a mostly snake-like body, and he's a few inches taller than me. He has the same ugly-as-

121

hell features as every other demon I've come across. Horns, yellow eyes, flaming blood-red skin, slathering pit bull-like jaw, talon-like claws. In his case it looked almost comical, given the extremely preppy clothes he was dressed in—Polo shirt, a white sweater tied around his neck, slacks, and oxford shoes. I didn't bring my iPhone to school with me, so I couldn't figure out his human appearance, but from the way I caught some of the girls looking him over, I knew he appeared to be good-looking.

This demon has been sent to keep watch over me. And of course, to test me. How can I possibly go to school every day and not only have to see him, but have him sitting so close to me that I can smell that noxious sweet sulfur odor that comes off of all demons? And knowing that those damn yellow demon eyes are on me constantly? How could anyone possibly do that without going insane? But I don't have a choice—if I switched high schools to Newton South, or even just some of my classes, the demons would know. But if I cracked under the demon Devin's watch, they'd know that, too. I was being put in an impossible situation, yet somehow I kept my composure while I was in Devin's presence, acting as if he was only some preppy kid that I didn't give a shit about. But how long would I be able to keep it up, especially knowing that one slip-up and I was as good as dead?

This had to be connected with Vincent Gilman. Most likely after they killed Gilman they searched his apartment and found out about the message board. They knew he was in communication with someone else who saw demons, and that had to be why they searched my home. Because I was one of their suspects. But this meant that there were others on their list. If I was the only one they suspected, they wouldn't have bothered to plant a demon in my school—they would've simply found a way to get rid of me like they did Gilman. And just like with Gilman, they would've made my death look like an accident. The fact that they were going to all this trouble made me think something big enough was up that they couldn't risk killing me and bringing the police into it unless they were certain I was the one they were looking for. It made me think more about what happened in Brooklyn, and whether the *something big* was connected with the abductions of Ginny Cataldo, Trey Wilkerson and God knows how many other four-year-old children they might've stolen from other states and brought here.

After the initial shock wore off, another thought stunned me. I had assumed that these demons came from some sort of hellish region or another dimension, and that when they slipped into this world they were able to create a kind of hypnotic trance that fooled almost everyone into seeing them as human. But for whatever reason, I and a few others, like Virgil, weren't susceptible to it, and saw them instead as what they really were. My theory explained why the demons I've encountered all live alone without any immediate family. But how could the demon Connor Devin be masquerading as a fifteen-year-old kid? Did they send up other demons to also masquerade as his parents? Or does this demon thing work in a completely different way? Maybe instead of the demons being actual physical demons, it's something else. Maybe it's more of a spiritual thing, where a demon spirit takes over a human host, and somehow what I'm seeing is what they're like inside—sort of like their essence. I realized that I'd have to look into Connor Devin's home situation. I was going to have to see whether his parents were demons, too. The thought of having to do that made me sick, but I had no choice.

I was a nervous wreck by the time school ended. Seeing Sally helped, but she sensed something was wrong and tried to get me to talk about it. First I tried telling her it was nothing, just schoolwork, but she knew me well enough already not to believe that, and kept pushing me. I was just too exhausted from the day's events to come up with a convincing lie, and instead just got quiet, which really pissed Sally off. Instead of the two of us going to the golf course like we'd been doing, she had me stop the bike so she could get off. I got off my bike also, and for a couple of blocks walked my bike alongside her, but Sally just kept getting angrier and angrier at me for not telling her what was bothering me, and my mind just wasn't working well enough to come up with a good lie. After we walked another block together (although not really together because the gulf growing between us seemed like miles) she told me in a voice icy enough to cause frostbite that she wanted to walk by herself without my company. There was nothing I could say to her, so I got on my bike and rode off. I felt kind of dead inside, like maybe things were over between us. I probably would've been crushed by this if I wasn't so confused and worried about the demon Connor Devin.

I don't want to make a joke of this and quote Al Pacino from *Godfather III*. I know it's clichéd and it's been done to death already, but it fits my situation so well right now that I have to do it. *Just when I thought I was out those damn demons had to drag me back in!*

I'VE BEEN PREOCCUPIED ALL DAY, BOTH ABOUT WHAT TO DO about the demon Connor Devin and also what to say to Sally so I don't lose her. During dinner my parents made several comments about how preoccupied I looked, and it didn't help that they had to repeat those comments several times before I realized what they were saying. The first time I grunted out something unintelligible. When they pressed me for an answer, I told them I was trying to figure out how to solve my math homework. They seemed to buy that. Even with their high income jobs, they're not the most astute people around.

I figured out what to tell Sally. I didn't like the idea of lying to her—the thought of doing that made me queasy inside, so I played around with telling her a variation of the truth, something like how the new kid made me feel uneasy. But I realized that wouldn't work. Either she'd press me about why he made me uneasy, which would eventually force me to lie to her, or worse, she'd confront the demon at school, or otherwise tip him off, which would put her life in danger. So instead I came up with another variation of the truth. That I suffered from depression at times. It wasn't that much of a stretch. Those demons depress the hell out of me. I called Sally up twenty minutes ago to explain myself to her. The line got deathly quiet as I told her this. I could barely stand it, my heart racing as I waited for her to say something. Finally, she asked me why I didn't tell her that earlier.

"I was afraid you might not want to be involved with me if you knew that," I said.

"Do you think I'm that shallow?"

This wasn't said out of anger, but more hurt. Like I didn't trust her. Her reaction surprised me, and I stammered out that that wasn't it. "I just don't want you thinking less of me. This isn't an easy thing to tell people."

"Henry, I won't think any less of you. I wish you had told me this this afternoon, but I'm glad you trust me enough to confide in me with something this serious." She hesitated before asking me whether I'd told my parents.

"No. If I told them they'd take me to a psychiatrist and have me all drugged up. I'm trying to figure out a way to solve this myself."

"Is anything helping?"

"Well, yeah. Seeing you again has helped."

"Be serious."

"I am. There are other things I've been doing, too, and it's been getting better. I'll talk to you more about it tomorrow. Maybe at the golf course?"

"We'll see." She hesitated, then asked how long I'd been suffering from this, and I told her since I was thirteen. So while I wasn't entirely truthful with Sally, it wasn't really a lie either. At least it seemed to solve the problem between us. I also figured out what I was going to have to do about the demon Connor Devin. I was either going to have to get him kicked out of school, or failing that, I'd have to kill him. Not that I had any moral issue with killing a demon. I just had no idea how to go about doing it. So for now I'll focus on the first approach.

Tuesday, September 27th 6:15 PM

I T'S IMPOSSIBLE FOR ME TO EXPLAIN JUST HOW MUCH IT SUCKS having a demon shadow you for almost an entire fucking day. I just can't describe what something like that does to your emotional and mental well-being. And what makes it all that more unbearable is knowing that the demon is there to study me and is just waiting to see if he can trip me up. The only way I was able to keep things together today was to tell myself over and over again that his days were numbered.

No surprise that he's in my Italian class, too, and the cherry to top it off—the teacher assigned him to sit next to Sally. I could barely stand the thought of that, and I heard him trying to hit on her a few times. Of course what I really heard were his animal hisses and snarls, which were barely understandable as words. Sally was polite to him but made it clear she had no interest. As angry as I was over this, I was also relieved that I hadn't said anything about Devin to her. He knew she was my girlfriend, and he was testing her, trying to determine from her response whether I'd told her about him. At least he didn't get anything from that.

The whole day was close to intolerable having him always nearby. Even during lunch he chose a table near us. A flock of girls who didn't know better joined him, and I had to listen to his demon hisses and snarls as he played his part and flirted with them. Maybe he was doing more than just playing his part. Maybe he'd use the opportunity to despoil as many of these girls as he could. I wanted to know what he looked like to his crowd of new admirers, so I took his picture with my iPhone while he wasn't paying attention, and it turns out he looks enough like Justin Bieber that his creators must've used Bieber as a model to craft his human appearance.

As you can probably guess, dealing with the demon Connor Devin left me in a rotten mood, and it was Ralph Malphi's bad luck that he finally found me in the boy's room late that afternoon. It was just the two of us in there—I was at the sink washing my hands when he came in, and as he recognized me, a big ugly grin filled his face. He pushed the door closed behind him and came charging at me, announcing how he'd been looking for me and how he was going to teach me a lesson for messing with him.

I guess he thought I would just stand there and let him pound on me or whatever he was planning on doing. But while he might've had two years and eighty pounds on me, he didn't know about my athletic abilities. I may not have competed in anything in some time, but quickness and agility could go a long way. Also, while Ralph Malphi might've looked like a gorilla, he looked as much like a soft and privileged rich kid, while I'd been spending my winters shoveling snow and my summers mowing lawns, which hardened me and made me stronger than he probably guessed. Third and last, I'd spent two and a half years dealing with demons, which hardened me far more than anything else ever could've. There wasn't a chance in hell someone like Malphi would've ever worried me.

I waited until he got within a few feet of me, and then I flew at him furiously, first kicking him in the balls, then grabbing his fat head and slamming it against one of the sinks. He went down to the floor hard before he ever knew what happened, and I went down with him, punching him in the ear over and over again until he was crying and begging me not to hurt him anymore. If it wasn't because of the demon Connor Devin putting me in such an awful mood, I would've eased up, but instead I kept at it, letting him know I'd cut out his eyes and fuck each of his empty eye sockets if he even as much as looked at me again.

I had him so scared that he pissed his pants. I'm not kidding; a puddle of urine leaked out under him. I got off him then, not wanting to get my own pants soiled by him, and gave him a few kicks to the ribs. When I left the boy's room, he was a bloody, urine-soaked mess, curled up in a fetal position and still crying like a baby. I didn't feel sorry for him in the least. For him, bullying and terrorizing other students was a game. For me survival had become something far more serious. He picked the wrong person to bully. It was bound to happen eventually.

My encounter with Malphi occurred near the end of the school day. I got some of his blood on my hands, but I'd been able to shake the demon Connor Devin off of me by then, which was lucky, since he probably would've smelled Malphi's blood on me. A minute later, I was able to wash it off in a different bathroom without anyone noticing. Otherwise, not even a drop on my pants or shirt. If anyone other than Malphi had found out about what happened, nobody mentioned it to me. I don't think Malphi reported it—I'm pretty sure I left him too scared and embarrassed to do that. If he did report it, nobody called my house, at least not yet. I guess I'll find out more about it tomorrow.

It was raining when Sally and I left school. Not a hard rain, but hard enough where we couldn't go to the golf course, so I rode Sally home. During the ride I told her about Malphi. I was keeping enough secrets from her regarding demons and

Connor Devin that I didn't want to keep any additional ones. Still, though, I downplayed what I did to Malphi, although I did tell her that he was crying by the time I left the boy's room.

"You're making this up," she said.

"Would I make up something like that?"

I held my right hand back so she could see the bruises on my knuckles.

"Wow," she said, "Malphi's a senior. And he's so huge and scary-looking."

"Not huge and scary-looking enough to tangle with the likes of me!"

Sally got quiet after that. Nor did she say anything about the depression I supposedly suffered from. Instead, she just held me tighter. I felt her shiver, but it might've only been because of the rain and not from what I had told her.

Her mom was home, so all we could do was study Italian together at their kitchen table. Sally's mom hovered nearby and kept a watchful eye on me, just as the demon Connor Devin had done all day, but she also made us hot chocolate, which is something Devin never would have done, so I can't complain too much.

I TOOK THE BUS TO SCHOOL TODAY. LAST NIGHT I TRIED TO find the demon Connor Devin's home address, but had no luck finding any Devins living in Newton. I wanted to see if he took the bus, and if he did, what direction he came from, so I got to the stop early this morning before either Curt or Wesley. Malphi, too.

Wesley beat both Curt and Malphi to the stop, and when he showed up, he gave me this scared, worried look and told me Malphi was still making threats about me. "Maybe you shouldn't be taking the bus right now?" he said.

I told him straight-faced that I'd take my chances and asked him if he saw Malphi on the bus home last night. Wesley shook his head and his mouth continued to twitch in this nervous and worried way. He was trying to think of some argument to give me, but nothing came to him.

When Curt showed up a few minutes later he gave me an exaggerated double take. "Whoa," he said, "you're taking your life in your hands coming here. And not much chance on this short notice that I'll be able to conjure up *Cthulhu* to save your ass."

"Don't know what you're talking about."

"Malphi. Big muscle-bound ape. Been clamoring for your scalp."

I gave him a confused look that was every bit as exaggerated as the double-take he had given me.

"Your funeral," Curt said pursing his lips and shrugging in an unconcerned manner, but he contradicted his nonchalant attitude when he started to fidget nervously.

Malphi arrived at the stop ten minutes after Curt. He looked battered and bruised with his right ear swollen to almost twice the size of his left. He also looked shrunken, with this defeated air about him, like a whipped dog. When he saw me he flinched and averted his eyes. Wesley and Curt both caught this and gave me an astonished look, and then I saw the machinery clicking on in their eyes. Their expressions shifted to show their curiosity, but neither of them asked what was going on, or whether I might've been responsible for the damage that was so obviously done to Malphi. Malphi himself stood frozen facing the street, as if he were afraid to let his eyes wander and catch a glimpse of me. One of the ideas I'd been playing with to get rid of the demon Connor Devin was coercing Malphi into blaming Devin for the beating he took, but as I watched him I decided I couldn't take that chance. Malphi was on the verge of crumbling apart, and I couldn't trust what he might say if pressed. So that idea was out, but I had others. One in particular that I liked.

The bus arrived without the demon Connor Devin making it to the stop. That was disappointing, but I took it in stride. I let Malphi get on first. He took a seat near the back of the bus and I took one near the front. I didn't want to push things with him. The reason I was able to get the upper hand over him so quickly was because he had been too cocky and careless with me. He was afraid of me now, which was good. If I were to push him into another fight, he'd be more cautious and there would be no guaranteeing the outcome. So as long as he kept away from me, I'd do the same with him.

When we got to the school, I hung around outside for a while hoping to see which direction the demon Connor Devin arrived from, as well as how he was getting to school. After I gave up, I went straight to my homeroom and found Devin already there sitting next to Sally in the seat I usually sat in. It might have been my imagination, but I could swear Sally flashed me a guilty look when I walked into the room. I took the other seat next to her and wondered about that look I thought I caught, like maybe she didn't mind the attention Devin had been paying her. When I looked his way he gave me what I guessed was a smirk. Demon jaws are so grotesque it's hard to tell for sure, but I was pretty sure that was his intention. Sally and Devin sat next to each other in Italian class, and maybe she was beginning to find herself attracted to him; maybe even developing some sort of crush. Since I saw him as he really was, to me he was ghastly looking, but I had to keep reminding myself of the way others saw him, which was with a Justin Bieber façade. I reminded myself again that his days were numbered.

Later at lunch, Sally seemed distracted, which made me feel sick to my stomach. So she was beginning to have conflicted feelings. Maybe she was already planning to break up with me so she could date the Bieber lookalike. There was no way I would ever let that happen. Not out of jealously, but to protect her. I couldn't let him spread his demon foulness to her. I would kill him if I had to, regardless of what the consequences might be. Somehow there has to be a way to kill a demon, and I would figure it out if I needed to do that for Sally's sake.

The rest of the day was just as miserable. Before my last class, Sally found me in the hallway to tell me that something had come up and she wouldn't be seeing me after school. That

I'd have to ride my bike home by myself. I didn't push her on what had come up. I didn't even have a chance to tell her that I hadn't ridden my bike, but had instead taken the school bus. Before I could process what she had told me, she was already moving away from me.

I was reeling from that encounter when I got to my classroom for my last class of the day and saw what I assumed was Devin smirking at me. I somehow kept things under control, but I couldn't concentrate on a word the teacher said. All I could think about was Sally falling into Devin's clutches and what he would do to her in all his horrific demon glory. How if he didn't kill her, he'd still be ruining her for the rest of her life, ripping and mutilating her insides and spreading his demon foulness throughout her. For a long moment the thought of all this made me feel like I was going to pass out, but again, I held it together enough not to show Devin what I was going through. While the teacher was scribbling something on the whiteboard with her back to the class, I took out my phone and texted Sally a message, asking her not to go out with anyone else, that if she's planning on doing that to at least break up with me first. I knew this wasn't the brightest thing in the world to do, but I couldn't help myself. The next fifteen minutes while I waited for a text back were absolute agony. Maybe I started sweating then. Maybe Devin even noticed, though I'm not sure. When Sally texted me back it was to tell me that she wasn't seeing anyone else and that she had a school event to do. She didn't volunteer anything more.

After school I had planned to follow Devin and make sure he wasn't meeting up with Sally. I knew this would be risky. From over two and a half years of observing these demons, I knew they had an unusually strong sense of smell and that I'd have to keep a large enough distance between us so that he wouldn't know I was there. When the class bell rang the teacher stopped me by calling me over, and like an idiot I hesitated enough to where I couldn't pretend that I hadn't heard her. I should've just left the room, except Devin hung back to see what I would do, and that screwed me up. When I went to her desk she sat silently for a good half minute acting as if I wasn't there before reprimanding me for texting in her classroom. I had to promise her that I wouldn't text again before she let me leave. My heart was in my throat by the time I fled her classroom and was searching the hallway to see that Devin was nowhere in sight.

I raced around like a crazy person after that hoping to spot either Devin or Sally, and barely made it onto the bus. I had to get on to make sure that Devin and Sally weren't on it together, and I'd been racing around so much that I was out of breath and panting when I took an empty seat next to Wesley. A couple of minutes later, after my breathing had slowed down to something more normal, Wesley asked why I wasn't with my girlfriend. I know that the question was mostly innocent on his part, but it was like a knife to my heart. A minute later, after I hadn't answered him, he asked if I wanted to come over and look at a new batch of comic books he had picked up over the weekend. I told him I'd like to, but that I had a lot of chemistry homework I needed to do.

He smiled at that. "Since when did you become so dedicated with school?"

"My parents are on my back too much for me not to be. But I'll come over soon."

"Next time you're not with Sally Freeman?"

"That's right."

He smiled thinly, but swallowed back whatever crack he was going to make. Inside I was dying. I wanted to trust her, but all I could think was that she had lied to me and that right at that moment she was with the demon Connor Devin. I nearly ran off the bus when it came to our stop, and after nodding my *so longs* to Wesley and Curt, I called Sally. The call rang through to voice mail. I called her again and this time she answered.

"I told you I had a school project today," Sally told me, her voice with a distinctive chill in it.

"I know," I said. "I only wanted to say hi and tell you I was missing you."

There was a long pause before Sally said anything. During that time I strained to listen for any demon hisses or snarls in the background. I thought I heard some, but I wasn't sure. Finally Sally told me she had to get back to what she was doing.

"Wait," I near begged. I hesitated, a weakness all of a sudden making my legs feel like rubber, and a queasy sickness filling up my stomach. I knew how dangerous it would be to mention the demon Connor Devin to Sally—not just to me, but to her, as well. But I couldn't just let her go without warning her. "Can I tell you something without you telling anyone else?" I asked.

There was another unbearable stretch of silence on Sally's part before she asked me what I wanted to tell her, an increasing impatience in her voice.

"You have to promise you can't tell anyone. It's important. Please promise me this."

"Look, Henry, I don't have time for this—"

"Please, just promise me."

I could imagine how annoyed she must've looked right then. In my mind's eye I could see her eyes narrowed, her lips pressed tight together, her cheeks slightly puffed out, and that image brought a lump to my throat. "Go ahead," Sally said. "I won't tell anyone."

"There's no one around you who can overhear what I'm saying?"

"No."

She might've thought that was the case, but I didn't know if I could trust her on that. Demons have dog-like hearing. Maybe even better. If Devin was standing five or so feet from her, he'd hear what I was telling her. I took a deep breath and struggled over whether or not to tell her about Devin. The consequences were staggering if he found out what I was telling her, but the damage that he could inflict on her if I didn't warn her was even worse.

"You have to promise me that you'll keep away from Connor Devin," I said. "If you want to break up with me, then break up with me, but whatever you do don't get involved with him."

"Why not?"

"Because he's evil. He'll hurt you badly"

She laughed at that, like what I was saying was so outrageous that she couldn't help herself.

"Why are you saying this?" she asked.

For a long moment I stood tongue-tied as I tried to figure out how to explain to her that he was a noxious creature from hell only disguised as something human. Finally, I stammered out, "I can sense these things. You have to believe me and take what I'm telling you on faith. I know I'm right about him."

In a voice that was so flat and impersonal that I barely recognized her, Sally told me she had to go, then disconnected the call. I stood paralyzed as an overwhelming sense of devastation sapped the strength out of me. My head was swimming too much for me to understand right then what it was that had left me as such a wreck, but as I played back every word of my phone call with Sally I understood what it was. It wasn't just her tone or the indifference toward me that I heard from her, although that was a big part of it. It was that when I told her that she could break up with me if she wanted to, as long as she promised me she'd keep away from Devin, she made no attempt to tell me she wasn't breaking up with me.

I tried figuring out what had happened between us, and realized it could've been any number of things. My telling her that I suffered from depression, or my violently beating Malphi—I might not have told her how violent it was, but she had plenty of opportunities to see that he was badly battered and bruised when he came to school today. Or maybe demons have some sort of supernatural pull on girls they want to seduce. Or it could be nothing more than Sally being superficially attracted to Devin's human guise. Whatever it was I knew in my gut I had lost her. And I knew I needed to kill Devin. Not to win Sally back, but to save her. But I still had no idea how to kill a demon, and to figure that out I needed a miracle.

My mom's yelling at me now to come down for dinner. Actually, she's been yelling that for the last five minutes. I hear footsteps on the stairs; either hers or my dad's. I need to put this journal away for now. Later tonight I'll write about what could be my miracle.

THREE HOURS AGO I FINISHED THE SUSHI TAKEOUT DINNER MY mom brought home (I had cucumber, avocado, and asparagus maki rolls, and no fish—I'm still a vegetarian and am not budging on that), and would've written earlier about my possible miracle today, but Sally called me just after I had finished eating, and I've been playing back our conversation in my head over and over again, trying to divine any nuance or hidden meaning that I can. It's only been the last few minutes that I've been able to focus on anything else.

As soon as I picked up Sally's call, she launched in and told me how pissed she was at me—that I had no right being suspicious of her or checking up on her or thinking that she was seeing someone behind my back. She again insisted that she had stayed after school for a legitimate school project, but she didn't volunteer what it was, and I knew better than to ask her. I also knew better than to ask her why she didn't tell me earlier that she wasn't breaking up with me. At least she hadn't been with the demon Connor Devin. If she had, she'd either be dead or hospitalized. So after she bawled me out for my bad behavior, she asked why I thought Devin was evil.

"It's not something I think, it's something I know."

"You haven't even talked to him, have you? Why would you think he's evil?"

"Sally, please, you need to take this on faith. This is something I know every bit as much as that you're the most beautiful girl I've ever seen."

"Thank you, Henry, but that's not good enough. You can't tell me that you can just look at Connor and know that about him. So what do you know about him that allows you to tell me that he's evil?"

I couldn't think of how to answer that, and after an awkward, painful silence that seemed to last forever, she gave up waiting for me.

"Henry," she said, her voice turning patronizing, "if you're saying this about Connor because you're jealous, you have no reason to be. I'm not so superficial that I want to go out with him just because he's good looking."

I laughed at that. I couldn't help myself.

"So you think I *am* that superficial?" Sally asked, her voice quickly turning frigid.

"No, come on. I laughed because he's not as good looking as you think. At least not if you saw him the way I do."

"How do you see him?"

How could I tell her that I saw him as a god-awful demon? "This one thing, please, just trust me. Keep away from him. He's dangerous. It's not something I think, but something I know. If you were to dump me for anyone else, I wouldn't be saying this to you. But I don't want to see you hurt, and Connor Devin will hurt you if you let him near you." I hesitated for a moment, then found enough of my voice to ask if she was dumping me.

"No," Sally said. "But I can't deal with the way you're acting now. Not believing me when I tell you I'm staying after school to work on a class project, or saying that you can look at someone and know what's inside them, or telling me the crazy things you're telling me about Connor. Or beating up Ralph Malphi. The way he looks, you almost killed him! I like you Henry. I've liked you for a long time. But I need you to act normal. So we need to take a break, and after our break, you can't tell me any more of the bizarre things you've been telling me. And you can't act jealous anymore or keep making things up about Connor."

"How long is the break going to be?"

"I don't know. But when it's over, you can't act the way you've been acting, Henry."

After that I thought I heard her start to cry, and she quickly whispered goodbye and got off the phone, and I kept playing the conversation over in my head, trying to decipher every possible meaning that I could from it. Was she calling to tell me where we stood, or to find out what I really knew about the demon Connor Devin? And were we really on a break, or was she just dumping me? All of this left me agonizing, but it would've been much worse if something else hadn't happened today, something that gave me hope that I'd be able to kill the demon Connor Devin. It would be crushing knowing that if I killed him and got caught, I'd never see Sally again. But at least she'd be safe. At least I'd have that.

Let me explain my possible miracle. First, though, I need to go back to this afternoon after I'd gotten off the phone with Sally, when I begged her to keep away from Devin. For minutes after that call I stood still, too devastated and weak to even move. Then desperation slowly set in, and I knew I had to do something, anything, to figure out how to kill Devin. So I got on my bike and rode towards Boston.

I got to Cornwall's a little before five o'clock. I was

sweating after my bike ride—my face flushed as I locked my bike against an iron ring embedded in the brick outer wall of the building that Cornwall's was in. That ring must have once been used to hitch horses.

It had been weeks since I'd visited Cornwall's, maybe the longest I'd gone ASD. Dorthop was sitting at the cluttered oak desk by the front door where he always sat when I went there, reading one of his books and wearing the same dirty clothes he always wore. He looked his same disheveled and scowling self, with those same ridiculously thick forearms on display. Without looking up from his book, he said in a voice like gravel being scraped against a road, "I thought you gave up on this occult business and moved on to healthier pursuits."

"Nope, I've just been busy with school and stuff. Any new additions to the collection?"

For a minute Dorthop acted as if he didn't hear me as he continued to stare intently at his book. After he turned the page he grunted out that he'd added one new book recently. I waited for another half a minute, and once I realized he wasn't going to volunteer which book that was, I turned and headed for the secret alcove where he kept his occult collection.

"You won't find it back there," he grunted after I'd taken a couple of steps away from him. After first carefully placing an antique leather bookmarker to hold his place, he put his book down and shifted his gaze towards me. With his thick, heavy face straining as if he were exerting himself, he pulled a heavy set of keys from his pocket, then making more grunt-like noises, he bent forward so most of him was obscured by his desk. I heard a key turning a lock, then what must've been safe tumblers being worked, and finally a metal door being opened. Dorthop then straightened in his chair and placed an ancient, blood-red leather-bound book carefully on his desk, the title of which was engraved in gold leaf. I took several steps before I realized what it was. A copy of *L'Occulto Illuminato*. My voice cracked as I asked him if it was genuine. He didn't bother answering me.

"How did you get it?" I asked, my voice barely coming out as a whisper.

He smiled, exposing his few rotted teeth. "Uh, uh," he said, shaking his head, "That's not something I'm about to share with you or anyone else."

My palms were sweating like crazy, but my throat had become as dry as a handful of sand. I tried to swallow, but couldn't. I could barely even force out a whisper then.

"Is it whole? No pages missing?"

"No pages missing. None torn either. A perfectly readable copy."

"How much?"

His smile disappeared, his eyes quickly deadening. "Twenty-five thousand."

I knew I stood there blinking stupidly at him, but I couldn't help myself. It was as if I'd been punched smack in the face. I should've been expecting that type of price. I knew how rare the book was. But still, it didn't make any sense to me. He had to know I couldn't raise that kind of money, so why'd he even bother showing me the book? Simply to torture me? For a fleeting moment I thought of grabbing the book and making a run for it, but I knew I wouldn't get far.

"I can't get twenty-five thousand," I stammered out.

"That's too bad," he said. His expression remained detached, and he showed no indication that he felt badly at all. "I can sell *L'Occulto* like this for that price." He snapped two fingers, the sound harsh in the room, like bones being broken. "I know how much you wanted it, so I thought I'd give you first crack at it."

He was lying. He knew I wouldn't be able to pay twenty-five thousand, so he had to have another reason for wanting to show me the book, but I had no idea what it could be. I tried to wet my lips but all the moisture was gone from my mouth. I needed to think of something, anything. The book was too important to lose.

"How about I pay you a thousand dollars for a translation," I said. "That's all I have."

He didn't bother answering me. He gently picked up the book and put it back in the safe he had under his desk. I heard the metal door closing and the tumblers being spun. Whatever chance I had to try to overpower him and grab the book was gone. When he straightened back up in his chair, he resumed his reading as if he had never shown me a copy of *L'Occulto Illuminato*. I stood paralyzed, my mind racing as I tried to think of some way that I could get that book. After several minutes passed, he warned me that if I was thinking of breaking into his store for *L'Occulto Illuminato* I was out of luck. "Even if you got into my store, not a chance in the world you'd be able to break into that safe. It's cemented to the floor, so you ain't moving it either."

The thought had crossed my mind. A year ago I had bought burglar picks off the Internet, and I'd been practicing picking locks. It seemed like a prudent thing to do—it could very well be a skill that I might need in my battle with these damn demons. Over the last year I'd gotten pretty good at it. But even if I could pick the desk cabinet door lock to gain access to his safe, I had no idea what I'd do next. A thought did come to me. Kind of a sickening thought, but it was the only way I saw to get *L'Occulto Illuminato*.

"I could trade you for it," I said. I hesitated for only a moment before adding, "A first edition of *Spider-Man*."

He looked up from his book then and studied me carefully. "Mint condition?" he asked.

I nodded. All of Wesley's dad's comic books were in mint condition. All stored away in plastic bags. Wesley wasn't allowed to take that one out of the bag, but he showed it to me once, and I remember the cover looking like it was brand new. I had no idea what it was worth, but I guessed from Dorthop's interest it had to be worth at least twenty-five thousand.

"Bring it here tomorrow," he said.

"Can you give me two weeks?"

He stared bug-eyed at me, his thick lips turning downward into a frown making him look like a bullfrog. He knew then that I didn't have the comic book in my possession and that I was planning to steal it.

"You have it here by Saturday, or *L'Occulto* will be sold elsewhere by Sunday."

There was no point arguing with him. I was going to have to steal a comic book that was worth forty thousand dollars (I looked up the price when I got home), or *L'Occulto Illuminato* would be lost to me forever, and along with that, any chance I had of protecting Sally and understanding what these demons were up to and what I could possibly do to stop them. Ideas started percolating in my head how I was going to do this, and none of them made me feel particularly good. I nodded glumly at Dorthop and started towards the door. I took several steps but then had to stop. I had to ask him if he had read any of *L'Occulto Illuminato*. For a moment I didn't think he was going to bother answering me, but then he shifted his gaze up to give me a cold, dead stare.

"I don't read any of that shit," he said, "I just sell rare books. That's all I do."

I didn't know whether I believed him, but it didn't matter if I did or not. I had two days to commit grand larceny and betray a friendship, and while I like to act like Wesley is only someone I pretend to be friends with to keep my parents off my back, since realizing what I have to do I've also had to admit that that's not really true. The reality is that Wesley *is* a friend, and I hate what I'm going to have to do to him. Over the last few hours I've even come up with a plan of how I'm going to do it. It's not foolproof by any means, but it's the best I've been able to come up with.

It's eleven forty. My parents are probably fast asleep, but I'll give it another hour before heading out. Earlier after school ended—when I was racing around like a crazy person looking for Sally and Devin—I placed a small piece of paper between the lock and door frame of one of the school's side doors. If nobody discovered it, I should be able to get in the school that way. Then it's a matter of using my burglar picks to see if I can get into the Administration office. It's the only way I can think of to find out the demon Connor Devin's address.

T HIS WILL BE A SHORT ENTRY. I HAVE THE DEMON CONNOR Devin's home address.

Devin shouldn't even be going to school in Newton. He doesn't live here—he lives in Waltham, but someone with some clout must've arranged it. Later I'll have to visit each member of Newton's school committee and see if any of them are demons. Much later, though, after I've dealt with far more pressing issues.

Getting inside the school was easy. Nobody had found the door I had tampered with, and if the school had an alarm system, it was a silent one, and it didn't bring any police. It took me all of three minutes to pick the lock for the administration's office door and less than a minute to get into the locked file cabinets. And then all of another two minutes to get Devin's address before racing out of there. The adrenaline rush of doing this has left me feeling like I'd chugged a couple dozen double espressos. There's no way I'm going to be getting any sleep tonight, but that's okay. I have a lot of extra Italian studying I need to do.

I POISONED WESLEY THIS AFTERNOON AND STOLE A FORTY thousand dollar comic book. But before I write about that, let me go back to yesterday.

As I had expected, I was far too wired after breaking into my high school's Administration office to consider sleeping, so instead I spent three hours pushing ahead in my Italian studies, and then two hours on the computer researching different ways to poison Wesley. I ended up with a list of reasonable options, and topping my list was psilocybin mushrooms. From reading about what the effects would be, it seemed like a good choice. It'll make Wesley feel ill, but shouldn't cause any long-term damage—plus, after looking around some more, I have a good idea about where I can buy some. There were other options for poisoning Wesley, but psilocybin mushrooms seemed like the safest bet for both of us.

When seven o'clock rolled around, I left the house as if I was going to school, but I skipped the bus stop and took the subway into Boston instead. I had to try to find those mush-rooms, which I did, but I also needed time to test them on myself to make sure they would work the way they were supposed to. Besides, after not sleeping, I would've been worthless at school. But even if I had slept a full night, and didn't need to find a drug dealer, I still would've skipped school yesterday. I wasn't up to seeing Sally after our last phone call.

I took the subway to North Station, and from there walked to Charlestown and to a street corner where my research told me I'd be able to buy drugs. The area was pretty seedy, but after almost three years of dealing with demons, not much scares me, and within a half hour I'd bought myself a small bag of psilocybin mushrooms. The dealer was a half foot taller than me, rail thin, with a hollowness to his eyes and a feral look about him. From the way his eyes dulled to a glassy sheen, I knew he was sizing me up, trying to decide whether to attack and rob me instead of selling me his drugs, but the dullness faded as he came to the decision that that might not be the best course of action. Once I had a small baggie of dried mushrooms in my pants pocket, I walked back to North Station and took the subway home. I needed to take the mushrooms myself not only to better understand their effect and the portion that I would need to give Wesley, but to make sure they were genuine and that I hadn't been ripped off by this guy. If I had, I'd move on to one of the other substances on my list, several of which I could buy at a hardware store.

It was eleven o'clock when I got home to an empty house, and there was a phone message from the school to my parents to let them know that I hadn't shown up that day. I erased the message. If they followed it up with a letter, I would take care of that, too.

I picked out half the number of mushrooms that were recommended on the website I had found, ground them up into powder, added it to a glass of water, and drank it. Ten minutes later my stomach started cramping and I felt a chill, like I had a bad case of the flu, and over the next twenty minutes it only got worse. Then I started feeling the effects of the hallucinogenic. That was the one kink in my plan. I wanted Wesley to think he had caught the flu or had gotten food poisoning, but I decided the hallucinations wouldn't matter. He'd have no idea about what he was given and he was such a dweeb, he'd probably think any hallucinations were because of a fever.

For the rest of the day, I put on some music, lay on my bed, and felt the effects of the mushrooms. At some point Sally called me on my phone and left a message wanting to know if I had ditched school because of her, and if I had I should grow up. I didn't want to talk to her then, but that wasn't why I didn't answer my phone. When I pulled it out, I saw all these different colored lights shooting out from it. It was pretty wild, and I was mesmerized by it.

I was still high by the time my parents came home, and I was also hungrier than I could ever remember being in my life. I was so hungry that if they had plated a piece of raw steak or calf's brains or any other disgusting type of meat, I would've scarfed it down without any hesitation. Fortunately my mom had picked me up some vegetable lo mein, and I forced myself to eat it at a normal pace instead of inhaling it like I wanted to. I don't think my parents suspected that I was high. I think they were too wrapped up in their job and career discussions. If they did suspect anything, they didn't let on.

I don't think I came down from that high until midnight. I decided I'd better give Wesley no more than half of what I took myself. Once I was sure my parents were asleep, I ground up a portion to give Wesley, put that in a plastic bag, then hid the rest of the mushrooms for later. I had plans for them.

So that was what I did yesterday. Now for today. Well, you already know what I did, but here's how it happened. First, I took the school bus this morning for the obvious reason that I needed to take the bus home after school. That was part of the plan. Making sure I was on the bus home with Wesley.

This morning Malphi was waiting at the stop looking every bit as battered as he had two days earlier. He was still avoiding eye contact with me, which was good, and things went without incident. When the bus came and we boarded, I bypassed Curt to sit next to Wesley and led him into talking about his latest comic book buys. I did this casually and without letting on to what I had in mind.

I skipped homeroom. I still wasn't up to seeing Sally. I also skipped the cafeteria at lunch for the same reason. The day dragged badly, and it didn't make it any easier having the demon Connor Devin on my tail all day, but at least I lost him for forty-five minutes during lunch, and I needed that break badly. The only way I made it through the day without cracking up was to focus my thoughts on getting *L'Occulto Illuminato* into my hands.

When school ended, I caught up with Curt and Wesley on the bus and again led Wesley into talking about his latest comic book buys. When we got off at our stop, I held my breath waiting for Wesley to invite me over to look at them. For a moment I didn't think he was going to do it, which would've forced me to make the first move, which I didn't want to do, but just as I was giving up hope he flashed me this sheepish grin and extended the invitation. I think I surprised him when I told him sure, why not. What Wesley did next caught me off guard. Curt was hanging around close by, and Wesley asked him if he wanted to join us. If Curt accepted, my plans would have been ruined. Fortunately, I'd managed to hurt his feelings by spending so much time talking comic books with Wesley that he dismissed the idea, claiming he wasn't about to waste a Friday afternoon reading Dark Knight comics with a couple of geeks.

The next big hurdle was Wesley's mom and his sister, Allison. His dad made a lot of money—I'm guessing more than my parents combined, and his mom didn't work. When I'd go over there she'd often hover around us, and that would've screwed everything up today. I wasn't so much concerned about Allison. She was only ten and painfully shy, and she probably would've spent the time I was there hiding in her bedroom. Fortunately, neither of them were home.

After we got to his house, we stopped off first in the kitchen, where Wesley brought out two glasses and a container of chocolate milk. The guy's fifteen years old and he still drinks chocolate milk, but I held my tongue and didn't mention how pathetic that was. I waited until he poured one glass, and then asked him if he could make me an espresso instead. Wesley blinked stupidly for a moment before telling me that he's not allowed to have coffee.

"That's a shame," I told him. I pointed out the espresso machine his parents had on the countertop, which cost at least as much as a Honda Civic. "You're parents have a top of the line Nuova Simonelli. That's about as good as it gets."

"I'm not making you an espresso," Wesley said. "They'd kill me if I touched that. And they don't want me drinking coffee."

"Again, that's too bad, but my parents make me a double espresso every morning."

"I'm not touching the espresso machine. And neither are you."

"Fine," I said, since I didn't want an espresso anyway. I didn't need to be more wired than I already was. "Can you check the fridge, maybe find me a soda?"

Wesley made a face, but did as I asked. When he had the fridge open and his back turned to me, I slipped the dose of powered mushrooms into his chocolate milk and stirred it with my finger. I had the baggie put away and my finger dried off on my pants while he was still reciting the different soft drink choices. None of them were typical sodas like Coke or Mountain Dew but expensive, natural sodas. I told him I'd take a ginger beer. That's what it was called—*ginger beer*, not ginger ale.

It was maybe twenty minutes later, while we were sitting around Wesley's room reading comic books—Wesley with the latest *X-Men Legacy* me with *Hellboy*—that Wesley started to shift around uncomfortably. He had gotten pale and drops of perspiration were beading along his forehead, and he was making a face like he had a stomach ache. I think he was too absorbed in his comic book to realize that he was in pain, but after a couple of more minutes he put down his X-Men and clutched his stomach.

"I don't feel too good," he told me in a weak and trembling voice.

Before I could say anything he scrambled to his feet and rushed out of the room, knocking over his glass and whatever was left of his chocolate milk. Once I heard what must've been a bathroom door slamming shut, I moved quickly. Wesley and his dad had shown me a number of times the 'collection room'—a room on the first floor that had been converted to what looked like a small comic book store. I'd brought my burglar picks with me, as well as a pair of sheer leather gloves, and I took both of these out of my backpack and moved fast out of Wesley's room. Once I was in the hallway I heard Wesley in the bathroom moaning and retching at the same time. I slipped on the gloves and nearly flew down the stairs taking several at a time. The door to the comic book room was unlocked and when I entered it I saw the shelves and turnstile displays that you'd find in any comic book store. Those shelves and displays weren't where the first edition of *Spider-Man* was kept. I knew that from the time Wesley showed it to me. The rarest and most expensive comic books were locked away in the closet. It didn't take me long to get the closet door open—the lock was easier to pick than the one for the high school's administration office. Inside the closet were several large file cabinets. I remembered which one the Spider-Man comic book was in, and I had that unlocked quickly, too. Inside of it I found two comic books with Spider-Man on the cover, both in thick plastic bags and stiff cardboard for backing. *Amazing Fantasy* #15 was one of them—it showed Spider-Man swinging through the air holding a bad guy. The other one was what I had expected; the first edition of *Spider-Man*, which showed Spider-Man trapped inside of a glass casing with the Fantastic Four members surrounding him. I stood confused, not sure which one to take since the Amazing Fantasy had an earlier date stamped on it, but when I heard a car pulling into the driveway, I made my decision and placed the Amazing Fantasy comic back in the cabinet, locked it up, then locked the closet door. I was amazingly calm as I did all this and then raced out of the room with the first edition of *Spider-Man* tucked under my arm. As I made my way to the staircase leading to the second level, I caught a glimpse through the front window and saw Mrs. Neuberger and Allison walking up the path to the front door. I had no idea whether either of them saw me, but I also had no time to worry about it. Next I was sprinting up the steps two at a time. Wesley was still in the bathroom making retching noises, although now it sounded like he was sobbing with his retching instead of moaning.

I had the stolen Spider-Man comic book stored away in my backpack and was back in the hallway knocking on the bathroom door and calling out to Wesley so that I would look concerned, all by the time Mrs. Neuberger opened the front door. She must've heard me because she yelled out in an alarmed voice, "Wesley, is that you?"

She had ran to the staircase, and I could see her wide-eyed and frantic at the bottom of it staring up at me. "Mrs. Neuberger, it's me, Henry Dudlow. Wesley and I were reading comic books when he got sick all of a sudden."

She was up the stairs fast after that, brushing past me, knocking on the bathroom door and calling out, "Wesley, dear, are you okay?" I was amazed at how much concern she showed. I doubted my mom would've been thinking of anything except how my being ill was inconveniencing her.

A moan came from the bathroom in response, and Mrs. Neuberger didn't wait any longer before opening the door. Wesley was sitting on the marble floor by the toilet, one arm hung loosely around the bowl. He turned to face his mom, his skin greenish, his eyes red and puffy. A thick strand of saliva and vomit hung from his mouth. "I don't feel good," he told her, his voice like a little kid's.

She helped him to his feet, washed off his face, and it was only as she was walking him out of there that she remembered I was there. "You better go home now, Henry," she said, stiffly, as if she were prescient enough to know that I was to blame for Wesley's condition. I told Wesley that I hoped he felt better soon, then I got my backpack from his room and squeezed past him and his mom in the hallway so I could head downstairs and let myself out. If Mrs. Neuberger saw me through the window earlier, she didn't say anything about it or ask me what I was doing downstairs. Allison was standing in the foyer. Like Wesley, she was small for her age and had a slight build. Mousy brown hair, small button nose, not very much chin. She stared at me fixedly as I made my way toward her so I could get out the front door.

"What's wrong with Wesley?" she asked.

"I don't know. He just got sick."

"Did you do something to him?"

"No."

She gave me a look like she didn't believe me. I pretended I didn't notice it, got past her, and left the house.

This all happened an hour and forty-five minutes ago. Over the last two days I've bought illegal drugs, poisoned a friend, and stolen a forty thousand-dollar comic book. You'd think after all this I'd be feeling anxious, or worried, or numb. That this would have some effect on me, especially with the way Mrs. Neuberger looked at me or the accusation Wesley's little sister Allison threw out. Nope. I feel nothing but calm. I don't want to say this was simply a matter of the ends justifying the means, or something else trite like that. This goes well beyond that. I didn't ask for the responsibility that's been dumped on me, and there's no longer any running from it. When I tried, the demons made it personal by sending one of their own to spy on me in the form of Connor Devin, and now that they're trying to drag Sally into it, I have no choice about what I have to do. I'm in it for the long haul now. I'll probably end up the same as Vincent Gilman, but still, I have to do whatever I can to stop these demons. First, I need to get Dorthop's copy of *L'Occulto Illuminato*. At least that will give me a fighting chance. After that, I'll do whatever it takes to get rid of Connor Devin. I can't have him shadowing me at school all day, and I certainly can't have him moving in on Sally. And I need to concern myself again with the two little kids who were taken: Ginny Cataldo and Trey Wilkerson. As much as I wanted to convince myself otherwise, I know in my gut that the demons are behind their abductions, and that something big is in the works.

I HAVE *L'OCCULTO ILLUMINATO*.

My hands have been shaking ever since I got it.

You can probably guess I was up early this morning, and by eight I was out of the house and riding my bike towards Boston. I wanted to get out of there while my parents were still holed up in their bedroom so they couldn't interfere with my plans, but I also wanted to get to Cornwall's as early as I could.

I arrived at the store a few minutes before ten o'clock. They were supposed to open at ten, but the door was already unlocked, and as I walked in and saw Dorthop looking as rumpled as he always did, sitting at his usual spot behind the front desk already engrossed in a book, I had the sense the store had been opened for hours. I also had this odd feeling then that Dorthop never left the place.

Dorthop paid no attention to me as I walked up to him, opened my backpack, and took out the binder that I had the first edition of *Spider-Man* stored in for protection. It was only after

I had the comic book out of the binder and laid flat on the desk in front of him that Dorthop shifted his eyes to me and acknowledged that I was there.

Dorthop had thick, meaty hands but he displayed a surprising grace and nimbleness as he removed the comic book from the plastic bag and examined it, gently turning each page. Once he was through with his inspection, he told me that I stole the comic book.

I saw no reason to deny the obvious.

"Of course, I did," I said. "You knew I would. You knew I would have to steal something to get you twenty-five thousand dollars."

His gruff rock-hard exterior softened. Maybe even something like compassion flickered for a moment in his eyes. I expected him to ask me if I really wanted to go ahead with this and that it wasn't too late for me to return the comic book. Instead, he said, "I had to test you to see how badly you wanted it. *L'Occulto Illuminato* can't just go to anyone."

He mostly disappeared behind his desk as he pushed his chair back and bent forward so he could unlock his safe. When he straightened back up, he scooted his chair forward and placed *L'Occulto Illuminato* in front of me, his gruff exterior was back, his eyes the same cold slate gray as before.

Did he know that I saw demons? Maybe, but I didn't really care. Now that I had *L'Occulto Illuminato*, I was done with him and his store. I placed the seventeenth century book on demonology into my backpack and left the store knowing I'd never be back. I didn't say anything further to Dorthop when I left, and he didn't say anything else to me.

I had my reason for riding my bike to Cornwall's instead of taking the subway. I had this odd feeling that maybe a demon would be able to sense the presence of *L'Occulto Illuminato*, and I didn't want to be stuck waiting in a crowd or on a subway car and come across one or more of them and be vulnerable. At least with a bike I'd have a better chance of escaping them. Now I'm home with the one book that gives me a chance against these demons. *L'Occulto Illuminato* is bound in red leather, and I'm trying hard not to imagine that it came from the skin of a demon. The book is over four hundred years old, and I think I can still detect a faint demon odor from it. That onion, sulfur odor that they all have. In a way, the thought is nauseating, in another way, it gives me hope. If the skin of a demon was really used, then they can be killed. But I don't want to imagine that I'm touching demon skin when I hold this book.

I've read the first page. The pages seem to be made of parchment. Calf-skin? Some other animal? The text is written by hand in brownish-red ink (animal blood? human blood?), I'm guessing by the author, Lazzarro Galeotti. It's carefully scripted, and legible, but it still makes for difficult reading given how archaic the language is. I was unable to find some of the words used in my Italian-English dictionary, or through Internet searches, and had to guess at their meaning from finding similar Latin words. The thought of having this book in my possession terrifies me, but also gives me a hope that I haven't had since that moment I first saw the demon Hanley without his human disguise.

The only thing else worth mentioning in this entry is that I tried calling Wesley to see how he was doing. It wasn't just to put on an act; I was genuinely concerned. His mom answered and wouldn't put Wesley on the phone, claiming that he wasn't available to talk to me. While she didn't come out and blame me for what happened, her voice had this chilly, accusatory tone to it. But I'm sure if she suspected anything, it would be that the two of us were doing drugs together, not that I slipped Wesley a Mickey so I could rob them. And if they knew that Wesley had ingested psilocybin mushrooms, they would've been on the phone with my parents. If they had discovered that their Spider-Man comic book had been taken, I'm sure the police would've already been sent after me. Fat chance they'd be able to prove anything now. But her tone made me realize that I'd better get my baggie of remaining psilocybin mushrooms out of the house and well hidden until I need it.

Sunday, October 2nd 1:45 AM

I'M EXHAUSTED. GOD, I'M SO BLEARY-EYED RIGHT NOW I CAN barely focus on writing this journal entry. I spent the last five hours since dinner (sausage pizza for my mom and dad, mushroom pizza for me) translating *L'Occulto Illuminato*, and before that I'd done another five hours of translation. I wish I could keep going, but even if I could see straight, I'm too wasted and can't think properly. It's hard work given how archaic so much of the book's language is. At least I got the first forty-three pages done.

I know I might be a little loopy after ten hours of translating *L'Occulto Illuminato*, as well as everything else I've been through, but I can honestly say this book is the genuine gospel as far as demons go. Lazzarro Galeotti says that he was twelve when he first saw a demon. This was in his native Florence. At first he thought he was suffering from madness or witchcraft, but when he noticed that others around him appeared normal and that it was only this one creature—the neighborhood butcher—that he saw as a demon, he began to suspect something else was going on. Two things finally convinced him that he wasn't mad or touched by a witch's spell, and that this butcher truly was a demon: (1) The absence of any dogs nearby—I mean, you've got a butcher shop and no dogs anywhere nearby? What's the likelihood of that? (2) Catching sight of this demon's reflection in a piece of glass and seeing that his reflection showed him as human. After that Galeotti accepted that he had a special gift and that God wanted him to learn what he could about these demons, so that he could be of service to future generations.

The way Galeotti described this butcher demon is the same as the way I see them. And it's not just his physical description, but also that sweet onion sulfur smell and the inhuman guttural sounds that they make. Galeotti described how he once tied a rope around a dog's neck so he could take the dog to see this demon. Once they got within a hundred feet of the butcher shop, this scrawny mongrel, as Galeotti described the animal, started fighting with every ounce of strength it had to keep from being pulled any closer. The dog fought so hard that its heart gave out and it dropped lifeless onto the brick street. This distressed Galeotti enough that he never tried this experiment again.

That's as far as I've gotten so far, but Galeotti makes references early on that he had discovered the true nature of these demons and why they were among us. He also writes about how he discovered the secret to killing a demon, and hints that the leather used for the book's binding is indeed demon hide. This is really nauseating, but also pretty exciting because it means that the demons aren't invincible, and I have some hope now.

As thrilled as I am to finally have my hands on *L'Occulto Illuminato*, I can barely keep my eyes open. You can probably tell from this journal entry that I almost nodded off several times while writing it from the pen marks that were made as I jerked awake. I hope to get up early tomorrow to continue my translation, but for now I just need to crawl into bed.

I WAS PLANNING TO WRITE A JOURNAL ENTRY YESTERDAY AFTER a solid five to six hours of more translation, but it just didn't work out that way. I guess I must've been really zonked from working on *L'Occulto Illuminato* the night before because I slept over thirteen hours and didn't wake up until after three o'clock Sunday afternoon. I was furious with my parents for letting me sleep that late, but they simply shrugged it off, completely unconcerned, and told me that they thought I needed a good sleep.

I had yard work that I needed to do for several of my clients, so that shot most of the day, and only left me a few hours at night to do any translation since my parents insisted that I hit the bed by eleven. I didn't argue with them. Three hours of translation exhausted me almost as much as the ten hours I had done the day before, plus I wanted my wits about me for today. So let me talk about today before I go into what I learned from the additional thirty-seven pages of *L'Occulto Illuminato* that I translated the last two nights.

165

Let me start from the beginning, although none of this will get that interesting until later.

I really didn't want to take the school bus this morning—mostly because of Wesley—but that's exactly why I knew I had to take the bus. I had to see if he was going to be coming to school today, and if he did, how he'd react to me. Also, I couldn't let it look like I was hiding from him, and had to play dumb as if I had no idea what made him sick.

Wesley was at the bus stop. He avoided eye contact with me and acted as if he didn't hear me when I asked how he was feeling. He didn't even bother grunting out a response. So he must have decided that I was the one who poisoned him. Fuck him. If his parents knew he had ingested psilocybin mushrooms, they would've called my parents by now. So they had no idea what it was that made him sick. All they had were their suspicions. So Wesley acted as if I was invisible while we were at the bus stop, and later once we boarded. I didn't care. What Wesley and his parents thought didn't matter anymore. I had *L'Occulto Illuminato* in my possession, and my destiny was already mapped out. Friends were no longer going to be part of the equation.

When I got to homeroom, Sally gave me the cold shoulder also, although she was willing to acknowledge me long enough so that she could accuse me of skipping school Thursday and homeroom on Friday to avoid her because I was too immature to deal with our temporary break, and that I had to quit acting like a jerk. I didn't argue with her. Of course, she was partially right, but that's not why I didn't argue with her. Maybe it wasn't already over between the two of us in her mind, but regardless, it was over. Now that I *L'Occulto Illuminato*, it had to be over. I accepted it, and because of it, all I felt any longer looking at Sally was sadness. Any past longing or desire was gone. All I could do now for her was make sure she was safe from the demons. And I was going to do that.

The demon Connor Devin's attitude toward me had changed subtly. I had to act as if I wasn't noticing him, but whenever I had my chance I'd catch a glimpse of him, and he had this more puzzled demon expression as he stared at me as if he sensed that something had radically changed but couldn't figure out what. Maybe he believed that *L'Occulto Illuminato* was only a myth, and that's why he didn't realize that what had changed was that I owned a copy. But there was no longer any question that I was going to have to get rid of him soon, and the first step was getting him kicked out of the school. Later, once the *L'Occulto Illuminato* provides me the secret of how to kill demons, I'll get rid of him for good.

So I watched myself and was careful and avoided as much as I could tipping my hand to the demon Devin. I saw Wesley a few times, once when I was with Curt, and Wesley again treated me as if I was invisible. All I could do was shrug at Curt as if I had no clue what was going on.

Once school was over, I rigged one of the side doors so it would stay unlocked—just as I had done before when I needed to break into the Administration Office—and took the bus home. I sat with Curt and didn't make any further attempts to talk to Wesley. Later, after I got off the bus, I bypassed the demon Hanley's house to get home (while Devin didn't realize what I had in my possession, I couldn't shake the thought that Hanley would smell the *L'Occulto Illuminato* from my skin). After dropping off my school books, I took my bike and rode to the demon Connor Devin's address in Waltham.

The address turned out to be a ratty-looking two family home. My plan was to hide out and see who was coming and going—demons or humans—but I quickly saw that this would be tricky, because the two houses shared a door. I gave it a try anyway, and after about forty minutes, I saw a woman with a dog on a leash leave the house. This made no sense. It just wouldn't be possible for a dog to live in the same building as

Devin. I was furious—I had lost valuable time that I could've been spending translating *L'Occulto Illuminato*, and it was all thanks to the high school administration's office incompetent record keeping. How could they keep such slipshod records for their students? I felt like an idiot. After the woman and the dog passed by me, I scrambled out of my hiding spot and stormed to the front door, my vision coated red I was so angry. The name on the mailbox was Chaske, not Devin. I rang the doorbell for that side of the house and a minute later a girl about twelve answered the door. She was about my height but much thinner than me, with long straight blond hair that framed a narrow face. She stared at me with this doleful expression, waiting for me to say something, but something about her took me aback—I was speechless.

The girl broke the stunned trance I had fallen into by asking what I wanted.

"I need to see Connor Devin," I told her, swallowing back my confusion and anger, trying hard to make my voice as innocent and pleasant as I could. "The school told me he's living here. Is he home?"

A subtle change in her eyes all but confirmed that something funny was going on. She shook her head and asked me to leave my phone number. "I'll make sure he calls you when he gets home," she half-mumbled.

"You're lying," I said. "He doesn't live here. I know that. I'm going to call the authorities and find out what's going on."

Her face went blank, and she turned quickly on her heels and yelled for her dad. After that she disappeared inside and pulled the door closed after her. Less than a minute later I heard footsteps thumping down a creaky wooden staircase, and a middle-aged man opened the door. He was thick and fleshy, and wore a stained wife beater and gray khakis. His chest had a caved-in look, his pot belly pushing out from his T-shirt as if there was a half-deflated basketball hiding under it. There wasn't much resemblance between him and the skinny girl from a minute earlier. Maybe a little around the eyes, but that was about it.

"What's this about?" he demanded, scowling harshly at me as if that would scare me away. Fat chance. I've been stared at by demons a lot scarier and more menacing than some balding middle-aged guy with a pot belly, and I've always held my ground.

"Connor Devin is supposed to live here. I know he doesn't, and I want to know where he lives."

"What? What do you mean he doesn't live here?" The potbellied man who was probably named Chaske (and who at this point I'm going to assume is named Chaske) scratched above his ear as if he couldn't understand why I was saying what I was. "Look, kid, I don't know what you're thinking, but Connor's not home right now, that's all. But why don'cha leave your name and number and I'll have him call you, okay?"

"Fine. Whatever. I'll call the police and have them look into this."

He tried harder to stare me down and bluff me, his eyes shrinking to hard black dots. He clearly didn't like having some fifteen-year-old kid putting him on the spot, but then he lost his nerve and his eyes wavered from me. At that moment his chest seemed to cave in all that much more. He looked away from me and pushed a hand through his thinning red hair, his mouth folding into a thick, fleshy frown.

"What's this about?" he asked.

"I want to know where he lives."

"You going to tell anyone about this?"

"No. I only want to know where he lives. That's all."

Chaske breathed in deeply and let it out in a tired sigh. "I don't know where the boy lives," he admitted. "All I've got is a phone number."

"How come the school has this address for him?"

He tried smiling at me, but it didn't stick. "It was arranged that way. From what I was told he needed this address so they could get him into that high school in Newton, so we're on the books as his foster house. We're trying to give the kid a break, that's all. So you sure you're not going to tell anyone about this?"

"You going to tell anyone I was here looking for him?"

He shifted his gaze back to me and shook his head, his expression defeated but also showing some wariness as he tried to figure out what I was up to.

"Who set this up?" I asked.

"I don't know." Chaske shrugged without much enthusiasm. "It was all done by phone. I don't have a name, just a phone number in case someone comes by looking for Connor."

"How much did you get paid for this?"

Again, he attempted to show me a weak smile. This time he was able to manage it. "Five thousand, plus monthly foster care checks. Times are tough, you know? But I was really just trying to give a kid a break and help him get into a better school. You going to bleed me for some of it to stay quiet?"

"No, but unless you were paid cash, you got a check. And there must've been a name on it."

He smiled kind of a weary smile at the thought of it. "Nah. Neither check or cash. Direct deposit straight into my bank account. So why the interest in this?"

I told him I had my reasons, then asked if he ever saw Connor Devin. Whether he ever came by the house.

Chaske shook his head.

"Why'd they pick you?" I asked.

He shrugged noncommittally. "Me and my wife have taken care of foster kids before. We're set up with the state for it."

There was no point in asking him anything further. I had him give me the phone number he was supposed to call if anyone came around looking for the demon Connor Devin. As I turned to leave, he asked again, this time with a pleading in his voice, whether I was going to rat him out about Connor Devin not living there.

"Not as long as you don't call that number and tell them I was looking for Devin."

So there I was. I still had no clue where Devin lived, but if I had to guess he was living alone like all the demons I'd encountered. Weird shit was going on with this. Demons, or humans in league with them, had arranged all this, and it must've been done for the reason I suspected—after killing Vincent Gilman and finding his messages to some unknown person who also saw demons they wanted Devin placed in my high school, so he could keep watch over me. The whole arrangement showed how well connected these demons were—they had to be, to be able to set this up.

And I knew why Devin hadn't been put into an actual foster home. These demons needed to live alone. Partly because they must desire it so they can do their rituals and eat their dog meat in peace, but also they must know they'd give themselves away if they lived in close proximity to humans.

So now I had a phone number that would lead me to Devin, or at least to whoever it was, demon or otherwise, who had set all of this up for Devin. I was tempted to call that number so I could hear whether a human or demon answered, but I knew that wouldn't be smart. I didn't want to tip my hand yet.

Even though I still didn't know where Devin lived, I'd been handed a way of getting Devin kicked out of my high school. Or at least a possible way. It wasn't foolproof. If I ratted out Chaske, it would cause a big stink, which would most likely end with Chaske being arrested and Devin booted out of Newton North, as well as an investigation into the demons or others who were behind everything. At least that's what could happen, but there were other ways of it playing out, including having it all blow up in my face. Chaske could end up describing me to the demons. Or the demons could be well-connected enough to get tipped off ahead of time so they could move Devin into Chaske's house before the authorities had a chance to investigate.

Even though it was risky to rat out Chaske, it was tempting. I found myself fantasizing about Social Services raiding whatever apartment the demon Connor Devin lived in now and finding half-eaten dog carcasses; and other horrific demon effects that Devin wouldn't have time to dispose of. So yeah, it would be risky and dangerous, but I still might've done it if I didn't have another plan in mind. Something I'd be putting into motion later tonight. The reason why I tampered with that side door earlier today before leaving the high school.

Okay, enough of that.

I promised earlier I'd write about what I'd been learning from *L'Occulto Illuminato*. In the additional pages that I've been able to translate, Galeotti writes about further observations of his since accepting that the neighborhood butcher was a demon. He found three other demons living in different neighborhoods in Florence, all of them living alone, all of them appearing as normal human beings when their images were reflected using a hand mirror. At some point Galeotti became convinced that these demons were butchering stray dogs for their food. That he'd spy on his neighborhood butcher shop, and even though these other demons lived in neighborhoods that had their own butcher shops, they'd come to this one, always at dusk, and left with bulky wrapped packages that Galeotti was sure were butchered dog carcasses.

Galeotti also wrote about a rash of young girls and prostitutes having gone missing—over twenty of them disappearing during a nine month period. The body of one of them was found. The girl was thirteen and her body was discovered in a wooded area five miles from the city. Her clothes had been shredded as if by knives, and an examination showed massive internal damage as if she'd been raped by a dagger. The city never solved the girl's murder or any of the other disappearances, but Galeotti was convinced one of the demons was responsible. Years after this incident when he was able to kill a demon and examine its body, he was even further convinced by the grotesquely misshapen form of the demon's sex organ and its knife-like serrated edges. This is what I had suspected, and Galeotti confirmed it.

(Note. Galeotti made the remark about killing a demon casually, as if it were nothing more than a passing reference. I reread that passage dozens of time to make sure I got it right, and there's no doubting it. *Galeotti killed a demon.* I knew it had to be possible to kill them, and Galeotti confirmed it, even if he did it in a casual reference. The thought of it left me lightheaded for several minutes. Somewhere in *L'Occulto Illuminato* Galeotti must describe how it's done.)

That's what I've gotten to so far. It's twenty past nine now. I'll be spending the next three hours doing further translation. Then I'm sneaking out of the house and putting plan '*Fuck You Demon Devin*' in action.

T HINGS DID NOT WORK OUT AS PLANNED. PUTTING IT LIGHTLY. Calling what happened a disaster would be more like it.

At first, things looked like they'd go smoothly. I snuck out of the house last night at one o'clock in the morning without incident, retrieved the baggy of psilocybin mushrooms where I'd hidden it, and rode my bike to the high school. The side door I had tampered with was still accessible. I'd brought my burglar picks and got into the demon's locker in less than a minute, hiding the baggy of mushrooms under a layer of garbage that lined the bottom of his locker. It smelled awful in there—I could only imagine the demonic items that he kept safeguarded in his locker during the day. I was home by a quarter to two and was able to get four and a half hours of sleep before getting up and sending an anonymous email to the school principal about Connor Devin selling drugs on school grounds, as well as having a stash hidden in his locker.

I felt a coolness in my head while I took the school bus

this morning. Curt sat next to me, and his voice was only a buzz as I nodded and pretended I was listening to him. I wanted to take the bus in so I'd arrive with everyone else. As I walked in through the main doors, I felt no nerves, instead only perfectly calm. Maybe my stomach tightened slightly when I saw the commotion going on in front of Devin's locker, but other than that, nothing. There were three police officers by the locker, and one of them had a Black Labrador on a leash that must've been a drug sniffing dog. Devin, the principal and the assistant principal were also there. What made it such a commotion was the way that dog was going nuts as it tried desperately to get away from Devin. The cop holding the leash was barking commands as he fought to control the dog, and the other two cops looked puzzled by the dog's frantic attempts to escape. All of us were being hurried along by teachers, so I couldn't watch this scene for more than a few seconds, but I did catch a look of intense hatred on Devin's demon face as he stared fixedly at the poor animal.

As I continued on to my homeroom I thought that would be that, and I was back to feeling absolutely calm, the tightness in my stomach gone. I enjoyed hearing the murmurs and whispers from my fellow students as they speculated about what must've been going on with Devin. At least I'd finally have Devin out of my hair and, more importantly, away from Sally. So it was a shock when ten minutes later the school principal and a cop escorted Devin back to the homeroom, a nasty smirk twisting the demon's face as he cast a glance at me. I should've expected what was going to happen next, but I was being too dense, and I was completely stunned when the principal called out my name. When the homeroom teacher pointed out who I was, the principal used his hand to motion me over, and in a voice that was way too calm, he asked me to join him. I was led out of the classroom and back toward my locker. The other cops were waiting there, along with the drug-sniffing Black Labrador, who had calmed down by this point, and stood attentively facing my locker, his snout right up against it. I was still too dumb then to have figured out what had happened, and it was only when the principal had me open my locker and the dog bulled straight into it sticking his nose into a stack of papers on the bottom of my locker, that it started to dawn on me how Devin had turned things around. Not right away—I was in too much of a state of shock for that, but at some level I began to realize what had happened.

Where I had screwed up was discounting the unusually powerful olfactory senses that these damn demons possess. They're like dogs that way. The demon Connor Devin must've sniffed out the baggy of mushrooms I had planted in his locker, and either guessed I was the one behind the deed, or maybe even detected my scent on the baggy. After that he picked my lock, just as I had done, and returned the favor by planting the drugs in my locker. Then, after the police found his locker clean of anything illegal, Devin must've told them that he heard a rumor about me dealing them. Maybe the police believed him, maybe not, but it was settled once they took their drug-sniffing dog to my locker.

You can probably guess everything that happened afterwards. I was brought to the police station, where I had to sit in a small room until my dad came to the station, and as you can probably guess, he was not happy. The police wanted to question me, but my dad the lawyer refused to let that happen, so I was then booked on a couple of different charges, including bringing illegal drugs onto school grounds. After that I had to sit in a holding area until my dad was able to arrange for me to be released to him. Neither of us spoke when we walked from the police station to where he had parked the car, nor while he drove us home. He sat frozen, unable to look at me, his face blanched of any color. It wasn't until he pulled into our driveway that he told me how disappointed he was in me. He couldn't even look at me as he said it, his voice cold and foreign, like he didn't know me. Or knew me, but felt only disdain.

"I had no idea those drugs were in my locker," I told him. "Someone planted them there."

"You expect me to believe that?" he asked, his voice even harsher than before.

"I don't care what you believe. You can have me take a lie detector if you want. I'm not lying."

He didn't bother responding verbally to that, just shook his head, his teeth clenched so tightly that I could hear them grind. Or maybe I was only imagining them grinding from the way he looked like he wanted to kill someone. We walked up the path to the front door in that same stone cold silence as earlier, and when he opened the door my mom was there waiting for us, her expression crestfallen, her skin ashen.

"How could you do this to us?" she asked me in a hurt voice. "How could you humiliate us like this?"

"He's innocent," my dad told her, his voice dripping in sarcasm. "Someone planted the drugs in his locker—at least that's what Henry's claiming."

I didn't say anything. My stomach had knotted up so much I had to fight to keep from doubling over. All I wanted to do was get away from them and be alone in my room. But as I tried to walk past her, my mom grabbed me by my shoulders and turned me so I had to face her.

"Look at me!" she insisted. "Do you have any idea what you've done to us? How everyone in the neighborhood will be talking about our drug-dealing son? And do you have any idea what this has done to you? How this has affected your life? How impossible it's going to be for you now to get into a top college?"

There was a near hysteria in her voice and her eyes were liquid and shining with a touch of madness. Veins stood out along the side of her neck and ruined her mouth. She looked ancient right then. Ancient and crazy. All I wanted to do was break free of her, but she had her fingers gripping me like a vise. I found myself losing control as I met her wide-eyed stare.

"I'm telling the truth about those drugs being planted in my locker," I said. "When the police investigate this they won't find a single witness that ever saw me sell drugs because I never did. But you're so willing to believe the worst of me!"

"That's not true—"

"Of course it is. You don't think I noticed all the hints and the insinuations the two of you have made about me in the past, like whether I'm gay? To put your mind at ease, I'm not, and as proof, I've been fucking the brains out of Sally Freeman for weeks."

That was a stupid thing for me to say, but I was out of control right then, sick with worry and fear. Not out of anything mundane, like the drug charges, or the fact that I had disgraced the family, or that I wouldn't be able to get into an Ivy League college anymore (not that there was ever a chance that I was going on to college anyway, how could I with what I had to do?). No—all I could think about was that the demons would be after me now. After I'd tried to frame Devin, they'd know that I was the one in contact with Vincent Gilman on that message board, and it would only be a matter of time before they'd break into my house and do to me what they did to Gilman. It wasn't the thought of them coming after me that scared me, but the thought that I had failed and let the world down. I finally had *L'Occulto Illuminato* in my possession, and I had to blow everything with a stupid, idiotic ploy. At that moment I was completely lost in an ocean of fear, self-pity and disgust, and so I said something really stupid.

My mom flinched as if she'd been slapped. Her mouth dropped open and she let go of her grip on my shoulders, her hands sliding off me as if she'd lost all her strength. Out of the corner of my eye I caught sight of my dad, and he looked like he wanted to punch me. I'm not exaggerating; his right hand had curled into a fist. I turned away from both of them and ran upstairs to my room, taking three steps at a time. This all happened forty-five minutes ago, and neither of them has bothered coming after me or knocking on my door. A while ago I smelled food downstairs, but they didn't bother calling me down for dinner. That's fine. I'm not hungry anyway, and I probably want to see them even less than they want to see me.

So now I'm suspended from school for an indefinite period of time, because the school takes drugs and especially drug dealing very seriously. Maybe they'll kick me out for good. It doesn't matter. None of it matters anymore. On the bright side, I won't have Devin dogging me all day, and I'll have more time to concentrate on *L'Occulto Illuminato*. I need that time now more than ever. I have to learn how to kill these demons before they come after me.

Of course, it's possible they won't come after me. Devin might've only guessed that I planted the drugs in his locker, and he might believe my animosity towards him is due to jealousy over him trying to steal Sally from me. I know it's only a small probability, but still, maybe the demons aren't yet convinced that I'm the person they're after. Maybe if I do get kicked out of school, Devin will disappear back into the woodwork where he came from, and Sally will be safe. What would be the point of them keeping him there if I was gone?

I checked my cell phone a few minutes ago, and there were a dozen or so text messages from Sally, and almost the same number of voicemails also from her. I'm not up to reading or listening to them yet. I might just delete them without bothering to read or listen to them. Whatever strength I can muster I need for these damn demons, and I don't think I could take being scolded by her now.

It's funny, Curt never leaves text or voice messages— something to do with an inbred paranoia on his part, but this time he left a voice message. Like with Sally's, I didn't listen to it. Nothing from Wesley.

I'm sure Devin is feeling pretty smug and pleased with himself right now. Maybe he feels as if he's discredited me enough so even if I did ever tell anyone about demons, no one would believe me, especially if they thought I had a history with hallucinogenic drugs. The more I think about it, the demons will have to keep him in school until they know whether I've been expelled or simply suspended. What Devin and the other demons don't know is that I know he doesn't live at that address in Waltham, where the school thinks he lives. It would be risky, but if I could find out where he's living, I could send the authorities swarming over there to discover whatever horrors he has lying around. I have the slip of paper on my desk right now; the one I had written that phone number on that I had gotten from Chaske. I need to figure out what to do with it. This time, though, I won't be as hasty as I was with planting those drugs.

My phone's ringing again. It's Sally. I'm going to turn off the phone without answering. I don't want to hear her voice right now.

I need to get back to *L'Occulto Illuminato*, but my mind's racing too much to concentrate on it. I'd hoped writing this journal entry would've helped calm me down, but it hasn't.

T WENTY MINUTES AGO WESLEY CAME BY THE HOUSE TO ACCUSE me of spiking his chocolate milk with psilocybin mushrooms. I denied it, but he was persistent.

"The whole school is talking about the police finding mushrooms in your locker," he said.

I had brought Wesley into the kitchen, but he had refused my offers for a snack or anything to drink, or even to sit down, and stood glaring at me with this angry, pinched expression. His skin had paled to the color of milk. Even though it gave him a psychological advantage, I took a seat at the table after I started brewing a pot of coffee. Espresso has started making me jittery, so I've switched to drinking plain coffee.

"Those mushrooms were planted in my locker," I said in a weary tone, which has become much more weary over the last three days after all the heart-to-heart talks I've been having with my dad where I've been constantly having to repeat my innocence.

Wesley snorted at that. "What a coincidence," he forced out, his mouth pinching even tighter. "Mushrooms being planted in your locker and also ending up in my chocolate milk when it was only the two of us together."

"What makes you think it was funny mushrooms that made you sick and not spoiled milk?" I asked with a sigh, my tone even wearier. Wesley's eyes narrowed into angry slits and his hands curled into fists. He looked comical with his jeans and shirt too tight for his pencil-thin body, and here he was, ready to launch himself at me. I'd snap him in half if we got into a fight. He had to know that.

"After they were found in your locker, I looked them up on the Internet," Wesley said, jutting his weak chin at me, his breathing having become more ragged, as if he were fighting to keep from flying at me with fists and feet. "The way they affect you, that's what I was poisoned with."

"Yeah? Did you also look up botulism? The way you were throwing up, that's what I would've guessed."

"You poisoned me! With mushrooms!"

"Why would I do that?"

"Because you thought it would be a big joke. That's why you agreed to come over to my house to read comic books. So you could get me high on mushrooms and laugh about it later. You didn't count on me getting as sick as I did."

"Is that what you really think of me?" I asked.

The hurt tone in my voice must've taken him aback. It was genuine and he knew it, and he reacted to it by blinking stupidly a couple of time, the pinched tightness of his mouth loosening. I really was surprised that he'd think so little of me. That I'd slip him mushrooms for a reason as sick and cruel as that.

"Okay, I don't know why you did it, but whatever your reason was, I know that's what happened." He was trying to sound insistent, but he had lost a good deal of his conviction.

Even with this newfound doubt, he still had his hands clenched into tiny fists.

I let out another heavy sigh and pushed myself away from the table and onto my feet. "If you want to throw a punch at me, go ahead, but I'll break your jaw," I promised him. "You were supposed to be one of the few friends I had left, and you're going to believe the worst of me like this. Fuck, man, I expected better from you."

Now I had him totally confused. Not convinced, but confused enough so that he didn't throw the punch he'd been dying to throw at me. He probably would've only hurt his hand if he had, at least if he was successful and connected. I doubt Wesley had ever punched anyone before.

I told him he'd better leave, and I showed him to the door, and that was how it went with Wesley.

I'd mentioned in an earlier journal entry how Sally left a bunch of text messages and calls on Tuesday. I ended up deleting them without reading or listening to them. I didn't feel up to hearing any more of her disappointment in me, and even though I knew it was over between us, I didn't actually want to hear her say it. Well, they continued, and against my better judgment I picked up a call from her last night. There was so much hurt in her voice when she asked me how I could've been selling drugs on school grounds. I gave her the same tired spiel about the drugs being planted in my locker. Then added how my dad had been looking into what happened.

"What my dad found out is that the police were brought to the school because of an anonymous email sent to the principal that Connor Devin had drugs stashed in his locker. It was Devin that then brought the police to my locker, saying that he had heard I had drugs."

"So?"

"The school is doing an investigation, and so far they've found no one else who had ever seen me with drugs or heard that I was dealing them. Which you know is true. So why would Devin say that?"

I held my forehead in my hand as I waited for Sally to say something. I felt so damn tired right then. Exhausted, really. Like all I wanted to do was lie down on my bed and close my eyes. That was it. Just be able to fall asleep and never have to wake up. That would've been something. To never have to worry about demons again.

But that wasn't going to be the case.

When it became obvious that Sally wasn't going to connect the dots to where I was trying to lead her, I did it for her. "He hid them in my locker," I continued. "Either Devin was tipped off about the police coming or he made the anonymous call himself."

"Why would he do that?"

"So he could frame me and get me kicked out of school."

"That doesn't make any sense." Sally hesitated, and I could imagine her brow creasing as she bit at her thumbnail, trying to make sense of what I was saying. That image brought such a heaviness to my chest that I had trouble breathing. "Why would he want to do that?" she asked.

"Because he knows that I know he's evil, and he probably also wants to get rid of me because he knows we're together, and he wants you."

"He's not evil." Her tone had changed subtly as if she were flattered that I had suggested Devin wanted her. I kept forgetting about his Justin Bieber façade. Still, the thought that she'd feel flattered by that made me a little nuts. "Please, Henry," she added, "Stop saying that about Connor."

"He is evil. Didn't you see the way that drug-sniffing dog reacted to him? That poor animal was just about killing himself trying to get away from Devin."

"That dog must've smelled drugs elsewhere, like your locker, and was only trying to get there. That's what was going on. So please, quit saying Connor is evil. It makes you sound crazy."

She could've ripped out my fingernails and it wouldn't have hurt as much as hearing her say that. My voice sounded very strange to me as I told her, "I didn't know those drugs were in my locker. If it wasn't Devin, then someone else planted them. If you don't believe me and are unwilling to trust me, we might as well call it quits right now. So do you believe me?"

Sally hesitated for a brief moment, and then, in a soft, halting voice she told me she believed me. I was pretty sure one of her reasons for calling me was to end things between us, but it must've stunned her that I was willing to put our relationship on the line the way I did. I think I did it because I must've been trying to just get things over. Make it kind of like with a Band-Aid; have it ripped off quickly so it would hurt less. It surprised me that she didn't take advantage of the opportunity I gave her to end things easily, but it didn't matter. Whether she wanted it to be or not, it's over. Once they put Devin in the school to spy on me, it was over, and there was no denying it any longer once I got my hands on a copy of *L'Occulto Illuminato*. My life is now all about the demons. It has to be. It's the burden I have to bear, especially now that there's a good chance that the demons are on to me.

What I told her about the school's investigation was true. Even during my last heart-to-heart with my dad, it sounded like he was beginning to believe me and suspect something fishy was going on. It didn't add up that Devin would be the only one to hear about me having drugs in my locker, unless the school officials think that the other students they're talking to just don't want to rat on me. But what it comes down to is that my parents have money and the school officials probably believe that Devin being a supposed exchange student from Waltham doesn't (although I'm sure the demons could raise a substantial amount), so in the end they'll side with me and probably suspect Devin of planting the drugs, as I've been saying all along. Maybe they'll even end up kicking him out of the school.

So that was how it went with Sally. She believed me about the drugs, or at least said she did. She wasn't ready to end things with me, even though they were already ended. And in her own way, she confirmed to me that she wanted Devin. Which meant I was going to have to make sure Devin was gone sooner than later.

I also got a call from Curt last night. He sounded like he was in awe when he told me I was now a legend. I told him I wasn't anything; and once again repeated that tired mantra of the drugs being planted in my locker.

"It's because of those cops bringing that dog. What a scene. Wow, though, no matter how it turns out, you're now a legend here. Worthy to be one of *Cthulhu's* soldiers."

"Does he pay well?"

Curt chuckled at that. "Next time I see him I'll ask."

I told Curt I'd see him again soon at school once all this was straightened out. Of course, I was hoping it wouldn't be straightened out anytime soon. More than ever, I need the time now to translate *L'Occulto Illuminato*, especially since the demons aren't going to waste much time coming after me. I'm surprised they haven't already—maybe they're still not fully convinced I'm the one they're after. The one who had been in contact with Virgil.

I should talk about the latest section of *L'Occulto Illuminato* that I've been translating. I can barely read it without breaking into a cold sweat. But I still have pages to go with it, and even when I finish, I'll have to double-check my translation before I write about it. It's too important. I can't afford to get it wrong, especially with the risk of demons coming for me soon, I might not have a chance to correct what I wrote.

I'm staring again at the phone number I got from Chaske as I try to decide what to do with it.

MY DAD'S NOW FIRMLY IN MY CORNER. DURING DINNER TONIGHT he became nearly epileptic as he ranted about the lawsuits he was going to file against the school, the principal, the city, you name it. He got so excited that bits of food spat out of his mouth, which was something I never thought I'd see from him.

"It's outrageous the way they handled it," he declared angrily to me and my mom, little specs of meatball and spaghetti flying out of his mouth. His face reddened for a moment as if he were choking, but I guess he was just swallowing down his rage. He raised his fork for emphasis, a piece of meatball attached to it. "Completely outrageous the way they made a spectacle of arresting Henry," he continued. He stopped for a moment, his jaw muscles tensing and his lips flattening out into thin hard lines, then he went on, "They had no corroborating evidence, just the word of one student—the very one they were investigating! And since then they haven't found a single student who could corroborate what this Devin kid is saying. Which is exactly what Henry's

189

been claiming would be the case. Someone planted those drugs in Henry's locker. Probably that Devin kid. It all adds up that way."

My mom didn't look too convinced of my innocence, but she didn't argue with him. I'm sure that with my dad arguing my case and with his threats of lawsuits, the school will be reinstating me soon and my charges will be dropped. Maybe this will cause them to look into the demon Devin more closely, and maybe even get them to find out he doesn't live at that Waltham foster home like he's supposed to. Of course, Wesley could start telling people that I spiked his chocolate milk with psilocybin mushrooms, and that might throw a wrench into everything. But maybe not. He wouldn't have any proof at this point, and with him being such an odd duck, people would probably be suspicious of his motives—maybe think he was making those claims to get attention. No, there's little doubt I'll be back in school soon, which is unfortunate. I need more time with *L'Occulto Illuminato*, especially after what I had just finished translating. I have to hope it takes my dad at least another week before he's able to get me back into school, but a week wouldn't be enough time for what I need to do. Even a month probably wouldn't be enough time.

Before dinner I finished translating the latest section I'd been working on, and I spent the last seven hours verifying my translation. There are no mistakes, no doubting what I've come up with. This section is absolutely chilling, and it explains what Clifton Gibson was doing in Brooklyn, and why Ginny Cataldo and Trey Wilkerson were taken. And not just them, but all the other little kids the demons must be stealing. I know of two others: a three-year-old girl just shy of her fourth birthday was taken in Maine a few weeks ago, as well as one in Rhode Island. Their abductions didn't make the local news here, but I found out about them through Internet searches that I've been doing since finishing this latest translation, and I'm convinced that demons are behind them. I'm also convinced that there will be other abductions of not-quite-four-year-olds. There will be thirty-nine abductions in this area, and thirty-nine in four other areas around the world—more if any of the children die before the demons can finish their rituals.

So in addition to the time I need to finish translating *L'Occulto Illuminato*, there's also a good chance I'll have to sneak away to New York for a day. I hope that won't be the case, because it will be dangerous in its own right, but there may be no way around it.

So now about the recent section I translated. The one that explained what Clifton Gibson and other demons were doing in Brooklyn, and what must be going on in Boston now. And four other cities around the world—cities where if you connected them with Boston added in you'd form a five-pointed star. That's why they were able to move their rituals from Brooklyn to Boston. Because they're close enough so that that star would still be formed. Let me explain. The section I translated outlines the rituals these demons need to perform to open the gates to hell.

The rituals are complicated, but involve abducting thirty-nine children under the age of four, carving symbols into their bodies and skulls, and sewing their eyes shut and their mouths mostly shut. They sew their mouths mostly shut so the children can't scream, which would interfere with their rituals, but they don't sew them completely shut because then the children would die of dehydration and starve to death, and the demons need them alive between the span of two full moons so they can perform these horrible rituals. Oh, they can't cut out their tongues because that's for the very end. But if these rituals are performed in five cities around the world—and those cities form a five-pointed star—then the gates to hell will open wide and demons and other dark creatures will flood the earth. And it will be the end of man.

So as you can see, the ante has been raised. If I ever had a choice of ignoring these demons before, I don't any longer. I have to stop what's happening, and my head's spinning just thinking about it.

I'm too tired to do any more translating now, but I know there's no chance I'll be able to sleep. Before sitting down to write this last entry I tried sleeping, but when I closed my eyes all I could see was what these demons must be doing to all those abducted children right now. The very thought of it is both sickening and heartbreaking.

All I know is that I need to learn how to kill these demons before they come after me. And I need to find those children. I know they're somewhere in the Boston area. According to *L'Occulto Illuminato* the rituals must be held in five heavily populated cities that are also major cultural centers.

The only thing I have going for me is that the rules for opening up the gates of hell are complicated, and I've got time. At least two full moons' worth from when the last of the thirty-nine children are abducted. The one kidnapped in Rhode Island was taken two weeks ago, which would give me three weeks. I could have a lot more time than that—they still might be collecting the thirty-nine children that they need. But the problem is that since I don't know how many they've taken so far, I have to assume the worst: that they've already started their rituals.

So while it was purely accidental on the demon Connor Devin's part, he did me a huge favor getting me kicked out of school, and I have to hope it takes my dad longer than he expects to get me reinstated. I need all the time I can get now if I'm going to save this world from being overrun by hell.

THREE SIGNIFICANT EVENTS OCCURRED TODAY, AT LEAST AS FAR as these demons go. I'll write about them now from least to most significant.

First and least, I went to New York today and met with the detective in charge of the Clifton Gibson investigation. I spent all day yesterday agonizing about how to handle things. I needed to know for sure that what Galeotti described in *L'Occulto Illuminato* were the same rituals that the demons performed on those stolen children in Brooklyn. I needed to know that I could trust every word I read in *L'Occulto Illuminato*.

The police detective in charge of the Clifton Gibson case was named Joe Thomase. I learned that early on from my many Internet searches involving the case. Meeting him in person would be risky. If he arrested me, it would alert the demons that I was the one they were after. And the chance that he'd arrest me was real, since I would be telling him things that only Clifton Gibson and his co-conspirators would know, at least if *L'Occulto*

Illuminato accurately described the rituals that demons need to perform to open the gates of hell. But after running through different scenarios in my head, I couldn't see how it could work without meeting Thomase in person. So yesterday I rode my bike into Watertown, bought a disposable cell phone, and called Thomase's precinct. I asked the police officer who answered if I could speak to Thomase. The cop, in an impatient tone, told me Thomase wasn't in and asked what this was about. I told him I thought I had information about the Clifton Gibson child kidnappings. The cop sounded even more impatient as he told me to leave my name and number. I gave him a made-up name, and he hung up on me the second I finished giving him the number for my disposable phone. I waited two hours, then called back, this time telling the cop answering the phone to tell Thomase that I knew that thirty-nine children were abducted. The number of children found in that Brooklyn warehouse had been withheld in the news. I got a call back fifteen minutes later.

"This is Joe Thomase," the voice said. "Is this Martin Slater?"

I'd seen pictures of Thomase. A thin man with dark features and piercing eyes. The voice didn't seem to go with those pictures. It was an old man's voice. Gruff and hoarse. Maybe he smoked a lot.

"My name's not really Martin Slater, but I'm the one who called."

"You sound like a kid."

"I'm fifteen."

"Yeah?" If that surprised him, it didn't show in his voice. "How'd you know that thirty-nine kids were taken? Have you been in contact with Gibson?"

"No. I haven't been in any contact with Gibson or any of his co-conspirators."

"What do you mean co-conspirators? What makes you think others were involved?"

"It's something I know. Just like I know that they sewed those children's eyes shut and their mouths almost completely shut, and that they carved symbols into the children's torsos and skulls."

"Uh uh, kid. I'm not playing this game. You give me your name now. And a phone number for something that's not a disposable cell."

"I'm not doing that, but I can meet you in New York tomorrow."

There was a long moment of silence from Thomase, then, "Where?"

"Somewhere near Penn Station. I need to take the train to New York, so I won't be able to get there until one."

There was another long hesitation before he said okay, and gave me an address for a diner near Penn Station, along with his private cell phone number.

"You'll be there at one thirty?"

"I'll try. As long as the train's not late."

"You know the names of any of Gibson's co-conspirators?" he asked, not quite believing me, but not totally discounting me either.

"No, but there had to be others involved."

"Had to be, huh? You know that for a fact? How do you know that?"

"You wouldn't believe me if I told you. But I'll show you tomorrow."

I hung up and also turned off the disposable phone. I had ridden my bike several miles away from my home before I called up that second time. I didn't know whether the police could trace someone's location from a disposable phone, but I didn't want to take the chance that they could.

Last night I told my dad I would be leaving early in the morning to go to the Boston Public Library to do research for school. Even though I was suspended, I was still supposed to be keeping up with my school work. Telling him that short-circuited any grief my parents might've otherwise given me when I left the house this morning at seven. Buried in my backpack was a folder I planned to give to Detective Joe Thomase that I had spent hours preparing last night. My hopes were that that folder would keep me from getting arrested, but I ended up miscalculating badly.

I had a difficult time during those three and a half hours while I rode the Acela train from South Station in Boston to New York. I had brought along some Manga graphic novels to keep me occupied, but I couldn't concentrate on them as my mind kept drifting to what was going to happen later. I knew I was walking right into the lion's den. If Joe Thomase arrested me, I was done. The demons would find out about it, and they'd know my reason for looking into Clifton Gibson; because I'm the one who had been trading messages with Vincent Gilman, aka *Virgil*. There was a chance Thomase would want to arrest me, and as it turned out, a better chance than I had thought. It would all come down to whether he believed me or whether he thought I knew what I did because I was somehow connected to Gibson. Worrying about that made it difficult to sit still. Every noise had me jumping in my seat, and by the time the train arrived at Penn Station, my neck and shoulders were hurting from all the tension that had built up inside them.

I found the diner where Thomase wanted to meet me without any problem. He was sitting facing the front door. He looked older than he did from the pictures I had seen of him; his hair speckled with gray and thick lines now carved into his face. The Clifton Gibson case must have aged him. As soon as I stepped into the diner, he knew I was the one he was waiting for, and he crooked his index finger at me to signal me over. My heart leapt into my throat as I thought again about the consequences, and for a moment I almost turned and ran, but instead I forced myself to continue to his table, and took the empty seat across from him. He gave me a long hard stare, frowning as he sized me up.

"Kid," he said in that hoarse smoker's voice, "you could be in a lot of trouble. You better tell me right now how you knew the things you did."

"From a book."

"From a book?" Thomase arched his right eyebrow quizzically and his lips twisted into a *what-kind-of-bullshit-is-this* grimace. "What do you mean from a book? Are you telling me that Gibson put something out? Where, on the Internet?"

"No, nothing like that. The book I'm talking about was written in the seventeenth century. Let me show you."

I took out of my backpack the folder that I had prepared for him. It was thick, stuffed with hundreds of sheets of paper— copies of all of the pages of *L'Occulto Illuminato*, as well as a printout of my translation so far and the information I had compiled on Ginny Cataldo, Trey Wilkerson, and the other missing children. Thomase frowned as he thumbed through the stack of paper.

"What am I looking at?" he demanded, his grimace turning into a scowl. "It looks like some kind of foreign language."

"The book I was talking about. It's called *L'Occulto Illuminato*. Probably only a few dozen people alive have ever heard of it, and most of those believe it's only a myth. I thought so too until a few weeks ago when someone emailed me photographed images of the book cover and all the pages you're looking at. The book is written in Italian, an archaic form of it. I've also included what I've been able to translate so far. If you look at the last ten pages of my translation, you can see what I've circled in red."

Thomase was thumbing through the pages, his grimace growing more severe. He still hadn't gotten to my translation and was looking at the pages photographed from *L'Occulto Illuminato*.

"Who emailed you this?" he asked.

"I don't know. It was done anonymously."

Thomase gave me a look as if he knew I was full of shit, but then was back to thumbing through what I had given him.

"Why would someone email you this?" he asked.

"Because of private chat rooms where I talked with other occult historians about how much I wanted to track down this book."

From the dubious look on Thomase's face, I doubted he believed me, but he kept thumbing through the pages in the folder until he reached my translation.

"You know Italian?" he asked.

"I took a crash course in it once I had those pages emailed to me. And a lot of the language used is archaic. For a good number of the words, I had to search for the Latin roots and still had to guess at their meaning."

Thomase grunted in response to that. He skimmed through the first two pages of my translation, his expression growing more dubious, then he skipped to the last ten pages so he could see what I had circled in red ink. As he read about the rituals these demons perform on the abducted children, his skin color grayed. After that he went back and more carefully read my translation from start to finish. When he was done he put the pages down on the table. He looked spooked.

"So he had accomplices," Thomase murmured. He wasn't really looking at me, at least not directly. I think at that moment he had forgotten I was there, and had murmured that to himself.

"That's right," I said. "According to *L'Occulto Illuminato* nine of them are needed to perform their rituals so that they can open the gates to hell. Clifton Gibson wouldn't have been doing it alone."

That snapped Thomase's attention back to me. His expression hardened as he stared at me. "Kid." he said, "there's no more joking around on this. I need your name and address now."

That stunned me. "Why?" I asked.

"Why?" He shook his head. "A hoax is being perpetrated on you, kid. That book is a fake. Whoever put it together knew what Gibson did to those children. I don't know why they'd go to all the trouble they did faking this so-called Occulto book and emailing you what they did, but that's what happened, and we need to have our computer forensics people examine your email."

Again, this stunned me. I hadn't anticipated this response from him, and found myself stammering as I told him that's not what it was.

"I lied before," I told him, desperately. "The book's real. I didn't want to admit I have a copy. I didn't want to have to bring it here. It's too rare and important to risk losing it by bringing it with me, but it's real. And what's in those pages I gave you are real."

"Kid—"

"No, it is. I know it is. And it's not a cult, if that's what you're thinking. They're demons. They really are. Clifton Gibson is a demon, and there are other demons involved. Take a DNA sample from him. You'll see."

Thomase wasn't buying it. I could tell he believed I was sincere in what I was saying, but from the humoring look he gave me he wasn't buying one word of what I was telling him.

"I see demons," I went on, talking fast and furiously as I tried to get out the whole story before he arrested me. "I do, I really do. They look exactly the way they're described early on in *L'Occulto Illuminato*, and there are some illustrations that show them. I came to New York when Clifton Gibson's trial was going on and I was able to get into the courtroom. He's a demon. And there were other demons in the courtroom, too. Two others who must've been part of Gibson's demon coven, or whatever a group of demons is called."

Thomase was losing patience with me. He felt sorry for me—I could tell—but he was probably convinced I was mentally unstable, and he was losing patience fast.

"I bet he didn't have fingerprints," I said.

That struck a minor chord with Thomase. "You somehow found out about that, huh?" he said. "Look, kid, it doesn't mean anything. Sometimes they use acid to get rid of their fingerprints. Gibson isn't the first pervert to wipe off his prints with a chemical agent." He glanced at his watch and let out an impatient sigh. "About time we get going, okay, kid?"

"Don't you understand why I'm doing this? It's not just so you can find the others involved with Gibson, but because they're doing it all over again in Boston! Look at the other pages I included in the folder, the ones about the almost four-year-old children who've been abducted. By the time they're done there are going to be thirty-nine abducted, and these demons are going to be doing the same horrible things to these children as the ones you found in Brooklyn. If you send police to my home, the demons are going to know that I know about them. And nobody will be left to stop them."

Thomase gave me this sad, almost exhausted look and started to push himself to his feet.

"I know you believe all this, son, probably why they chose you to send this bullshit to—"

"What about dogs? Were you able to see the way dogs react to Gibson?"

That slowed Thomase down. He must've seen something. Maybe they brought police dogs to that warehouse in Brooklyn. Whatever he saw, this slowed him down.

A waitress at that moment was walking past Thomase carrying a full tray of food. I wasn't going to let Thomase bring me to his precinct and send cops to my home. I'd be dead if either of those happened, especially with Hanley watching my house, so I used the opportunity that presented itself to me. I pushed this white-haired grandmotherly-looking waitress into Thomase. The tray of food went all over him, and the waitress knocked him into another table, then the two of them fell onto the floor. The whole thing made quite a racket and drowned out most of Thomase's swearing. I didn't stick around to hear too much of it as I ran out of there as fast as I could. If anyone ran after me, I had no idea. I kept running and didn't stop until I was six blocks away.

Even though I had bought a round-trip train ticket, I didn't want to risk going back to Penn Station. Thomase knew I had taken the train to New York, and I couldn't take the chance of him sending cops there to look for me. So I threw away the return ticket and made my way to Kennedy Airport in Queens. It would be risky enough flying home since I just about told him I had come up from Boston and he could be sending cops to Kennedy, too, but I didn't see what choice I had other than trying to hitchhike home.

If Thomase had sent cops to the airport, I didn't see them. I only had to wait fifteen minutes from the time I bought my ticket for the three o'clock shuttle to when I was allowed to board—and I did this while standing near the gate for a flight heading for Miami—but I was still sweating like crazy. After I got on the plane, my heart pounded like a drum as I waited for cops to come after me, but none did. Even after the plane took off, I was still waiting for someone to arrest me, at least for the first five minutes or so. I was lucky all the way around, especially that I had brought enough money to buy the plane ticket, since I wasn't expecting to have to. I was home well before my parents, so even that worked out.

Now for the second significant event. When I got home I checked the message board where I'd earlier traded messages with Virgil. I don't know why I did that—just something nagging at me to check it once more—and sure enough, there was a new message from Virgil. Except it wasn't from Virgil since Vincent Gilman was dead; instead, it came from a demon trying to smoke me out. The message had this fake Virgil telling me that he was able to verify the demon I had sent him, and he gave me a name and an address for a demon for me to verify in return. It was a trap. If I went anywhere near that address, I'd be dead. But it showed that the demons forced Gilman to tell them about the message board before they killed him. It also showed that they were getting anxious to hunt down whoever Gilman had been corresponding with—namely, me. Something big was happening soon; something like opening the gates to hell, and they didn't want to risk some unknown demon spotter screwing things up for them.

Finally, the most significant event. It's got to be a whopper to top those two, right? Well, it's more subtle, and anyone reading this might disagree with me on how significant it is, but to me, it is. When I was at Kennedy Airport, before I headed to my gate, I used a payphone to call the number that Chaske had given me. A demon answered. It wasn't Devin but a different one. Even though their voices are all guttural hisses and snarls, I can still tell demons apart by their voices. I disguised my voice as best I could and mumbled something about a wrong number before hanging up. Even though I knew there had to be a network of these demons, this confirmed it for me. I also knew in my gut that this was the central point for this demon network; that through this demon I could find all the others in the Boston area. And I had the address. After I'd gotten the number from Chaske, I was able to perform a reverse phone number lookup through the Internet and get the address. It was for a single family home in Lynn. These demons might be clever, but they're not very tech savvy—at least they don't realize the kinds of things you can find on the Internet.

Right now I'm both excited and really antsy. Logically, I know there's no way for Thomase to track me down to Newton—maybe he knows I took the train from Boston, but it's a large area here. I don't think he took a picture of me, so worst case, he might be able to commission a police sketch. And would he really go through all this trouble to hunt me down over a closed case? Still, even though it's crazy to worry about Thomase, I can't help it. If he shows up at my home, it's over. But then again, maybe he won't even try looking for me. I think something clicked with him when I brought up the dogs. He must've seen something. Maybe he's looking at the pages from *L'Occulto Illuminato* in a different light—maybe he'll try to get a DNA sample from Gibson. The demons might be able to disguise themselves so that only a few like me can recognize them, but how could they disguise the way their DNA is analyzed?

But as I said, I'm also excited, and that's because I know that demon in Lynn will lead me to all the others. I have enough proof now that *L'Occulto Illuminato* is on the level—it has been right so far about everything regarding these demons, even the rituals that they perform to open up hell. Now I have to hope it shows me how to kill them. I need to start killing demons.

I KNOW HOW TO KILL THEM. AT LEAST I DO IF *L'OCCULTO Illuminato* is right. Late Monday night I got to the section where Galeotti describes how to kill demons, and I've been translating like a fiend ever since. The good news: it's not as hard as I thought. The bad news: there's one serious gotcha that I'm not sure how I'm going to get around. But before I get into the details, I have some other stuff to cover. One item in particular that could be a nuisance. Maybe much worse than that.

First item. No sign of Thomase or any other cop looking for me. I'm pretty sure I'm in the clear. For the last two days I've been worried that a police sketch of me would show up on the news, but it hasn't happened yet, and at this point I can't see it happening. I'm sure it would be an uphill battle for Thomase to spend any of his department's money hunting me down, and I'm also hoping that he's now thinking *L'Occulto Illuminato* might be genuine and not some bizarre and elaborate hoax concocted by associates of Gibson, like he first thought. Maybe he's even researching it and learning more about it. Worst case, he sends a police sketch of me to police departments in the Boston area, and that's not going to do him any good. I look like too many other fifteen-year-olds, and there's no picture of me on file at any police station. Any fingerprints he pulls from the folder I gave him aren't going to do him any good either. Mine aren't on file anywhere. When they booked me for possession of those psilocybin mushrooms, they didn't fingerprint me. I don't why they didn't, but they didn't. Maybe because I was a juvenile, or maybe because of my dad, but for whatever reason, they didn't bother doing it. If they had, I'd be sweating bullets right now, because as careful as I might've been in handling that folder and all its pages, I still could've left prints.

Second item. My dad has a hearing set with the school on Monday. He's probably going to have me reinstated imme- diately afterwards since the school's investigators haven't been able to find any corroborating evidence that I've been dealing drugs. Also, he's probably going to get the police charges dropped, since there's no way they could prove the drugs weren't planted in my locker. This is all unfortunate, because it means that my available time is quickly coming to an end. Now that I'm finally learning how to kill these demons, I wish this suspen- sion would go on longer.

Final item, and the one that could cause me serious grief. Wesley's dad came by last night accusing me of stealing his Spi- der-Man comic book. Yep, a flat-out accusation.

Mr. Neuberger, like Wesley, is kind of goofy looking. Scrawny, with tight curly hair, thick glasses and this general awk- wardness about him. Him standing next to my dad, it's a bit of a joke, with my dad lucking out in every possible way geneti- cally, and Wesley's dad severely shortchanged and just how you'd imagine the dictionary definition of a 'schlemiel' to look. To be fair to him, even though he's not tall, broad shouldered, good looking, and impeccably groomed like my dad, up until last night he was always good to me—always kidding around and genuinely decent. If I could've ripped my dad off instead of Mr. Neuberger to get my copy of *L'Occulto Illuminato*, I would've gladly done so.

Mr. Neuberger was livid when he came by our house last night. My dad sensed something was wrong right away, and instantly put up his lawyer shields. A distinct coolness came off him as he politely invited Mr. Neuberger into our house. I knew what was coming, of course, so it didn't surprise me when Wesley's dad asked to speak to me and my dad in private. Once we were alone, he cleared his throat and in a gravely severe voice that I earlier wouldn't have imagined possible from him, told my dad that we had a serious issue to discuss.

"And what would that be?" my dad asked with his polite coolness.

For a moment Mr. Neuberger stared at his hands, his lips pressed so tightly together they nearly disappeared. Then his eyes shifted up to meet mine. The look he gave me was one of mostly disappointment. Maybe a little anger and betrayal thrown in.

"On September thirtieth, Henry was over at my house, and I have reason to believe he stole a comic book."

My dad nearly laughed at that. "A comic book?"

"A mint condition first issue of *Spider-Man* valued at forty thousand dollars. I believe that would be grand larceny."

My dad physically bristled as he regarded Mr. Neuberger. "What evidence do you have?" he demanded, his tone now ice. But if he thought that would make Wesley's dad back down, he was mistaken. Mr. Neuberger didn't even blink.

"That day Wesley and Henry were hanging out in Wesley's room when Wesley became violently ill. I now believe he was poisoned with psilocybin mushrooms—the same drugs your son was arrested with at school. Henry used the opportunity of my son being incapacitated in the bathroom to steal my first edition of *Spider-Man*."

"I see," my dad said. "Was Wesley tested to see if he had ingested psilocybin mushrooms?"

"No, unfortunately not. At the time I didn't have any reason to think that he was poisoned. But looking back at Wesley's symptoms and what later happened with your son, it makes sense."

"So you have no evidence that he was poisoned with mushrooms. Do you have any evidence that your comic book was stolen that day? Surveillance video, anything?"

Wesley's dad didn't bother to answer that.

"Was this priceless comic book just left in the open?"

Wesley's dad showed a sick grin. "No it wasn't," he said. "It was locked away. Both in a room and a file cabinet."

"And were my son's fingerprints found?"

Mr. Neuberger shook his head slightly, his sick grin intensifying, like it would have to be chipped from his face with a hammer and chisel.

"I see," my dad said. "Henry is now a criminal mastermind. He poisons your son so he can break through several locks, all undetected by anyone. Is that what you're accusing him of? What would you say if I told you the school's investigators now believe that Henry never dealt drugs and that those mushrooms were planted in his locker?"

Mr. Neuberger's sick grin hardened even more, his eyes now every bit as cold and harsh as my dad's attitude towards him.

"I know Henry did this," he said. "My daughter saw him running up the staircase. He must've just stolen the comic book, and when he heard my wife drive up he ran up the stairs."

"Really? Is that supposed to prove something? That your daughter might have seen Henry going up a staircase?"

"She saw him. Through the front window."

"And when was this? When she was sitting in the car?"

"No, when she was walking up the pathway."

"This really is outrageous, Walt," my dad said, shaking his head, his expression incredulous. "You have no idea when your comic book was stolen. You have no evidence that your son was poisoned, just as you have no evidence that Henry did anything. All you have is that your daughter might have seen my son on a staircase. And from this you're going to level these kind of accusations against Henry? Especially with these false accusations he's having to deal with at school?"

Mr. Neuberger took in a deep breath, and slid his stare from my dad to me. "Henry," he said, "I'm not interested in pressing charges. All I want is my comic book back."

"I'm sorry," I told him. "I wish I could help you, but I didn't take your comic book. You can search my room if you want. And if you think I stole and sold it, the only money I have is what I've been making with my lawn mowing and snow shoveling business."

I was taking a bit of a chance offering to let him search my room—both because of the occult book collection he'd find, and also this journal. Maybe if he saw this journal he'd get the idea of insisting on reading my entries around the time I stole his Spider-Man comic book. But I didn't think my dad would put up with something like that, so I gave as innocent a look as I could manufacture. He wasn't buying any of it, though.

"Why'd Allison see you on the staircase?"

I scrunched my nose up as if I was trying to remember back a week ago. "She probably did see me," I said. "I was getting worried about how sick Wesley had gotten, and I was thinking of heading downstairs to look for a phone number for his mom. I don't remember going downstairs. I was too worried about Wesley to remember things exactly, but I think when I heard a car pulling in, I just wanted to check on Wesley again."

"You're lying."

"You better be careful with your accusations," my dad warned him.

"I'm not lying," I insisted. "That's what happened. And those drugs were planted in my locker." I paused as if I was in deep thought. "It's funny," I said after a while. "I hadn't even thought of the possibility that Wesley might've been the one to put those drugs in my locker, but he does have a spare key for it, just like I have the spare for his. Wow. . . Maybe if he really did get sick on those mushrooms like you think, maybe he did all this himself, you know, so he could frame me and steal the comic book so I'd be blamed for it."

Mr. Neuberger's eyes went dead when I said that. It was as if he decided right then that I was nothing but a lying piece of scum and he wasn't going to waste any more time with me. It wasn't as if I had stolen his comic book for my own personal gain. It was so I could stop the demons. If he thought his first edition *Spider-Man* was worth more than keeping the gates of hell from opening up, then fuck him.

Mr. Neuberger looked away from me to shake his head sadly at my dad. "I tried doing this without police," he said. "But I guess I've just been wasting my time."

"You better be careful, Walt," my dad said. "You better have a lot more evidence than you showed me here if you're going to bring the police into this, at least unless you want to be sued."

At that point Walt Neuberger left. Maybe he went to the police afterwards. If he did, they haven't contacted us yet. I can't imagine they'd get involved. Maybe as a courtesy, they'd come by for a talk, even ask if they could search my room, which is making me think I should find a hiding place for my occult books and this journal until all this blows over. But even if they came just to appease Mr. Neuberger and didn't get anywhere with their investigation, this could still be very troubling. It wouldn't do me any good for the demon Hanley to see cops coming over to the house, and it would also interfere with my plans just as I'm learning about how to kill these demons. As far as my dad goes, he dismissed Mr. Neuberger's allegations as ridiculous, even choosing to ignore my inane explanation of how Wesley might've been behind planting the drugs and stealing his dad's comic book.

Okay, that covers the three items I needed to report. Now, how to kill demons. For the most part it's not as hard as I would've thought. First, I need a one-foot-long dagger—the material doesn't matter as long as it's sharp. Which is good, because at first I was worried that I'd need a solid gold dagger like the one Galeotti used. But anything—gold, silver, iron, steel, whatever—will do the trick.

Once I get the dagger, I'll need to etch a series of symbols into the blade, which I also think is doable. According to the book, these symbols will mesmerize a demon long enough for me to get a fatal strike in.

Finally, the part that has me stuck. The blade must first be washed in virgin blood and then baked. If it wasn't for Sally, I'd still be a virgin and this would be easy enough to do. Curt and Wesley have to still be virgins, but there's no way I could approach Wesley now, and I doubt I could ask Curt, either. Besides, they might not be virgins as far as *L'Occulto Illuminato* is concerned. It's possible that masturbating could violate their virgin status, at least in terms of this ritual for killing demons, and I'm sure they've both been yanking themselves raw.

So that's the problem I have: how to get virgin blood. From the web? Maybe eBay? But how could I trust what I end up with?

I'll worry about that problem later. For now I'm going to head into Boston and buy myself a very sharp, foot-long dagger.

I GOT MY DAGGER FROM A CREEPY SHOP THAT SPECIALIZES IN swords and knives. Need a twelve-inch blade? Not a problem. I went with a stainless-steel knife whose handle had the best feel, and it only cost me twenty-seven dollars. I also bought an etching kit from a hobby shop. After dinner, I stayed holed up in my room reading the directions on how to use the etching kit, and once I heard my parents in their respective bathrooms, I waited twenty minutes and then set about etching the symbols outlined in *L'Occulto Illuminato*. If you ask me, I think I did a pretty damn good job. Now all I need to do is wash this knife with virgin blood and bake it, and I'll be ready to kill me some demons!

Alright, I admit it, I'm excited by the idea of it. I've been living under the oppressive weight of these demons for too long, and it's liberating to know that there's something I can do. I even have an idea about how to get a hold of virgin blood. It's risky—man, is it risky—but it's the only thing I can think of. Later this

213

morning I'm going to try it, and if all works well, I might get to kill my first demon as early as tonight.

Now I need to get some sleep. Surprisingly, I'm not as wired as I would've thought. It's as if I can see that everything is coming to an end and that all I'm doing is playing the part I was meant to play. Fate, I guess. Right now I'm just feeling bone tired, and I actually think I'm going to be able to get some sleep once I crawl into bed and close my eyes.

I'VE WASHED MY DAGGER IN VIRGIN BLOOD AS DESCRIBED IN *L'Occulto Illuminato* and I'm now baking it in my parents' top-of-the-line Thermador oven, which I'm sure is quite a bit better than what Galeotti had available back in his day. I'm scared to death, but also excited about what I'll be doing soon, and I've already picked out the first demon I'm going to kill— and no, it's not Hanley. As much as I'd like to kill him, he's going to have to be last for obvious reasons.

You're probably wondering why my handwriting is so shaky right now. I can't help it. Adrenaline is pounding through me like you wouldn't believe, and it has nothing to do with thinking about how I'm going to be killing demons. What's got my hands shaking like I'm a nervous wreck is replaying in my mind what I had to do to get the virgin blood that I needed. I still can't believe I did it.

Okay, I've taken a few deep breaths, and as you can probably tell from my markedly improved handwriting, I'm shaking but not nearly as bad I was a few minutes ago. Let me take a few more deep breaths and hold them longer this time and see if I can calm myself completely.

Better. Much better now.

So, where did I get my virgin blood? The most obvious place. Namely, from a hospital. I mean, what better place to get blood?

I didn't want to go to any hospitals nearby in case I ran into someone I knew, so I went into Boston. Once there, I wandered around until I ended up in a children's cancer ward and found a kid who was completely out of it, so I could sit by his bed as if we were relatives and I was visiting and nobody would question me. At times I would get up as if I was heading to the bathroom or going out to get myself a soft drink. What I was really doing was surveillance—giving myself a chance to observe what was going on and trying to piece together the nurses' and doctors' routines. At no time did anyone act suspiciously towards me or question why I was there; instead the nurses and everyone else I met were extra nice to me. They must have appreciated that I was spending time visiting one of their sick patients.

It didn't take me long to identify who the best sources were for what I needed. I eliminated any of the patients who were twelve or older—I couldn't risk any of them having had sex, which was possible even at that age. After an hour of waiting and watching, I saw a nurse making her rounds and taking blood from some of the children. When this same nurse took a sample from an eight-year old girl that I had targeted, I snatched it from her cart while she was busy with another patient. She didn't see me do it, and even though my heart was thumping so loudly in my chest that someone should've noticed it and suspected something was up, I was able to walk out of there with the blood without anybody stopping me.

So how do I feel about stealing blood from a sick eight-year-old? Any guilt at all? None. Not a single bit. All I feel is incredibly relieved and happy that I pulled it off. The nurse who took the blood will wonder how she'd misplaced the sample— she might even decide that some sicko stole it. Too bad. And as for the girl, she'll have to give another sample. A small price to pay to keep the gates of hell from opening up. Anyway, I made a note of this eight-year-old girl's name, and when this business with demons is all done I'll send her a box of candy or something to make up for the inconvenience.

The blood should be baked onto the knife by this point. Soon there will be one less demon in the world. Either that, or I'll be finding out the hard way that *L'Occulto Illuminato* is full of shit, at least as far as killing demons goes.

I DIDN'T KILL ANY DEMONS LAST NIGHT. I HAD THE KNIFE ready and was all set to head out when I chickened out. As soon as I reached the front door my knees buckled and I became paralyzed with fear over the thought of what I'd be doing. More than that. It was almost like a hand had pushed its way into my chest and grabbed my heart and squeezed it into pulp. For a long moment I couldn't breathe, and then I started hyperventilating to the point where I almost passed out.

During the two and a half years that I've been dealing with demons, I've never felt fear like this before. I tried to understand it, and eventually realized it was because I didn't fully trust *L'Occulto Illuminato*. Maybe Galeotti believed he was describing the way to kill these demons, but had accidentally left something out—something that he hadn't even been aware of. If Galeotti was wrong, or if he'd left out even a tiny step, I'd be helpless against any demon I went up against, and the thought of that was terrifying. Or maybe I got one of the symbols on the blade wrong,

219

or maybe I mistranslated the *'killing of demons'* section of the book. But what could I do other than blindly accept what Galeotti had written? Or trust that I've prepared the knife properly and have translated Galeotti's archaic text correctly?

The terror never quite left me yesterday. It faded to where I could breathe again, so that I no longer felt like my heart was being squeezed by a fist, but I didn't feel strong enough to go after any of the demons. The way I was feeling yesterday I would've had a hard time going up against either Wesley or Curt. I kept trying to convince myself that I'd do it later that night after my parents went to sleep, but even if the police hadn't come over to the house, I still don't think I would've been up to it.

And yeah, a policeman came over to the house while we were having dinner. Before I get into that, though, when my dad came home, he gave me a quick double take and asked if I was feeling okay. I guess I was looking much paler than normal. My mom also gave me a concerned look and felt my forehead to see if I had a fever. It had been years since she had done something like that, but that's how bad I was looking. Later, while we were having dinner—Korean takeout that my mom had picked up— the doorbell rang, and a police detective stood waiting outside. He had been sent by Wesley's dad, and wanted to know if we'd cooperate and let him search for the stolen Spider-Man comic book. Fortunately my dad got all huffy and refused, letting the detective know that without a search warrant he wasn't going to be searching anywhere within our home. This detective made some veiled threats about how he could've cleared this issue up quickly if my dad had been reasonable, but now he was thinking I was guilty because of the way my dad was stonewalling him. If he was trying to scare my dad, it didn't work—in fact, it probably had the opposite effect of making my dad even more determined not to cooperate in any way. Still, I probably turned several shades lighter as he was making his threats. I had the knife hidden in my closet, but probably not well enough, and all

I could think about was what would happen if my dad acquiesced and this cop found it. A knife caked in blood, hidden in the closet. Fortunately my dad held firm, but the incident made me realize the cop could easily come back with a search warrant, which meant I needed to get the knife out of the house.

That was yesterday. Today was a very different day.

At around six thirty this evening I killed my first demon, and I feel mostly calm about it. Somewhat disappointed maybe, and the reason for this I'll explain later, but still, mostly calm. Let me start from the beginning.

I decided the first demon I was going to kill would be the one in Revere—the one whose address I had given Vincent Gilman, or Virgil, as I had known him on the message board. I chose this demon for several reasons. First, Revere is far enough away from Newton that it shouldn't draw any attention to me. Second, so that I could avenge Vincent Gilman—after what he went through his whole life to battle these demons only to die the way he did, he needed to be avenged. And third, when I scouted this demon's address months ago, I noticed that his property was isolated enough so that I would be able sneak into his house without being seen by neighbors. This was mostly true of all the demon addresses I had scouted, including Hanley's house, but I particularly liked the way this house was situated, and I knew this demon's work schedule from my earlier surveillance.

It was six o'clock when I got to his house, and it was easy enough to hop a backyard fence and break in through a back door. Since he was a demon, I didn't have to worry that there might be a family or anyone else living with him. And he certainly wouldn't have a dog, unless he had one caged up so he could butcher it later, which he didn't. I found myself surprisingly calm as I waited in that empty house.

This demon went by the name Todd Robohoe. He was a big one, maybe the biggest demon I'd seen yet. With the human form he took, which I was able to see using my iPhone camera, he looked like an NFL offensive lineman. Thick neck, thicker body, square jaw, his blond hair cut down to a buzz cut. Of course, this was an illusion. In reality, he was as butt ugly as any other demon. Maybe even more so as there was something about his eyes that was particularly chilling. As I waited for him, I realized that one of the reasons I chose him—at least on a subconscious level—was that I knew if I could kill him, I could kill any of the other demons.

At six twenty-five I heard an angry demon snarl from outside the front door. I was waiting in his kitchen which was in the back of his house, but he must've smelled me from where he was. As I've mentioned before, these demons have exceptionally powerful olfactory senses. As the front door was flung open and then slammed shut, this demon roared out in that hissing and crackling voice that they have that I picked the wrong house to break into. His exact words were: *You stupid asshole, you fucked up breaking into my house 'cause I'll be eating your brains tonight.* Maybe he would've too if I hadn't killed him. Maybe that's what they eat when they don't have dog meat available.

It sounded like a rhinoceros rumbling towards me, and from the way he came charging into the kitchen, he knew I was there; again, either he smelled me or he could hear me breathing. Whichever it was, I didn't bother to ask him. When he saw me, his ugly demon face twisted into an ugly snarl; the same vicious type that you might see on a rabid pit bull. Then he spotted the knife I was holding and his expression turned more into an amused smirk.

"You think that knife is going to do you any good?" he asked, his voice that same weird heavy mix of hisses and pops as all the other demons.

"I'm hoping so," I said.

He took a step closer, then stopped as he noticed the symbols etched onto the knife's blade. Maybe he didn't stop voluntarily, maybe the symbols held a power over him. Whichever it was, a look of stunned surprise came over his face, his beady yellow eyes popping open and his grotesque, muzzle-like jaw falling slack.

"It's been washed and baked in virgin's blood," I told him, my voice sounding unnatural to me, as if it weren't my own. At that moment I might've been scared shitless, but I was also overwhelmed by a flood of adrenaline and all the anger and disgust I'd been feeling for two and a half years towards these demons. All of it left me trembling in a near homicidal rage. "*L'Occulto Illuminato* is real," I forced out. "It's not a myth like you demons might think. And if you haven't figured it out yet, I own a copy."

He took a frantic step away from me, and then fell backwards as if he had slipped on ice. While still on his back, he tried crawling away like a crab, but as I got closer his strength seemed to ebb out of his body. It had to be the symbols etched onto the knife. A look of horror shone through his gaping expression as I straddled him with the knife raised to plunge into him.

"You're insane," he blubbered in those demon hisses and snarls. "Don't do this!"

He raised one of his claws to try to stop me. The knife sliced through his flesh as if it were made of butter instead of leathery hide, and I continued thrusting the knife downward until the blade went through his throat and the tip stuck into the floor underneath him, just as *L'Occulto Illuminato* had described. With very little difficulty I soon had his head severed from his body.

The stench that poured out of him was awful. Like burning sulfur and vomit and decayed flesh all mixed together. I had to struggle to keep from throwing up, but at least the demon was dead.

Now for the disappointing part. I had assumed that when I killed the demon that his human façade would disappear and he would show himself to the world as what he was, and because of that I had used my phone to record the killing. Of course, when I looked at the dead demon, that's exactly what I saw, as well as the black blood pooling from his severed neck. But when I looked at him through the iPhone display, he retained his human disguise even while in death, and the color of his blood was the same dark red that you'd expect from a human. It hadn't occurred to me that that would happen, and it was deeply deflating to see that was the case. I had convinced myself that with this one killing, I would be able to prove to the world what these demons were.

I erased the video after watching it, disappointed that not even a glimpse of his demon form showed on the recording. Then I stood over the dead demon, staring at its corpse through the iPhone viewer and praying that it would transform into the same demon image that I saw when I looked at it directly. I did this for maybe ten minutes before giving up. I considered cutting it open. I knew a demon couldn't possibly have the same organs and biological make up as a human, but I just didn't have the nerve to do it. It took all my resolve to cut its head off as *L'Occulto Illuminato* demanded, and I had nothing left inside to do anything further. I had to hope that when they did an autopsy its human disguise would vanish and they'd realize they were dealing with something nightmarish from outside of this world.

I have to admit, when I watched the video of me killing the demon Todd Robohoe as if he were only a frightened man, I felt a twinge of uneasiness when I wondered if I could've been hallucinating all this demon stuff after all. I know it was crazy to think like that, but the situation I was in was so bizarre that a brief moment of self-doubt was natural. But then when I looked away from the video and saw the already rotting demon corpse by my feet and continued to smell that awful stench from it, any slight momentary qualms I'd had were gone. Convinced, I cleaned the demon blood from my knife blade using the method detailed in *L'Occulto Illuminato*.

When I visited the hospital the other day, I took a handful of latex gloves, and I had slipped on a pair before entering the demon Robohoe's house so I didn't have to worry about fingerprints. I opened his refrigerator and searched inside, and all it had in it were wrapped up cuts of meat. These were thick, uneven cuts, something that you might get if you butchered the animal yourself. I unwrapped one of the packages and knew from the smell that it had to be dog meat. I wrapped it back up and stacked it with the other packages. Same in the freezer: only thing in it were these thick, uneven packages of frozen meat. At least when the police investigate they'll wonder why Robohoe had only dog meat in his refrigerator and freezer. Maybe if they dig up his backyard, they'll find the remains of all the dogs he's butchered.

I gave his cabinets a quick look and found no other food, and the kitchen drawers were mostly empty. They didn't even have the usual homeowner bills that my parents were always collecting, which made me wonder if there was one central demon paying their bills. I did find a sheet of paper with phone numbers, and one of the numbers struck me as familiar. Once I checked my phone, I realized why—it was the phone number that Chaske had given me, the one that he was supposed to call in case anyone tried contacting the demon Connor Devin. The same number I had called when I was in New York. I entered the other numbers into my iPhone and searched the rest of the house, which didn't take me long given that it was a small two-bedroom ranch. One thing was obvious right away: there were no personal effects—no books, CDs, photos, knickknacks, nothing! There was a big screen TV set and a recliner in what would've been the living room, and I found a stack of hardcore porn DVDs piled next to the TV. Really nasty looking stuff—at least the ones with labels and pictures. Now I know that demons like porn, and the nastier the better.

The bedroom had a large king-sized bed and a closet full of clothes and shoes. My skin crawled as I entered the room—as if something unholy and evil permeated it. I soon found myself drenched in cold sweat, but I forced myself to search through the closet and eventually I found these odd and ancient-looking trinkets. I had no idea what they were since I hadn't found anything like them mentioned in *L'Occulto Illuminato*, but I still had a third of the book to go through. I took photos of them.

When I walked into the basement, I felt like I was walking into a slaughterhouse. There was a stench of death there, and I knew this had to be where Robohoe butchered the dogs that he rounded up. I didn't find any direct evidence—no pools of blood or dog carcasses or anything like that, but I knew this was what he used his basement for.

I didn't stay long in the basement—I would've gotten sick to my stomach if I had. I'd spent long enough in that house, so I left through the kitchen door into his fenced-in backyard and hopped the fence. That took me to an empty lot overgrown with weeds. From there, I broke into a jog, and twenty minutes later I was back to where I had earlier hidden my bike, the latex gloves I had worn discarded along the way.

That was over three hours ago. Before I came home I secured my knife in a plastic bag and buried it in the same secluded woods along the golf course where Sally and I used to go after school. There was little chance any golfer would hit a stray ball anywhere near where I hid the knife, so I didn't have to worry about anyone stumbling upon it. Not only were the woods secluded, but they were up on a hill with the course greens far below.

I got home forty minutes ago. My parents were furious with me for being out so late without calling. My mom was eyeballing me extra hard trying to figure out if I'd been doing drugs. I told them that I had studied all day to keep up with my schoolwork, and that at five decided to go for a bike ride to blow off some steam. My mom didn't believe me. She didn't say anything, but from the way her mouth tightened it was pretty obvious. Whether my dad did or not, I couldn't tell, but he clearly wasn't happy with me.

"Where'd you ride your bike?"

"To Cambridge. I rode along the Charles River for a while, then stopped off at Harvard Square, had falafel, hung around some more, and rode home."

"You couldn't think of calling?"

"My battery had run down and I couldn't make a call. Sorry."

That was a lie. All he had to do was ask to see my cell phone and he'd know I was lying. But he didn't ask for it, and instead stood staring at me as he tried to size me up and decide for himself whether I was lying. Of course, I must've looked like I'd done a strenuous bike ride, which I had. Newton to Revere was about twice the distance as Newton to Cambridge. I also hadn't eaten anything since lunch, but I told him that story about the falafel so my mom wouldn't put out anything for me to eat. After killing the demon Robohoe, there was no way I would've been able to force down a bite of food. After a minute or so, my dad grudgingly decided to accept my story, although he still complained about me being out as late as I was.

"I really don't want you out riding your bike in the dark like this," he said. "It's not safe."

I had to bite my tongue to keep from giggling. Riding my bike late at night was the least of it. Anyway, these demons all had day jobs, so unless I only killed them on weekends, I was going to have to be out in the evenings, which meant getting home late. And also riding my bike, since I wasn't about to take public transportation after killing a demon. But there was no point arguing any of that with my dad, so I nodded in agreement and politely asked if I could be excused. Then I went upstairs to my room so I could write this journal entry.

So I've killed my first demon. And as I said, I mostly feel calm about it, although the whole experience seems too surreal to have actually happened, like it's something from a dream or a movie. I know that it really did happen and that it's not something I imagined or am deluding myself about. I also know that I should be a little worried that I left a clue of some sort behind that could lead the demons back to me. Maybe even simply my scent. But I'm not worried. Maybe I'm too numb right now to feel worried.

I'm certainly not worried about the police, either. Even if someone saw me leaving the house, they wouldn't have been able to see me well enough in the dark to describe me. And likewise, the Revere police wouldn't be able to connect the demon Robohoe's murder to some high school kid living in Newton. No, I had nothing to worry about with the police. The demons, though, were another matter. But fuck them. I was sick of worrying about them.

I DIDN'T KILL ANY MORE DEMONS THIS WEEKEND. IT WAS PARTLY that I didn't feel up to it and partly that I wanted to see how the demon Robohoe's murder would be reported. So far there was nothing in the newspapers or on TV. If they'd found his body, it would be a big story. It would have to be with the way I cut off his head, and with his refrigerator and freezer filled with dog meat. They'd then dig into his background and realize that he just showed up one day without any parents or relatives or a birth certificate or anything else. And when they performed an autopsy, they'd learn the truth about him: that there was nothing human about Robohoe.

I guess I should've expected that his body wouldn't have been found yet. He wouldn't have any family or friends visiting, so why would his body have been found? At some point next week, his employer will send the police over there, but until then I have to be patient and resist the temptation to call the murder in anonymously.

I wonder if the demons know. They might. I checked the message board a half hour ago and found another bogus message from *Virgil*, this one posted early this morning. It was another attempt to smoke me out by sending me another address for a demon for me to verify. And guess what address they gave me? My demon neighbor from a few doors down, Hanley. So either they're onto me and are just being cute, or it was a bizarre coincidence. But if they sent it because they suspect me, then they're expecting some sort of reaction from me, which they're not going to get.

I know I've wasted two days that I could've been out killing demons, especially since I could be reinstated back in school Monday, which would mean an end to all this free time. I also expect it will be much harder to kill them once they find out about their brother demon, Robohoe. They'll know for sure then that *L'Occulto Illuminato* exists, and that whoever it was that Vincent Gilman had been in contact with is now hunting them down. But I couldn't attempt killing another demon feeling the way I do. I'll feel better soon. I just need another day or so, although I can't help feeling time is running out. There haven't been any more stories in the papers or on TV about little kids being kidnapped, at least not since the one that was taken from Rhode Island over three weeks ago. They must have their thirty-nine stolen children by now, and I could only have ten days left—that's when we have our next full moon. I need to start killing demons. I know that. And I need to find out where they've hidden those children.

So it's been a weekend of sitting and waiting and trying to keep myself on an even keel. My dad's mostly been okay this weekend—he's looking forward to winning a battle tomorrow with the school, and has refused to consider that those drugs could've been mine or that I had anything to do with stealing the Spider-Man comic book. My mom, though, hasn't been showing the same trusting spirit. I catch the way she looks at me when she doesn't think I'm watching, and I know she suspects the worst of me. Maybe not that I went out Friday to cut the head off a demon, but I'm sure she's convinced that I'm guilty of everything else I've been accused of. I guess she's just more perceptive than my dad. But I'm sure she's not giving me the benefit of any doubt as far as my motives go. I'm going to make sure this journal and my books are well hidden. I wouldn't put it past her to search my room looking for evidence against me.

At least that police detective hasn't shown up yet with a warrant. I'm sure he needs more solid evidence than Mr. Neuberger's accusations, so it's very possible he won't be showing up. I hope not.

I'VE GOT A LOT TO REPORT, ALTHOUGH NOT THAT MUCH ABOUT demons. Some, but not much.

First, while not much of a surprise, my dad was successful in getting me reinstated back in school. Not only that, he got the police charges against me dropped. The school's investigation found no one who could corroborate the demon Connor Devin's claim that I had been dealing drugs, or that I had ever done drugs, or was ever seen in the presence of drugs, which made it highly suspicious that he brought the police to my locker. Although the principal didn't come out and say this, it sounded like he believed Devin planted the drugs in my locker and that the school was currently investigating him. I badly wanted to tell him that Devin wasn't living in Waltham, regardless of what his supposed foster parent, Chaske, might've been telling them, but I wisely held my tongue and didn't blurt this out, since I had no reasonable way of explaining how I knew this.

My hearing started at nine and only lasted fifteen minutes, and it wouldn't even have lasted five minutes if the principal hadn't

233

spent most of the hearing apologizing to me and my dad, promising that the school would fully investigate how those psilocybin mushrooms ended up where they did, and stumbling over himself to tell us how he was satisfied that I wasn't involved and that I was only an innocent party in the matter. My dad was in full lawyer mode throughout with his chest puffed out like a rooster's and his expression what you'd see on a shark. I thought he was going to threaten lawsuits, but instead he accepted the principal's ass kissing, as well as his promise that my teachers would work with me to catch me up on my lost class time. Stiffly, but still somewhat magnanimously, he accepted the school's apologies on my behalf. Somehow I kept a straight face through it all.

With the hearing ending at nine fifteen, I missed homeroom and the beginning of my first period class. It felt weird being back in school, like I no longer belonged there, or more specifically, that I belonged there even less than I ever had in the past. When I walked into my first period classroom twenty minutes late, the teacher stopped talking while I took my seat. I could feel the eyes of all my classmates on me, and the stone silence that had fallen over the class was broken by a rush of whispering that went back and forth among some of the students, mostly mean little things about me as they speculated about what a loser and oddball I was, and what my dad must've paid the school to get my suspension lifted.

The demon Connor Devin was there as I expected. I tried hard not to pay any attention to him, but I couldn't help catching this odd look that he gave me, his demon face twisted partially into a nasty smirk and partially frozen in indecision, as if he were trying to make up his mind about something. It made me think that even though there hadn't been anything in the news yet about the demon Robohoe, his fellow demons knew about it, and Devin was trying to decide whether I could've been the one to kill and decapitate his fellow demon.

I felt an almost unbearable uneasiness while I sat in the

class, and I was unable to pay attention to anything the teacher said. I felt this not only in my stomach, but deep in my groin, almost as if a needle had been shoved in there. It wasn't just because Devin sat directly behind me and I could feel his dead yellow eyes boring into me, trying to expose the truth about me. No, that had little to do with how I was feeling. It was more that Devin was a reminder that I needed to be out there killing him and his kind instead of wasting time sitting in classrooms. Even though I'd been aware that I might only have ten days left before it would be too late, that thought had been mostly an abstraction and I'd been in denial about it. Sitting there, though, it struck me how close we could be to the gates of hell opening and the world ending as we know it. And instead of doing what I could to stop this Armageddon from happening, I was sitting impotently in a classroom, listening to a pear-shaped sixty-something-year-old man drone on about algebra, as if that would make any difference when the demons started roasting us in the fires that would leak out from hell.

I should've been paying more attention later when I was walking to my next class, but I had fallen into a deep funk over the whole being stuck back in school business, and I was so stuck in my own head that I had lost any sort of awareness of what was going on around me. Next thing I knew I was smacked hard in the side of the head—hard enough where the blow knocked me against a locker and I crumpled to the floor. Dazed, I looked up to see Ralph Malphi leering at me, his hand squeezed into a big, ham hock-sized fist. Devin was alongside him, showing an ugly demon grin. Devin said something to Malphi, but with the way my head was ringing I couldn't make out any words from his demon hisses and snarls. Whatever he said, it got Malphi laughing. The big ape put a thumbnail against his throat and drew a line as if he were slicing it, letting me know that I was dead as far as he was concerned. After that there were some more demon hisses and snarls from Devin that I couldn't decipher, and then more laughing from Malphi as the two of them walked off.

So the two of them were now friends. It figured. I'm sure it was Devin who helped Malphi build up the nerve to go after me. I considered charging Malphi then. It would be the last thing he'd expect—at that moment he thought he had turned the tables on me and had me afraid of him. If I went after him, I'd get a shot at one of his vulnerable areas before he knew what hit him, and they'd end up having to pull me off of him. But if I tried something like that, Devin, who had those razor sharp demon talons, as well as his inhuman demon strength, would've killed me and claimed it was an accident. That he was only trying to get me off of Malphi.

I took a deep breath. That had to be why Devin egged Malphi into attacking me. So that I'd go after Malphi and he'd have his chance to kill me *accidentally*.

I watched as the two of them walked away together, Devin and Malphi; one butt-ugly demon and one almost equally butt-ugly Neanderthal-looking human. Quite a pair.

I wish I could kill Devin next, but I can't do that. Killing Devin could very well convince the demons that I'm the one they're after. Because of that, he and my down-the-street demon Hanley have to be last. But I'm really looking forward to killing both of them—especially Devin.

I took another deep breath. If Devin wasn't around to interfere and I had retaliated against Malphi the way I wanted to, I would've been suspended from school. No doubt about it. And it would've backfired on me. Knowing my parents, that would've been the last straw for them, and they would've shipped me right off to military school, probably the very next day. A shiver ran through me as I thought about what the consequences of that would've been. Thank God I had stayed down on the floor! The whole thing was a wakeup call. I need to stay focused on what's important. I can't let Ralph Malphi, the demon Devin, or any of the other demons sidetrack me. Too much is at stake, and there's so little time left as it is.

• • •

I almost left the high school campus during our lunch break. The last thing I wanted to do was sit around the cafeteria and catch other students sneaking peeks at me as if I were some kind of freak, or listen to their snide whispers about me. But the simple truth was it had been over ten days since I'd seen Sally, and I felt this tightness growing in my chest over that. As much as I wanted to tell myself it was over between us, I was anxious to see her, and maybe even more anxious to see how she'd react to seeing me.

I made sure to get to the cafeteria early and loitered around watching for her. When she walked in it was with the demon Connor Devin, the two of them together as if they were girlfriend and boyfriend. I have to admit, it didn't surprise me. I kind of figured as much with her not calling me in over a week.

Sally was even more beautiful than any other time I'd seen her—her eyes sparkling and her skin radiant as she said something to Devin, all the while a heart-stopping smile breaking out over her face. I wondered if they'd gone out yet. Clearly they hadn't had sex—if they had, Sally would be dead with Devin's razor-sharp demon cock slicing her up internally. But Devin didn't want to kill her yet. He wanted me to see them together so he could see what I'd do about it.

I stood watching them. Devin had to know I was there—even if he hadn't seen me yet, he must've picked up my scent, but Sally was oblivious. I wondered if she had tried holding his claw yet, and if she had, how she possibly could've done that without cutting her hands to ribbons. Those damn claws or talons or whatever those demons have are like stiletto knives, but they've already proven that they possess an amazing dexterity with how they're able to dress themselves without destroying their clothes and even tie Windsor knots, so I guess it's not too hard to believe that they can touch someone without ripping that person's flesh. I still couldn't imagine how Sally or anyone else could possibly touch one of those things and think that what they were touching was remotely human. Maybe the magic or mass hypnosis or whatever it is that disguises their physical forms and their voices and odors, also disguises the way they physically feel to people.

Sally finally saw me. As soon as she did she averted her eyes from mine, and her mouth kind of crumbled. In a matter of seconds her skin went pale white, and then to dark red. For a long moment she seemed stuck, like she didn't know whether to pretend that she hadn't seen me or whether to acknowledge me, or maybe simply run away. Fuck, watching how uncomfortable she looked brought a small lump to my throat.

That bastard of a demon, Devin, immediately put on the sensitive guy act, and whispered something to her. I was standing too far away from them to hear anything more than snarls and hisses, but I knew he was pretending to be supportive, and he probably told her that it would be okay with him if she had a few minutes alone with me. Fucking bastard. I was really going to enjoy killing him.

Whatever it was he said to her, Sally nodded in a painfully fragile way and then smiled the most brittle smile I had ever seen as she walked over to me.

"I didn't know you were back in school," she said, her voice barely above a whisper. "How'd that happen?"

It was over. Whatever longing or desire I'd had before was dead now, as well as the anxiousness I'd been feeling just minutes earlier. I still found her amazingly beautiful, and I still cared about her and I didn't want to see her hurt, but more than anything I felt an aching sadness knowing that it was dead between us.

"Can we go somewhere private to talk?" I asked.

She hesitated. She didn't want to go anywhere with me. Was she afraid of me now? How fucking ironic would that be! She's on the verge of dating a demon, but I'm the one she's afraid of!

"There's no one around us," she said. "We can talk here."

No we couldn't. Devin could hear every word I said from where he was standing.

"Please?" I said. "I only want to talk with you for ten minutes. I'll be nice. I promise."

She didn't want to, but she relented and gave me a short nod. I led the way out of the cafeteria and then out of the building, and we walked together towards the baseball field. I could feel Sally's discomfort as we walked, but I waited until I knew we were a safe distance away before I said anything.

"It's like what I told you before. Those drugs found in my locker weren't mine, and the school now believes that," I said. "They're also convinced your friend, Connor Devin, was the one who planted them there."

"That's not possible," she insisted. "Connor never would've done something like that."

Of course I knew that's exactly what happened since I planted the mushrooms in Devin's locker first, but I wasn't going to tell Sally that. She was staring at me so intently right then, as if she thought she could read from my expression whether I was lying or not, and I had this feeling that she'd probably be able to do exactly that. Fortunately I was able to tell her the truth, although admittedly, while omitting certain facts.

"Devin's such a choir boy? He egged Ralph Malphi into punching me in the side of the head when I wasn't looking. You want to feel how swollen the side of my head is?"

Sally didn't say anything. Only looked at me as if I was lying to her.

"Forget it," I continued. "You don't want to believe me about Ralph Malphi, fine. But the school believes that what I told you is what happened, and I do, too," I said. "Why else would he have brought the police to my locker? He had no reason to think I had drugs there. No one else in the school ever saw me using or dealing drugs."

"Because you're such a choir boy yourself?"

"Compared to Devin, yeah, I am."

"Look, Henry, if you're trying to break us up by telling me this—"

"So you are going out with him?"

"We haven't done anything yet, but it's none of your business whatever happens between Connor and me." The discomfort Sally had been showing earlier was gone, replaced by a white hot defiance. "Henry, you and I, all we did was hook up a few times. That's all. You don't own me. I'm sorry that it didn't work out between us, but it didn't."

God, she was so beautiful right then. I wished that I could still feel something romantically for her, but I couldn't. My future was mapped out already. I had to kill demons as long as I was able to, and because of that there was no possible future for me with Sally, or with anyone else. But I still cared about her. Deeply. I made up my mind then.

"What I'm telling you now is between us only," I said.

She hesitated, and then in a whisper told me 'okay'.

"I mean it," I said. "If you tell Devin any of what I'm about to tell you, I'll be dead shortly afterwards."

A film fell over her eyes then as if she was remembering that I was crazy. At that moment she was only humoring me. Nothing I told her was going to have any impact, but I ploughed ahead. I felt as if I had to do something to try to protect her from that demon.

"What I told you about him earlier is true," I said. "I know you don't believe me. I know you think I'm mentally ill, but what I'm saying is the truth. And I'm not saying this out of some deluded belief that I can win you back. As much as I wish it was otherwise, I know it's over between us, and it is as much for me as it is for you. But I care about you, and I don't want to see you hurt. And he'll hurt you. And I don't mean by breaking your heart or anything like that, but he'll physically hurt you in horrible ways. Like I told you before, he's not what you think he is. He's something evil. Something inhuman."

The way her eyes had glazed over, she was only patronizing me. She didn't believe a word I was saying. How could I blame her? Still, though, I could feel a rush of anger warming my face.

"Go ahead, tell him what I just told you. I'll be dead soon afterwards, and at least that will prove to you I'm not crazy. Or better yet, get a dog anywhere near him and see how the dog reacts."

That patronizing look that had settled on her face quickly vanished. She turned to me, startled. So she had already seen that happen.

"Why, what would a dog do?" she asked, pretending badly that she didn't already know the answer to that.

"Easy enough to find out," I told her.

We turned back towards the school. The demon Connor Devin was leaning against the school building, maybe a hundred yards away. A chill ran through me causing me to shiver. It was dumb talking to Sally with my back to the building like I did. I should've been looking out for that demon, should have made sure he was nowhere in sight before I said anything to her. I just had to hope that we were far enough away that Devin couldn't hear us, even with his super sensitive demon hearing. I could sense that Sally wanted to ask me more about why dogs did what they did around Devin, but she saw him, too, and that stopped her. She was beginning to believe me. I could tell from the way her mouth pinched tight as she looked at Devin. I reached over and took hold of her hand and gave it a small squeeze. She didn't pull away. Instead, she gave me back a slight squeeze in return.

While I know it's going to be dangerous because of how it could alert the other demons as to who they're looking for, I'm going to have to kill Devin as soon as possible. I can't wait until the end anymore. It would be far more dangerous to wait now. He'll sense something's up with Sally, and even if she doesn't say anything to him, he'll figure out what I told her. So

I'll be killing him as soon as I find out his address, and I have a good idea how to do that.

Later, after we went back inside, I took a table by myself in the corner of the dining hall while Sally and Devin sat by themselves at a table on the opposite end of the room. I was trying not to openly stare at them, but it was clear that Sally's attitude towards Devin had turned more guarded. I must've been looking again in their direction because Curt surprised me by sitting at my table. I didn't notice him making his way over, so when he sat down I jumped a little in my skin, as if someone had snuck up behind me and yelled boo.

Curt, in his normal Goth attire and his face as round and fleshy as ever, gave me a sympathetic smile. "Hey, man, if I'd known you were coming back to school today I would've called you and warned you about that. Over the last week, the two of them have become an item, but I didn't want to tell you about it and bum you out any more while you were on suspension. It figures, huh? In the end that's what they go for, preppy Justin Bieber look-alikes. If you ask me the guy's a dick with the personality of a brick."

"Nice rhyme," I said.

"I thought you'd like it. It's a tough break about Sally. She's very cute. I feel for you, man." Curt shoveled a mouth full of macaroni and cheese into his mouth and took his time chewing and swallowing, then edged closer, a glint in his eyes. "Henry, man, you've become legendary in this school. You should hear all the stories circulating about you. Fuck, even if you lost Sally, there are other girls here who are going to want to fool around with the school's badass."

I was going to shake my head and make some comment about how ridiculous that was about me being remotely thought of as a badass, but he already knew I had beaten up Malphi that day weeks ago, and besides, I had to be the only one in the school to kill a demon, so who was I to argue that point with Curt? He took another bite of his lunch, then edged closer.

"How'd you beat the drug rap?" he asked in a low whisper, his manner conspiratorial.

"Not too hard," I said. "After the school investigated the incident, they realized I had nothing to do with those drugs. That someone planted them in my locker."

"Really?" He looked disappointed on hearing that I wasn't quite the badass he was hoping I was. "Why would someone do that?"

I shrugged. I didn't want to say anything more about the demon Connor Devin to him. I had made things dangerous enough for myself by telling Sally what I did.

"You got any ideas who might've done it?" I said, as if I was really interested in what Curt might think.

Curt sat back and rubbed his chin as he pondered the subject, then flashed me a guilty look. "This might sound crazy," he said, "but Wesley really hates your guts right now. I mean, with a passion. You gave him the spare key to your locker, didn't you?"

"Yeah. But why are you saying Wesley hates my guts?"

"Because that's what he told me when I asked him if he wanted to join me at your table. What's up with the two of you? You fuck his sister or something?"

"Come on, she's ten years old."

"His mom then?"

I didn't bother responding to that.

"Whatever you did, you really pissed him off."

"I really have no idea, I'm serious."

Curt wasn't anywhere near as intuitive as Sally, so he couldn't tell that I was lying. He filled up his fork again with more food and chewed on it thoughtfully. "Whatever you did to piss him off, maybe he retaliated by planting those drugs in your locker? It makes sense since he has a spare key. I wonder how he got those drugs? I wouldn't have thought he was capable of it." His eyes widened, and his face whitened with a nervous excitement. "The police are gonna talk to him," Curt went on. "They'll figure out that he's the guy also since he's been holding a spare key to your locker."

A cool numbness filled my head as I realized Curt could be right. At the moment, the school and the police were thinking it was Devin, but once they realized Wesley had my spare key, they'd probably figure the two of them did it together, or at least that's what they'd be figuring before they talked to Wesley. But what then? Would they believe Wesley that I drugged him with psilocybin mushrooms so I could steal a forty thousand dollar comic book? Would they then go back to thinking those drugs were mine after all?

My head started hurting thinking of all that. No matter what, even if they went back to believing those drugs were mine and that I stole that comic book, they wouldn't have any evidence and they wouldn't be able to do anything. They probably wouldn't even be able to kick me out of school at this point. My parents wouldn't believe them, at least not without any solid evidence. Well, maybe my mom would, but not my dad. Word would get back to Sally, though, and she'd start thinking again that I was a complete lunatic and that I made up everything I did about Devin. Right now she was having her doubts about him, but once she heard that the police were investigating me again, she'd forget all about how dogs reacted with Devin, probably go into deep denial about it. And then she'd be telling Devin what I told her.

Fuck.

I had to hope that the police didn't talk to Wesley, or if they did, that they didn't believe him. This had the potential of blowing up in my face.

I must've gotten very quiet after that, because Curt asked me what was wrong, was I thinking also that it had to be Wesley? I told him that I couldn't believe Wesley would've had the balls to do something like that, but I had a lot on my mind.

My cell phone's ringing. It's Sally.

More later.

I JUST GOT OFF THE PHONE WITH SALLY. SHE'S SCARED, AND SHE wants to know why dogs act the way they do with Devin.

"We did make plans to hook up this afternoon," she told me, her voice cautious, fragile. "This was when we met up right before lunch. After what you told me I couldn't do it. I started seeing Connor differently, like he was colder, harsher, if that makes any sense. So I made up an excuse why I couldn't get together with him. This look came over his face when I told him that really scared me, Henry. I think he would've hurt me, too, if there weren't other people around. He lifted his hand as if he was going to hit me, but then he caught himself and noticed all the other kids, and he changed the gesture as if he were only pushing his hand through his hair."

Another chill and shiver hit me. If Devin had struck Sally, he would've killed her. His demon talon would've sliced off her head. I also knew he'd been waiting until I was back in school before making his move on Sally. If she hadn't cancelled their plans, he would've made sure that I knew where and when their hook up was going to be so he'd have his chance to torture and kill me when I showed up to stop them.

"What did you see that scared you so much?" I asked, my voice only a whisper.

"This expression that came over his face. Something that wasn't human. Almost like a shadow that passed over him. I don't know, like this awful mix of fury and hatred and ugliness. What's wrong with him, Henry, and why did I see a dog almost choke himself to death on his leash trying to get away from Connor? And another one acted the same way when the owner tried to walk the dog near us."

It was too bad Sally hadn't looked at Devin's face when those dogs first showed up. She would've known then that something was very wrong about him.

"He's evil," I said. "If you had hooked up with him this afternoon he would've hurt you badly, maybe killed you."

She was quiet for a long moment as she thought about what I told her. When she spoke next it was to ask me what I meant about Devin hurting her. "Does Connor have really bad STDs or something?"

"No. He would've done terrible things to you if he had gotten you alone somewhere."

I imagined Sally taking Devin to those same secluded woods near the golf course where we had gone to those times when we hooked up, and I became nauseous as I pictured what Devin would've done to her.

There was more silence on Sally's part as she digested what I told her. Then she asked me again about the dogs, about why those two dogs acted the way they did.

"Three dogs," I said. "You're forgetting about that police drug-sniffing dog that was brought to the school."

"Okay, three dogs. Why do they act that way?"

"Because they sense what he really is and it terrifies them."

"Would this happen with any dog?"

"Yep, every single one."

"Henry, when I broke off my plans with Connor, he demanded that I tell him what you told me about him. He insisted that you had to have told me something, and that was why I was acting so nervous around him."

"Did you tell him?"

"No, of course not. I admitted to him that I lied about my excuse, and that I broke things off because I realized I still had feelings for you and didn't want to hook up with anyone else now. I don't think he believed me. Henry, I'm scared. I don't want to see him again. I don't think I could go to school knowing he's there."

"He won't hurt you now," I said, and I knew that was true. The demon Devin couldn't take the chance of hurting her after this, not with the demons so close to opening the gates of hell. They couldn't risk bringing any undue attention to themselves. It would be one thing sneaking Sally into the woods and doing horrible things to her and leaving her body torn up as if she'd been attacked and killed by wild animals—it would be another thing altogether to go after her now that she was onto him, especially since she might've told her parents and other people about him scaring her. No, he couldn't take that chance. And why would he bother with them so close to bringing us all to hell?

I asked, "Do you know where he lives?"

There was more silence from Sally before she told me that she didn't. "It's funny," she said, "but I don't have any idea." Another long pause, then, "Why do you want to know?"

"No reason. I'll see you tomorrow. And don't worry about Devin. He won't hurt you. I won't let him."

After I got off the phone with Sally, I thought about some of the things she told me, like her telling Devin that she still had feelings for me. That could've been meant only as an excuse on her part, but maybe it wasn't, maybe she really did have feelings for me. I decided I couldn't let myself go there. I had to let that part of me stay dead. I could care about Sally and want to protect her, but I couldn't let myself reopen any sort of romantic feelings towards her. Time was slipping away fast enough as it was.

I also decided I was going to have to keep my dagger with me at all times. There was a chance that the police detective would get his warrant to search my parents' house, but there had to be a bigger chance that one of those demons might try visiting me late at night, especially now that Devin was more suspicious of me than ever. At least the school doesn't have metal detectors like the ones in Boston, so I'll be able to keep the dagger in my backpack. No fucking way I'm taking any chances now.

I feel so tired that I can barely keep my eyes open, but I still have so much that I need to do tonight. Once my parents are asleep I need to go out and retrieve my dagger from where I hid it. I also have to make plans for tomorrow because I need to get back to killing demons.

Tuesday, October 17th 7:05 AM

MY PARENTS WENT TO BED EARLY LAST NIGHT. BY ELEVEN, THEY were finished up in their respective bathrooms, at least from what I could hear from the hallway, and soon afterwards the lights went out in their room. I spent the next fifteen minutes listening outside their door. After hearing nothing but the simulated ocean sounds that they use for sleeping, I decided it was safe, and I snuck out of the house. Once outside, I rode my bike to the golf course, then into the woods where I had hidden my dagger. At one point my flashlight hit some large weasel-like animal that I think was a fisher cat, but after it hissed out some god-awful cry at me, it slunk away.

It didn't take me long to find where I had buried the knife—I had used several rocks near a fallen tree as a marker, and even in the dark with only a flashlight I found it without too much trouble. I had buried the dagger in a plastic bag, and I'd just finished digging out the hole when I heard leaves crunching from a distance behind me. I pulled the dagger out of the bag and turned with my flashlight to catch Hanley's ugly demon face, his yellow eyes tinged with black demon blood and shining with violence. He was maybe a hundred feet away, but there was no mistaking what was in those eyes.

So he'd been watching my house and had followed me. He must've run after me on foot, or more accurately, demon paws, since he wasn't wearing anything other than a wife beater and a pair of boxer shorts, and had nothing covering his animal-like demon feet. Maybe he had spotted me from his house and ran out before he had a chance to put on some clothes, but I was sure these demons had tough enough hide that the cold October air didn't matter to him.

Hanley's eyes locked on me. He didn't say anything. He didn't bother with any pretense of acting human, like asking me what I was doing there or anything else. As far as he was concerned what was going to happen next was a done deal, and he came charging at me like a fiend out of hell, moving a lot faster than I would've imagined possible. He was no more than ten feet from me when I spun around to face him, the dagger gripped in both hands. Things changed quickly then. His demon jaw twisted to show a look of utter confusion, and his movements slowed tremendously, as if he were making his way through a vat of molasses. I don't think he saw my knife yet, but a confused fear showed in his eyes. As the fear spread throughout his demon face, he started to back away from me. He didn't get very far before tripping over a tree stump and falling onto his back. It had to be the symbols etched onto the dagger's blade. That had to be what robbed these demons of their strength. I couldn't help smiling realizing that.

Hanley hadn't given up quite yet. He tried rolling over onto his hands and knees so he could crawl away, but as I took several steps towards him, which brought the dagger all that much closer, his knees and arms gave out and he collapsed onto his belly. I moved forward a few more steps so that I was standing next to him. Weakly, he lifted his head up and I showed him the dagger. He made a gurgling noise at first, as if he were drowning, then groaned out in a weaker versions of his demon hisses and snarls, "Henry, I believe I'm having a heart attack. Please, get me help."

The scene was so ludicrous that I started laughing like I was insane. As I laughed, my body convulsed so hard that my stomach ached and tears streamed down my face. I couldn't help myself. I guess I was having some sort of breakdown, even though I didn't realize it at the time. But who could blame me? Here I had the demon Hanley following me into the woods, charging me to kill me, and then trying to pretend that he was only my down-the-street-neighbor instead of a homicidal demon even though he had to know that I could see him for what he really was. I guess he must've been confused over what was happening to him and was trying to play for time, hoping his strength would come back to him. What did he take me for, an idiot?

"I wanted to make sure everything was okay with you," he continued to croak out in his guttural demon sputtering with very little strength to his voice. There were long pauses from him as he stopped to suck in air. "Why would you be coming into the woods at this hour?"

My laughter quickly died down to a wheeze and then to nothing. I told him he had to be kidding.

"What do you mean that I'm kidding?" Another long pause as his breathing became more ragged. "Henry, try to understand that I need medical help. Please, get me a doctor."

I sat down on the ground next to him and gingerly rubbed my stomach. It was sore from how hard I'd been laughing. I used the back of my hand to wipe a few remaining tears from my eyes before turning to Hanley.

"You were spying on me from your house," I said. "When you saw me leave, you followed me here on foot, or whatever you demons have, and you ran almost as fast as I could ride my bike."

"What do you mean demons?"

"Shut up." I felt a coldness build up deep in my skull. Like I had eaten ice cream too fast and had the mother of all ice cream headaches. I squeezed my eyes with my thumb and index finger before looking back at Hanley. "I can see what you are," I said. "I've been able to see what you are for over two years now, so shut up."

"Henry, what you're saying doesn't make sense," Hanley croaked, his breathing getting more ragged, almost like a dog panting heavily. "You're delusional. I don't know what you think you see, but I'm flesh and blood like you, and I'm not any sort of creature or demon." More sucking in air, and more heavy breathing. "I glanced out my window and saw you sneaking out of your house, and I was afraid you were going to get yourself in trouble. That's why I followed after you, but I did so by car and not on foot. You think I ran after you? At my age? And you didn't hear me calling for you outside your house? Or when I saw you here in the woods?"

All I could do was smile listening to his demon lies. A hard smile that made my jaw ache. Even though he was breathing with great difficulty, he could sure talk a lot for someone who was supposed to be having a heart attack. Damn, these demons could be morons. I lowered the knife blade and shined the flashlight on it so he could see it clearly.

"In case you haven't figured it out yet, here's the reason you lost all your strength when you came near me and why you're panting now like a sick dog. *L'Occulto Illuminato* exists. I know that because I found a copy, and I prepared this blade as the book specifies. Do you see the symbols that I've etched into the blade? They make sense to you? And yes, in case you're wondering, the blade was washed and baked in virgin's blood, so it will have no trouble slicing through your thick demon hide."

"Henry, don't you hear how crazy what you're saying is? You're only imagining what you think you're seeing and reading. Please, try to understand that!"

Maybe if I could've heard him as a human I would've been able to hear the panic in his voice, but listening to his weakened demon hisses and snarls it was all laughable. Anyway, I was getting tired of the whole thing.

"This might've worked two years ago," I said. "Maybe you would've actually had me doubting what I see. But not now. Not with what I've learned. And not with the confirmation I've gotten from others who've seen the way dogs react to you demons."

"Boy, don't do anything stupid! Don't you understand you're delusional about all of it? Even what others are telling you?"

Finally I heard the panic in his demon hisses and snarls. For some reason I wanted to hear that before I killed him. Anyway, it was pointless gong on any further. Just to make sure of that, I pushed the blade about two inches into the back of his neck. He let loose a howl that would've made that fisher cat envious. He squirmed as he struggled to push himself to his hands and knees but couldn't, and fell flat again to the ground, howling all the while. It lasted for maybe a minute and I waited until the howl died off into a whimper before asking him about all the children that they'd been stealing. At first he ignored me, but after I stuck the blade in another inch, I asked him again where the children were being kept.

"I'll see you in hell," he forced out in a ragged demon breath.

As I said, it was pointless trying to get anything from him, and I pushed the blade all the way in, and proceeded to cut off his head. We were on a slight incline and his head rolled a few feet away. For the hell of it, I took out my iPhone, and looked through the viewfinder to see that he retained his human disguise in death, just as Robohoe had done. Not that I expected anything different.

For the little good it would do me, I covered his body and severed head with leaves. It could be days, maybe longer, before he was discovered, at least by the police. It was too late in the season for golfers, but even if it wasn't, no one would see him from the course below the woods. People do take their dogs for walks through these woods, and it was likely one of them would stumble on Hanley soon, but maybe not. Maybe a demon corpse would freak out a dog every bit as much as a live one.

While I have no idea how long it will take before Hanley's body is found, I do know I have nothing to worry about with the police. They might talk to me because I quit mowing his lawn, but I'll just tell them that Hanley propositioned me for sex and that I didn't feel comfortable working for him after that. That way the cops might end up thinking that his death was the result of a gay sex hookup that turned deadly violent. Maybe they'd even come to that same conclusion on their own. No, my problem wasn't going to be with the police, but with the other demons. Once they realized Hanley was dead and his body found this close to my home, they'd know I was the one who had left messages with Vincent Gilman. They might not know I had a copy of *L'Occulto Illuminato*, but they'd know something was up with the way I was able to kill both Robohoe and Hanley, and they'd be careful with the way they came after me. I don't have much time before that happens. Maybe a day, maybe two, which means I'm going to have to start killing a lot of demons in a very short few days.

When I returned home last night, I was able to sneak into my bedroom without my parents being any the wiser. No demon blood had splattered on me, or any other signs that I had killed Hanley. When I left Hanley's body, I carried my bike out of the woods and kicked at the leaves I had ridden over earlier, so hopefully the police won't find any evidence of a bike being ridden to the scene, and that's assuming that they find Hanley quickly— soon enough, those foot and bike tire marks will disappear entirely. I don't think anyone saw me entering or leaving the woods—at least I didn't pass any cars—and I tried to stay in the shadows and away from the streetlights as I rode home. I didn't see Hanley's car parked anywhere when I left the woods. I'm sure he was lying about following me by car, just as he had been lying about everything else.

My biggest problem, like I said, is going to be with the demons. They might already know about Hanley—maybe he called one of the other demons when he saw me leave my house, and they were expecting a report back. My bedroom door opens into the room, so before going to bed I shoved my chair under the door handle. Since I had my knife with me, if a demon broke through the door to get in, I'd hear him and have enough time to be ready for him.

As I wrote earlier, everything has to happen faster now with Hanley's death. I don't have ten days anymore to kill these demons, but only a few days now at the most, so when I got back to my room I took out all the addresses and notes that I had about these demons and made my plans.

It was past two o'clock before I'd finished organizing my demon-elimination plans and was finally ready for bed. I was amazed at how calm and serene I felt. In a way it was a big relief to have Hanley dead and to know that things would soon be coming to an end with these demons. It had been wearing on me knowing Hanley was living right down the street, knowing that he suspected me, and was spying on me whenever he had the chance. It was liberating, in a way, to know that all this was going to be over soon, one way or another. I fell asleep almost the moment I closed my eyes, and slept soundly until my alarm woke me up a half hour ago. I don't even feel groggy after only four and a half hours of sleep. Instead I feel energized, as if I'd been waiting my whole life for what's going to be happening later this evening.

Before starting this morning's journal entry, I checked online to see if there was anything about Hanley's body being found. There wasn't. Nothing about Robohoe's yet either. When I tracked him down a year ago, he worked as a bouncer at a bar. Two shifts, afternoon and late at night, which is why I knew he'd be coming back to his house when he did. Kind of ironic in a way. As a bouncer, he probably had the *second* most appropriate job that any of these demons had—after lawyers, of course. Maybe that's the reason the police don't know yet about Robohoe. In that line of work it's probably not unusual for someone to skip a night, or even a week, without calling in. At least I have to think that was the case. His absence from work so far isn't about to make his employer worried that something had happened to him, and he wouldn't be calling the police yet.

I thought about skipping school today so I could start killing demons right away, but most of these demons that I've tracked have day jobs, and it would be far too dangerous if I tried killing them at their work. If I didn't get caught, I'd at least be seen. Even if there was a way for me to safely kill some of them outside of their homes, I'd probably stick to my plan and go to school today. For one thing, Sally will need me at school. She won't be able to face Devin if I'm not there, and I don't want her freaking out. I want to provide her whatever comfort I can. And I want to make sure she's safe and that Devin stays the fuck away from her.

The night will come soon enough, and I'll be able to start killing demons then. If things go right, by this time tomorrow there'll be a few less demons fouling the Boston area. It won't be enough, but at least it will make a small dent. And with a little bit of luck, Connor Devin will be one of them.

I have to wrap this up. I guess I've been dragging it out knowing that this might be my last journal entry. I expect to be successful tonight, but you just never know. Things could go wrong, and if they do I'm dead. I'll probably be dead soon even if everything goes right.

I have to make sure someone reads this journal in case I don't survive my night of demon killing. I thought about leaving it on my pillow. I know my parents well enough to know that they wouldn't bother snooping in my room tonight, but there's a remote chance that the police detective could show up with his warrant, and if that happens I'm fucked. I guess we'd all be fucked. But even if that doesn't happen, it wouldn't do any good leaving this journal for my parents. They're so wrapped up in their own worlds that they probably wouldn't read it, or at least not soon enough to do any good. And even if they did, they'd be too concerned about their own reputations and what their neighbors and coworkers might think about them having a lunatic son to show it to anyone. So I decided to take a chance and give it to Curt to hold for me with the promise that he won't look at it unless something happens to me. So Curt, if you're reading this now, for God's sake, take this seriously and try to get the right people to look at it. If those demons aren't stopped, all of you will be fucked. Finding those stolen children will be the key. If that's done, it will disrupt their plans for opening up hell, at least for the time being. And Curt, this isn't some riff on Lovecraft or *Cthulhu*. This isn't a hoax or a fictional piece of writing on my part. To prove I'm serious, search the woods above the fourth green at Brandenberg golf course and you'll find Hanley's corpse and his severed head buried under leaves.

I thought about riding my bike to school, but I decided to take the bus instead. I don't want to be encumbered by my bike. And it will be too easy for someone to remember it if I leave it outside the houses of any of the demons I'll be killing. So tonight I'll have to rely on public transportation, though I said I wouldn't. But at least I have everything mapped out—bus schedules, subway lines, commuter rail. I should have no problem going from one demon's house to the next.

I'm taking the dagger to school with me. It will be hidden in my backpack, and there shouldn't be any problem with that. From this point on, the dagger will be with me at all times.

That's it for now. I've got to run to catch the school bus.

I CAN'T BELIEVE HENRY'S DEAD. EVEN MORE SO, I CAN'T
believe what he's left me to read. But it all makes sense.
His journal, his translation of that ancient book on demons,
L'Occulto Illuminato, *and even the book itself, with the creepy*
red material used for its binding. It's exactly the kind of thing
H.P. Lovecraft wrote about. He must've been one of those, like
Henry, who was able to see into that world.

I don't know why Henry didn't have them do DNA test-
ing on that binding. If it really comes from a demon, then that
would prove everything he's written is true, and maybe I can use
that to stop them . . .

I'm kidding, I'm kidding. The reason my handwriting looks so different is because I'm writing all this left-handed. There's a simple
reason why I'm using my left hand, and I'll get to it later. Interestingly, though, it turns out I've discovered that I'm more ambidex-
trous than I would've imagined, and not just with my handwriting.

That was maybe a little mean of me trying to fake you
out and make you think that came from Curt. Sorry. Blame it

on me being doped up to the gills on painkillers. But hell, forget about the painkillers. Anyone who has gone through what I have over the last sixteen hours would be more than a little punch drunk even without popping Vicodin. Or maybe even a little insane by this point. Or a lot insane. But forget about that for now. Let me start from earlier on. Maybe when I showed up at school yesterday. Yeah, that would be as good a starting point as any. Then I'll write about what happened later.

Actually, a better place to start would be when I was waiting for the school bus yesterday. With everything that happened later it's understandable that I momentarily forgot about beating up Ralph Malphi again, but I guess it shows my state of mind that I'd forgotten about something like that. Or maybe it just shows how insignificant it was compared to everything else that happened afterwards. But I should explain about what happened. People might bring it up later as a way to dismiss me as a crazy person. Besides, more than ever I feel like having an accurate and complete record of what I've been going through.

First, before Ralph Malphi, there was Wesley glaring at me as if he were some kind of hardass who was going to get in my face. He didn't, but that's the way he acted. Curt was standing by me, and he kept looking back and forth at Wesley and me, finally telling me how Wesley wanted a piece of me. "Dude, take a look at him and tell me that's not true."

I was trying hard not to look at Wesley, but allowed myself a glance, and yeah, that's what it looked like, though I mostly ignored it. I told Curt I didn't know what he was talking about.

Ralph Malphi, unlike Wesley, I couldn't ignore. When he arrived at the bus stop, he started leering at me right away, all full of himself as if he now owned me because he was able to smack me in the head Monday and get away with it. After a half minute or so of his leering, he built up enough courage to walk over to me, a big ugly grin in place. His leer had turned more into a sneer, and he demanded all my money for allowing me to keep my teeth. "Yo, prick face, you don't hand over your wallet and I'll have to knock out every tooth in your mouth for payment instead."

I didn't bother to respond. What would've been the point? I guess he had convinced himself that what happened in the bathroom was a fluke since he massively outweighed me and resembled a gorilla while at best I could've been a gibbon. He flashed an ugly grin to the rest of the kids watching, and announced how he'd take my backpack from me instead as payment because he was in such a magnanimous mood (the fact that he knew that word showed he'd been studying for his SATs). The dumb ape moved towards me then as if he were going to put me in a headlock, and I went at him fast, first ducking and elbowing him in the groin, then springing up and striking him hard under his chin with my palm. He tumbled backwards hitting the ground, his mouth a bloody mess—my palm strike must've made him bite either his tongue or his lip, I wasn't sure which, but it sure as hell bled a lot. It was just too easy, and he had no chance after that.

I didn't want to get his blood on me. If I did I would have to go home and change, which would cause too many problems with my parents, so instead of falling on him and punching his face in like I wanted, I just started screaming at him as I kicked him in the ribs, calling him a *motherfucker* with each kick. I was too mad at him for making me do this to him for me not to. He curled up into a fetal position after my second kick, and even though I had sneakers on, I still managed to hurt him pretty badly. I got at least five kicks in before a couple of the other kids pulled me away.

Malphi lay on the ground moaning for a solid minute. When he finally pushed himself up into a sitting position, his eyes showed that he was both scared and dazed. He couldn't understand why I didn't just stand still and let him do what he wanted. There were a few tense moments before he got to his feet. If he went to school all bloody like that, there'd be questions—the principal would get involved, which meant I wouldn't be able to go to school as I'd planned because of the risk of them searching my backpack. But even if I didn't go to school, they'd still call my parents, which could also mess up my plans for later. Fortunately, Malphi was too humiliated by the beating I gave him in front of the other kids to hang around because he skulked away, his face screwed up as if he were struggling to keep from bawling. He was also too ashamed to make any more threats against me, or even to look back at the rest of us as he broke into a run and disappeared around the corner.

What I did to Malphi shocked the rest of the kids waiting at the bus stop—including Curt, who had suspected that I had beaten up Malphi earlier. Even Wesley had stopped his glaring and only stared in stunned amazement. The quiet that descended over the two dozen or so kids there was really quite something. Nobody spoke a word while we waited for the bus to show up.

Once the bus came, I sat up front with Curt, and the bus was filled with that same stunned silence. Even the students who had gotten on at earlier stops fell into it. It lasted maybe a minute before the whispering started. Curt just sat shaking his head before asking how I learned to do what I did.

"Don't know," I told him, not wanting to get into it.

"Dude, you were like a tornado the way you hit him. Malphi didn't know what happened. That was outstanding!"

"Whatever. I need a favor. How about I come over to your house after school and I tell you about it?"

"Sure, Henry, won't be a problem."

Word of what happened with Malphi spread quickly once we got to school, because when I got to my homeroom, Devin, who was already there, looked at me with bitter disappointment, his demon face locked in a dour frown. I took a seat as far away from him as I could. As soon as Sally came into the room, she hurried to sit down next to me and asked about what happened with Malphi, all breathless and excited. I kept it simple and told her how Malphi tried bullying me and I didn't let it happen.

"Wow. I heard other kids talking about it. You're becoming legendary here, Henry." She placed a hand on my arm as she smiled at me. Even with everything that happened afterwards, the warmth of her hand resting on my arm will be burned forever into my memory. As well as the way she smiled at me. The meaning was clear. As far as she was concerned it wasn't over after all. I felt my resolve weaken for a moment. She was offering me everything I desired, everything I could possibly want, but it wouldn't do either of us much good if the gates of hell were allowed to open. Somehow I knew that would be the last time I'd feel her touch, and I concentrated to commit every aspect of it to memory. Then I hardened myself to her. I had to, and soon her closeness barely even stirred anything in me, not even when she moved closer so she could whisper in my ear, her breath hot against my skin, her faint jasmine scent lingering in the air.

"I decided not to let Connor bother me. Whatever he is, too fucking bad."

God, I wished she hadn't said that. She whispered it so low that she probably didn't think he'd be able to hear her, but with his ultra-sensitive demon hearing he heard every word. I scribbled on a piece of paper that we should talk about Devin later. She smiled bravely as she shrugged, trying to show me how unconcerned she was, but I could see a hint of fear in her eyes. No matter what she said, Devin still had her freaked out.

Sally was the only reason I went to school yesterday. She needed me there so she could face Devin, and I needed to be there to make sure he'd stay away from her. I needed to make sure she'd be safe. Maybe I also needed to see her this one last day, especially since I didn't expect to survive last night.

I didn't risk looking at Devin. I knew he'd heard what Sally said, which meant he knew for certain that I was the one they were looking for. I didn't want to see that knowledge in his demon eyes.

After homeroom ended I caught a glimpse of Devin and the angry storm brewing over his demon face. It was little more than pure animalistic rage. I wondered how others saw him at that moment—did he still look like Justin Bieber? I felt a tenseness in my chest as I walked with Sally until we separated for our individual classes. Devin was only twenty feet or so behind us, and I didn't know what he was planning. One swipe of his demon claw would probably decapitate both of us. I held my breath until I knew he was following me instead of Sally. At least I knew she'd be safe for the time being.

An idea came to me. I slipped into the bathroom, and had my backpack unzipped and my hand clutching the dagger handle by the time Devin followed me in. There was only malicious intent as he came at me. I guess he'd decided to kill me then and there and take his chances of being discovered for my murder. Maybe he'd make sure there was no body left for anyone to discover. Could a demon devour a whole human body? Probably. Whatever he had in mind, he spread the nails on his right claw and moved towards me so quickly that I didn't have a chance to pull the dagger out from my backpack. As it turned out, I didn't need to. Even though the dagger was hidden from sight, the symbols etched on the blade did their job and Devin staggered and fell to one knee before he got within five feet of me. He had no idea what had happened to him. I could see the confusion in his eyes as he looked up at me. Then he lowered his face into one of his claws and let out a whimpering moan.

I could've killed him then. It would've been easy. But I'd have no way of getting rid of his corpse. And I'd be fucked once he was found.

I moved closer to Devin, and with the dagger's closer proximity to him he lost even the strength to stay on one knee, instead collapsing to the floor. His yellow eyes glazed as he stared at me, utterly baffled by what was happening to him. He had an almost beseeching look, as if he wanted to ask me how I managed to do this to him. I stepped over him and got out of there while I could still keep myself from cutting off his head.

There was no point in going to any of my classes, and I certainly didn't want to be in them with Devin sitting behind me and plotting how to kill me. I hid out in the library, and after each class I'd catch up with Sally to make sure Devin left her alone, which he did. At this point he was wary of coming too close to me. Maybe these demons knew about *L'Occulto Illuminato*, or maybe it was only a legend to them, if even that, but I doubted that Devin had any idea why he collapsed in the bathroom.

During lunch, Sally and I sat alone together. I should've left campus with her. It was stupid sitting there with her and exposing myself the way I did, especially with Devin sitting four tables away studying me with this intense furrowed look, as if he were trying to figure out what it was about me that made him collapse onto the bathroom floor without the strength to move. Ironically, it wasn't Devin that I had trouble with, but Wesley. I was so focused on watching Devin watch me that I didn't notice Wesley come over to my table. I felt a frostiness from his presence before I saw or heard him. When I looked to my right he was standing maybe two feet away from me trembling with what I guessed was a mixture of rage and fear. I didn't say anything to him and for a long moment he seemed incapable of saying anything to me. Then he called me an asshole, saying it loud enough so that people in the cafeteria turned to look at us.

A hotness flushed my cheeks, but I didn't respond to him. Sally asked Wesley what was wrong. I didn't want to hear his answer. I just wanted to be anywhere but where I was.

"What's wrong is your boyfriend is an asshole and a thief!" he shouted, his voice rising and cracking in his nervousness. "He came to my house so he could drug me and steal a forty thousand dollar comic book from my dad!"

"That's not true," I said. Out of the corner of my eye I could see Sally looking at me funny, as if she was trying to decide whether I was lying or not. Maybe trying to decide whether everything I'd been telling her was a lie. Goddamn Wesley for having to do this!

Wesley, enflamed, shouted back at me, "You're a liar! An asshole, a thief, and a liar!"

I turned to Sally to implore to her that what Wesley was saying wasn't true. "I don't have that comic book," I told her. "Wesley and his dad sent the police to my house with that same bullshit story, but I don't have their comic book and the police believe that I don't. They have to because they haven't bothered with a search warrant. And if they did they'd only be wasting their time because I don't have it."

There were flickers of doubt in Sally's eyes as she tried to read the truthfulness of what I was saying, and there was just enough of the truth in what I told her to leave her confused, or maybe even leaning my way. My attention was drawn away from her by something cold and wet slapping me in the face. I turned to see Wesley holding an empty cup, his lips twisted into a harsh, rigid smile. He had tossed his soft drink into my face. I could taste enough of it to know it was ginger ale. Ice cubes slid down my shirt and clattered onto the floor. I sat there frozen in my seat while ginger ale dripped from my nose and chin.

"Stand up," Wesley demanded, his voice quivering with his false bravado, his small hands balled into fists. He looked ridiculous as he challenged me. This awkward stick figure who'd probably never been in a fight in his life. He may have been picked on over the years, maybe been put in dozens of headlocks and thrown to the ground and otherwise treated like a tackling dummy, but I couldn't imagine Wesley actually ever being in a fight. He was scared to death as he waited for me to stand, but he wasn't about to back down.

I hated Wesley right then. I hated him for drawing all this attention to me and creating doubt for Sally. But what was I going to do? Beat him up? As angry as I was right then, I understood how betrayed he was feeling, so I just shook my head and told him I wasn't going to fight him. That just frustrated and enraged him even more. Here he had built up the nerve to do what he did and get in the first fight of his life, and I was refusing to give him the satisfaction even if it would only result in him badly losing that fight.

"You asshole coward!" he screamed, tears now wetting his eyes and worming down his cheeks. "You're nothing but an asshole coward!"

Maybe Wesley was planning to pull me to my feet and make me fight him, but he never had the chance. Mr. Landry, one of the phys ed teachers, had come running over to grab Wesley, and was quickly ushering him away from the table, ordering him to calm down and to get a grip. The whole time, Wesley twisted as much as he could to face me and scream at me that I was coward. Almost everyone in the cafeteria watched the scene as Landry forced Wesley out of the cafeteria. Devin didn't. A quick glance showed that he kept his stare focused on me, a bemused smirk twisting his demon mouth as he considered how he could use this. Once Landry and Wesley were gone, all the other kids sitting in the cafeteria turned their attention to me. The silence right then was so oppressive I could barely breathe against it. I told Sally I needed to get out of there, and that there were things I needed to tell her. She nodded, her mouth brittle and her eyes showing the dread she was feeling.

On the way out, I grabbed a handful of napkins and wiped off my face and neck. My shirt collar was wet and sticky from the ginger ale, but there was nothing I could do about it.

• • •

Sally and I walked out a side door and headed towards one of the empty baseball fields. I tried to think about what I could possibly tell her so that she wouldn't think I was crazy—or at least give me the benefit of the doubt. I couldn't afford for her to lose faith in me now, not with Devin still around and looking for any opening to get at me. Sally would be that opening, and Devin knew it.

Once we were alone by the bleachers and far enough away that Devin wouldn't be able to hear us even if he was lurking around outside the building, I asked Sally if she remembered reading about Clifton Gibson. The way her forehead wrinkled and her nose scrunched up, the name sounded familiar to her but she couldn't figure out where she had heard it before.

"Two years ago the police found dozens of little children in cages in a warehouse in Brooklyn, New York," I said. "Terrible things were done to those children, although the police never released specific information on what happened. Clifton Gibson was arrested and found guilty of the crimes."

Sally's complexion paled as she remembered. "Of course," she said, her voice thin.

"What I'm going to tell you now is going to sound incredible, but please believe there's a chance that it's true. The same thing that happened in Brooklyn is happening now here in Boston. Dozens of children are being stolen, and for the same reason." I took a deep breath and told her about Ginny Cataldo and the others that I knew about, and as I did so her face became blank. She didn't believe a word I was saying. I took another deep breath and carefully removed from my backpack my copy of *L'Occulto Illuminato*.

"This was written four hundred years ago," I mumbled as I hurriedly searched through the pages for the section that talked about the rituals the demons needed to perform to open up the gates of hell. Galeotti had drawn several detailed illustrations that showed children in cages and a few of the horrific acts that these demons would perform on these children.

Sally's knowledge of Italian was rudimentary at best given that she'd only been studying the language since the beginning of the new school year, and hadn't put in the hundreds of extra hours that I needed to, nor been exposed to the archaic language that the book used. Still, her eyes narrowed and her mouth became pinched as she looked over the pages. I could see her picking out words here and there, but it was those illustrations that absorbed her attention.

"Those monsters in these drawings . . . the book calls them *demoni . . . they're* supposed to be demons? Is that what you think Connor is?"

"The drawings are symbolic," I lied. I had to lie, otherwise she'd be discounting everything I was telling her. "Whether they're actually demons or an ancient cult who thinks of themselves as demons, it doesn't matter. I contacted Detective Joe Thomase, the lead investigator for the Clifton Gibson case, and I told him about the rituals outlined in this book. He confirmed to me that those same rituals were performed on those children, but he thought I knew about them only because Gibson had contacted me. But that's not what happened. I knew what was done to those children because it was described in this book. A book that was written four hundred years ago."

Sally studied the book more intensely. "*Porte dell'inferno?* What does that mean?"

"Gates of hell."

She shook her head and handed me back *L'Occulto Illuminato*. "You actually believe this?" she asked.

"I know there was a cult in Brooklyn that tried carrying out these rituals. I know there are members in Boston now doing the same."

Her eyes drifted from me. She wasn't believing any of this. "And you think Connor is one of them?" she asked, a coolness in her voice. I was losing her. Goddamn it, I was losing her. What I threw at her was too much.

"I know he is," I said. "Think about it yourself. The way dogs react to him. I can show you in the book about these *demoni* cult members and dogs. But think also what you saw in him the moment before you thought he was going to hit you the other day."

There was a flicker of doubt in her eyes again. She wasn't completely lost. I continued, telling her that the children would be found soon. "Within a week," I said. "And when they're found, stories will come out that the same horrific things that were done to those children in Brooklyn were done to the ones found in Boston."

"How do you know that?"

More of that flicker of doubt in her eyes. She was beginning to believe there was a chance that what I was telling her was true.

"I just know it," I told her. "So please, just give me a week, okay? If it doesn't happen, then you can consider me a lunatic."

That drew a slight smile from her. Of course, I didn't know that those children would be found within a week, but if it didn't happen then nothing would matter. I had to hope that when I was killing those demons, I'd find something that pointed me to where those children were being kept.

When we walked back to the building, Sally looked exhausted, maybe even more so than I was feeling. But she promised me that she'd give me a week before making up her mind about me, and that she'd keep away from Devin during that time. As we got within twenty feet of the school's entrance, she asked me about Wesley and his dad's forty thousand dollar comic book.

"You stole it, didn't you?" she said.

I hesitated only a second before telling her that everything I was doing was to find those stolen children and to expose the *demoni* cult members. A white lie, but in a way close enough to the truth if you replace *exposing* with *killing*.

"That's why you stole it," she said, "so you could buy that book you showed me."

Damn, she was perceptive. I couldn't answer her directly, so I just asked her not to say a word to anyone about everything I'd just told her. She promised me she wouldn't.

The rest of the day at school was mostly uneventful. No more run-ins with Wesley, but I'm guessing the school must've sent him home. Devin kept his distance. I checked in with Sally between classes to make sure that the demon was keeping his distance from her also, and I convinced her to take the bus home with me. She got off at the same stop with me and Curt, and she walked with me to my house so I could ride her home on my bike. She squeezed onto the back of my bike seat like she used to, and soon her arms were wrapped around my chest and her body pressed against my back. As we went past Hanley's house, there weren't any cops or police cars out front, so it was a pretty good bet they hadn't found him. Or if they did, they didn't know who he was. Of course, they wouldn't be able to identify him by fingerprints.

With Sally's body squeezed up against mine and with the feel of her breath on my ear, I soon realized I wasn't as dead inside to her as I had thought, that there were more than several cracks in the shell I thought I had formed. Before too long my throat felt as dry as if I'd swallowed a handful of sand and a throbbing started deep in both my temples. All I wanted to do was throw away my plans and spend the afternoon with her, but I had to accept that I couldn't allow myself to do that. I had to find a way to close myself off to her for good, at least at that level, and this time seal every single crack. It would make things impossible otherwise. I'd be dooming her and everyone else. As it was, after I left her off at her home, I became overwhelmed with this heaviness in my chest, and I just started crying like a little kid. It was embarrassing and I couldn't stop until I got within a block of Curt's house.

When Curt saw me, he knew I'd been crying but he mistook the reason for it. He gave me this knowing look as he shook his head, his lips pressed into a hard line.

271

"She dumped you for good, huh?" he said. "Man, that sucks. Was it because of the blow up you had with Wesley during lunch? I didn't see it myself, but I heard about it. I warned you he was pissed at you."

"Forget it," I said. "Let's go to your room. I've got two favors I need to ask you."

He raised an eyebrow at that, but he led the way to his room and waited until we got there before asking me what I needed from him. His room was pure Goth motif and smelled like stale cheese. It was cramped and messy with dirty clothes scattered about, and bookcases crammed with Lovecraft and other dark fantasy books. Metal skulls and monstrous creatures rested on these bookcases, and the walls were covered with dark fantasy posters. None of these creatures were as ugly or as dread-inducing as the demons that I had to deal with, though.

Curt cleared off some clothes from a chair so I could sit. Making sure that he couldn't catch a glimpse of the dagger that I had in my backpack, I took my journal and *L'Occulto Illuminato* from it and asked him if he could store them for me. He was curious—I could tell that from the way he eyed both of them and wetted his lips. He held a palm out so I'd hand them to him. I shook my head.

"That's part of the favor. You don't read either of these. At least not now."

"One of them looks ancient." He squinted as he tried to read the cover of *L'Occulto Illuminato*. "*L'Occulto*? What does that mean, occult?"

"Yeah. It's written in Italian, so it probably wouldn't do you any good to look at it anyway. So can I keep them here?"

He shrugged. "Sure, why not? The best place to hide them is in plain sight."

I couldn't disagree with him. He had hundreds of books crammed in those book cases, many of them leather bound and crafted to look every bit as ancient as *L'Occulto Illuminato*, as well as dozens of his own handwritten journals. I stuck them on the bottom shelf of one of the bookcases. They blended right in.

"As part of this favor, if anything happens to me, I want you to read my journal and do your best to get it and my other book to someone who can do something."

A queasy smile twisted his lips. "You're spooking me, Henry. What's this about?"

"If I'm able to tell you tomorrow, I will. If not, my journal will explain everything far better than I could now."

"So you're going to be all mysterious on me? Okay, whatever. You can tell me about it tomorrow."

"Okay. Now for the second favor. I'm going to tell my parents I'm spending the night here. If they call, cover for me, okay?"

He nodded, his round face beginning to look pasty, maybe nervous. "You're sure you don't want to tell me what's going on?" he asked.

"Not now. Maybe later."

With that I told him I had to get going, that I had a long night ahead of me, and as it turned out I wasn't kidding. Curt walked me to the door, his face having grown even pastier. He gave me a smile that looked like he was suffering from a bad stomach ache.

"You're not going to do anything stupid, are you?" he asked.

"What do you mean?"

"You know, like getting back at Sally for dumping you. You're not going to hurt anyone, are you?"

"Not a living soul, I promise."

Which was a promise I was able to make with all sincerity.

My hand's killing me. I need to take another Vicodin and a break. I'll be back soon, and will write about my night of killing demons.

I'VE BEEN PUTTING OFF WRITING ABOUT ALL THE DEMONS I killed last night. I guess it's because I haven't been feeling up to reliving it, but I really need to document what happened, especially since I don't know how much longer I'll be able to keep this journal going. I have a feeling things are rapidly coming to an end.

Let me begin with what happened after I left Curt yesterday. The subway and a bus took me to Lynn, and by five thirty I was breaking into the house tied to the phone number I got from Chaske. Like the demons Robohoe and Hanley, this one's house was also isolated and had a fenced-in backyard, and it was easy enough to hop the fence and break in through a back door. When these demons pick their houses, privacy must be an important issue. Probably so they can sneak stolen dogs into their houses without being seen. Also probably so they can butcher them without anyone hearing it.

The house was empty when I broke in, and I had time to search it. The inside was almost a carbon copy of Robohoe's.

No pictures or photographs anywhere, same stack of sickening porn by the TV, same bundles of mysterious meat in the freezer, same ancient and odd-looking trinkets in his bedroom closet. This time I took them. I was going to have to find out what they were. I haven't finished translating *L'Occulto Illuminato* yet, and if I have a chance before it's too late, maybe the book will end up explaining the significance of these trinkets.

When I made my way down into the basement, I had the same vibes as I did at Robohoe's—this was where he butchered the dogs he stole. One big difference between this house and Robohoe's was that this demon had a computer, and it wasn't password protected. I couldn't find any personal emails, but I found digital receipts for bills that he paid, and my original guess was right—this demon was paying bills for all the others. As I went through the receipts, I found bills paid for Robohoe's address, Hanley's and all the other addresses for the demons that I had located, as well as other addresses that I didn't know about. Searching further back through these emails, I also found bills paid for dog cages. Thirty-nine of them. And I found the address in East Boston where they were delivered. Some more searching and I found that the address was for a warehouse that this demon had rented over two years ago. The date when it was rented sounded familiar, and after a minute I figured it out: it was the day after that warehouse in Brooklyn was raided. That's why these demons were here in Boston. In case anything went wrong in New York, they'd be ready to act.

I thought about whether to call the police now about the warehouse, or to wait. If I called them now, these demons could very well scatter before I had a chance to kill them, or maybe something even worse would happen—if the police tried raiding that warehouse while the demons were gathered there, it could be a slaughter. I decided to wait until later. I didn't want to be responsible for sending any police officers to their deaths, and I didn't want to lose my chance to kill more of these demons.

When the demon came home, it was the same as with Robohoe. He must've smelled me from outside. He was shorter and broader, and he was roaring his threats the second he came charging through his front door, running at me like a bull. As he came within maybe five feet of me, his knees buckled, and he pitched forward. His front door was open, so I planted the blade several inches into his neck, then left him to close the door. When I returned I crouched next to him and pulled the blade out so that he could talk. I asked him what happened to demons when they died, whether they went back to hell or simply ceased to exist. He grunted out in his demon hisses and snarls that I'd be finding out soon. Another week at most.

"I don't think so," I said. "I know about your warehouse in East Boston. The one where you have all your stolen children. I'll be sending the police there soon."

Panic exploded in his eyes, and he strained desperately to get up, but the knife had him immobilized. I didn't see any point in prolonging this. There wasn't any chance he'd answer my questions. And even if he did, I didn't know what I'd ask him anymore, now that I knew where they had those children. Without wasting any more time, I plunged the blade into his neck and proceeded to cut off his head. After I finished, I used my phone to see what he looked like in human form, and he reminded me of some dull-looking accountant, bald and shapeless.

This demon was carrying a briefcase when he entered his house. I opened it and saw that I had hit the jackpot. He'd been carrying around in the briefcase a file with addresses for all the demons that he was responsible for. Forty-seven of them. There would've been forty-eight but Hanley's address had been scratched out. Interestingly, Robohoe's was still intact. Somehow they hadn't found out about him yet.

I had put on leather racing gloves before I'd broken into the house, so I didn't have to worry about fingerprints and didn't have to wipe anything off. I was going to leave through the back, but something made me open the front door a crack, and when I looked outside I noticed the late model Toyota parked in this demon's driveway. I closed the door and thought things out. If I went about my plan and used public transportation to get to each demon's address, maybe I'd be able to kill five or six of them that night, but if I used the Toyota I'd have a chance to kill many more. My dad would let me at times pull his car into the driveway and also back it onto the street, so I wasn't completely clueless about driving, but the idea of taking that Toyota out into the streets scared me more than killing demons. I thought about it and realized I needed to do it. If it was possible to get rid of more of them that night, I had to try.

I went through those forty-seven addresses and started connecting the dots—first finding the one closest to this demon's address in Lynn, then the one closest to that address, and so on, until I had them all mapped out. When I looked it over, I realized I could maybe get rid of as many as twenty of them. If things went smoothly, there could be twenty fewer demons by morning.

I searched the dead demon's pockets and found a set of car keys. With those in hand I left through the front door and moved quickly to the car. When I first got inside I started gagging. That sickeningly sweet demon smell of onion and sulfur had saturated the cloth seats, and it made me both nauseous and dizzy. I would've opened all the windows but I didn't want to draw the attention of any passing police cars—it would've looked funny to any cop if they saw someone driving around on a cold October night with the windows down. I quickly found that if I breathed in only through my mouth I could stomach it, but still, I put the air conditioner on full blast hoping that that would help alleviate the odor. Even if it didn't do anything with the smell, blasting cold air into my face helped clear my head and get rid of the dizziness.

As I mentioned before, the house was isolated from others on the street. It was set back from the road and the front was kept dark, so there was little chance anyone would see me, or at least see me well enough to be able to identify me. But I still knew I couldn't risk sitting there for long, and after figuring out the controls for the Toyota, I backed it out onto the street and drove off.

My knuckles were pinched white as I gripped the wheel, and my shoulders were tense and stiff. I was terrified—partly because I had never driven in traffic before, but mostly due to what would happen if a cop pulled me over. First, they'd find the dagger; second, they'd get the address of the owner of this car, and they'd find what they thought was a dead man with his head cut off. Maybe I'd be able to get them to check the warehouse, but maybe not. It was possible that by the time I got anyone to listen to me, the other demons would realize what had happened to their brother demon in Lynn and they'd move the stolen children to another location. It was also possible that I'd be locked away in a psychiatric unit and so loaded up with drugs that I wouldn't even have a chance to tell anyone about the warehouse filled with stolen children. So yeah, being on the road terrified me. I pulled the car into a nearby strip mall and took deep breaths until I could calm myself down. I knew if I continued to drive around in this terrified state, I'd be begging for a cop to pull me over. A self-fulfilling prophecy.

Once I was feeling a little more under control, I spent about ten minutes driving the car around the strip mall parking lot and getting used to it. One huge break was that the car had a GPS navigational system, and I plugged in the next address on the list, selected that I wanted to stay off of highways, and was able to find it easily by following the voice instructions.

Like Robohoe's and the last demon's house, this one was kept dark and was set back from the road. I parked a block away and broke into a jog to get back there. I didn't bother breaking in through the back. With this one, I just rang the doorbell. When the demon answered, I stepped towards him with my dagger and he immediately stumbled backwards as if his legs had given out on him. He collapsed on the floor, and I buried the dagger into his throat—then, after closing the door, I returned back to him. He was squirming a little, but not enough to keep me from cutting off his head. I didn't bother questioning him, because there no longer seemed to be any point, and I was out of the house in less than three minutes. Then I was driving to the next address on the list, even though it was for Robohoe's house in Revere.

I wasn't even that surprised when I made out movement from behind a curtain at Robohoe's address, and I did exactly the same as I did with that last demon.

A demon about the same size as Robohoe answered the door. He didn't really resemble Robohoe—he had different markings and a more pushed in snout. After I cut off his head I looked at him through my iPhone's viewfinder, and wasn't surprised by what I found. He had the same human disguise that Robohoe had. That was why there hadn't been anything in the papers about Robohoe's death—the demons discovered it first, disposed of Robohoe's body, and put another demon in Robohoe's place. It didn't matter. I spent no more than five minutes with Robohoe's replacement, and then I was on the road to the next demon on the list.

It went on like this until eleven thirty. By that point I'd managed to kill six demons, none of them taking more than five minutes, with most of my time spent driving to the different locations. In each case, the dagger cut through their necks as easily as if their demon hide were made of warm ice cream. None of them was capable of putting up any fight as the dagger robbed them of their strength before they realized what was happening.

Of those six demons, I knew three of them from my own hunting—the other three were courtesy of the list that the big cheese demon from Lynn had provided. When I got to the address for number seven, I found the house empty. At first this concerned me, as I was worried that the demons might've discovered what I was up to and were fleeing, but then I realized that this demon was probably participating in the midnight rituals that they were doing to open up hell, and so I decided to camp out inside and wait.

Nine demons were needed for their midnight rituals. If any of those nine were among the ones I killed, the remaining demons would soon suspect that something was wrong. So what would they do if any of their brethren were missing tonight? First, they'd call up other demons so that they could carry on with their rituals. But, what would they do after that? They'd obviously try to call the missing demons to find out what happened, and when they couldn't get in touch with them they'd start worrying. I started panicking as I realized they might move the stolen children then. Fuck. I should've thought about that ahead of time. I almost left to drive to the warehouse, but I forced myself to stay where I was. If they spotted me near the warehouse, that would cause even more problems.

I sat waiting at the demon's kitchen table so I could watch the front door. I guess I had gotten sloppy, expecting the same thing to happen that had happened with the other demons—for this demon to smell me from outside and to charge through the house without any consideration that he was in danger. At a quarter past three in the morning, something else happened. A loud crash made me jump in my seat. This demon had smelled me out and knew that I was in the kitchen, and since he'd been warned that something was up, was more cautious. Instead of coming through the front door he had crashed through a kitchen window, his claw raised to slice me in half. It scared the hell out of me, but as I turned with the dagger held out in front, his arm fell limp before he could do any damage, and he collapsed to the floor. Even though the house was isolated, I needed to get out of there fast because a neighbor still could've heard the window breaking. But I also needed to know whether they'd moved those children. I stuck the dagger's blade into the wooden floor less than an inch from this demon's ear, and I told him how he was going to be the seventh demon I killed that night. He grunted out a few obscenities, his demon voice coarse and weak, but didn't say anything else.

"That's all you're going to say? You're not even going to try to convince me that I'm crazy?"

His yellow eyes blazed hotly. "You'll be ours soon enough," he gasped out, his voice now little more than a series of wheezes.

"Maybe, but I don't think so. I know about your warehouse in East Boston, the one where you have the stolen children, and I'll be sending the police there."

His reaction gave it away. Panic set in as he struggled to get off the floor. They hadn't moved the children. If they had, I would've seen only contempt in his eyes. Since I didn't need anything more from him, I pulled the blade from the floor and cut off his head like I did the others. And then it was on to number eight.

The rest of the night went pretty much the same. These demons were more cautious now. They had been warned that something was wrong, but either through denseness or arrogance they hadn't figured out that they should be leaving their houses. They didn't know about *L'Occulto Illuminato* or how a specially prepared dagger could leave them collapsing helpless to the floor. So I was no longer ringing doorbells—instead I used my burglary picks to break into their houses. Some of them would try hiding so they could attack when I got close without realizing that once I got close enough they'd fall to the floor helpless. A few tried running away when they saw me, but in those cases I was able to throw the dagger and either hit them or hit close enough to them to also leave them helpless. By six o'clock in the morning I had killed fourteen of them, and while I was physically intact I had saved up enough nightmarish memories to last me a lifetime. Soon the remaining demons would be heading off to their jobs, or maybe scattering once they realized their brethren demons were being killed. I only had time for one more. I hadn't run across Devin yet, but I had a good idea which address was his. One of the houses on the list was in Belmont, and it made the most sense for Devin since that was the only address within a reasonable commuting distance of the high school. As I drove there I started worrying whether or not this was really where Devin was living. I needed to kill him, not only for my satisfaction, but for Sally's sake.

The address in Belmont was like all the other demon houses. A small, isolated ranch-style home, kind of a dump. I felt groggy as I broke in, and maybe that was why what happened happened. After killing all those demons last night without even working up a sweat, I guess I had started taking things for granted. After I stepped into the living room I caught something whizzing at me out of the corner of my eye. Before I had a chance to react, something hard hit me in the right hand, sending the dagger flying out of my grasp and clattering across the floor. I dropped to my knees and seized my injured hand, the pain immobilizing me. Red stars flashed for a moment, I swear to God, and I almost blacked out from the pain, but I fought to stay conscious, and the moment passed. I saw then that a baseball-sized rock had been thrown at me. And then I saw Devin from across the room grinning viciously.

I fucked up. I should've called the police before then. All I could think at that moment was how because of me fucking up they'd never find those stolen children in East Boston and that Devin and the remaining demons would continue with their rituals. That because of my fuckup, they were going to succeed in opening up hell.

Devin was enjoying how things had turned out, but he fucked up even worse than I did. He should've just killed me, but instead he decided he was going to have fun with it. Growling out in his demon hisses and snarls, he told me how he was going to make me eat that knife. And then he went to retrieve it.

That was it. I could see his legs weakening as he approached the dagger, and it was only after he collapsed to the floor that he realized that it was the dagger that stole his strength away.

I fought against the pain throbbing throughout my hand and seemingly my whole arm, and I pushed myself to my feet. I knew I had several broken bones, but I was able to use my left hand to cut off Devin's head. As soon as I did so, though, the pain must have finally succeeded in making me pass out, because when I woke up I had no idea where I was. All I knew was that my right hand hurt terribly. I still had my racing gloves on, and I touched my forehead with my left forearm and felt how clammy and sweaty my skin was. I knew I was in rough shape.

Then I saw Devin's severed head and I remembered about last night and all the demons I had killed. It took me a while before I could stand up. The first few times I tried, the room would start swimming on me and I'd have to sit down again. When I could finally get to my feet, I used Devin's phone to call the Boston police and tell them about that East Boston warehouse. I also told them about that demon in Lynn (although I didn't tell them he was a demon) and how if they searched his house they'd find evidence that he was behind the abductions. After that I left the house and just about staggered to where I had left the Toyota. Fortunately it was still there, and I drove to Curt's house so I could retrieve my journal and copy of *L'Occulto Illuminato*. Nobody was home, so I used my burglar picks to break in. After rummaging through his parents' medicine cabinet I found a half-used bottle of Vicodin and took several. When I made my way to Curt's room, all I felt like I could do was lie down. The next time I opened my eyes I saw that two hours had passed. I took some more Vicodin, and decided Curt's room was as good as any to write my journal entries.

Fuck, I'm so damn tired right now. I need to lie down and close my eyes. Only for a few minutes. Right after I pop a couple more Vicodins.

H HELL. IT TURNS OUT I WAS OUT FOR MORE THAN A FEW minutes. Curt woke me up a little while ago. He looked both startled and worried to find me asleep in his room. For a minute or so I was too groggy and out of it to explain that I needed to get my things back.

"How'd you get in the house?"

"No one was home." My vision was all blurry and I rubbed at my eyes with my left hand so I'd have a chance of being able to focus on him. My right hand was throbbing like crazy and I rested my arm on my stomach so my hand wasn't touching anything. "I let myself in. I guess I needed to take a nap. I hope you don't mind that I used your bed."

He didn't answer me at first. He was too upset or something. I couldn't quite read him, but something was going on in his head, like he was struggling over something.

He told me that I had to leave. He contorted his face as

if he'd been punched in the stomach and added that the police were after me.

"What do you mean?"

There was more of that punched-in-the-stomach face from Curt, then he told me he'd show me. I pushed myself off his bed, my legs weak and wobbly, and I followed him to his computer. He brought up the *Boston Globe's* website and was going to click on a story about a suspect for a grisly murder, but I stopped and asked him to instead click on the breaking story about children being rescued from a warehouse in East Boston. Curt did as I asked.

There were hints in the story of depraved acts and other torture, but the police kept most of the details out of it. Still, there was enough there to show that these were the thirty-nine children that the demons had stolen. The demons weren't going to be opening up hell in the next week or so. They were going to have to start all over somewhere else. The demons I didn't get a chance to kill would soon be scattering to other cities. Maybe they'd try New York again, maybe Philadelphia. It would have to be some East coast city so that it would form a five-pointed star with the others. At least for now they've been stopped.

After I read the story and fully digested what it meant, I let Curt show me the other story. It turns out when I drove into that strip mall after I killed the big cheese demon in Lynn, I was caught on video by a liquor store's surveillance camera. The video had a good shot of the Toyota's license plate, and a clear shot of me driving the car. I was amazed that the police were on the ball enough to track down the video, but they did, and since it had me stealing that demon's car, I was the main suspect for his murder. There was nothing yet about this demon being connected with the stolen children, but I'm sure there will be soon.

After I read the article and studied the photos that clearly showed me, Curt told me how everyone at school was talking about it. He told me how Sally broke down in tears when she saw it. I was okay with that. She'd see the other story about the children being rescued and she'd know I was telling the truth earlier. At least there would be that.

Curt looked glum as he waited for me to respond. Oddly, I felt okay with it all. I did what I had to do. And really, the fact that the police were on to me now didn't matter. Whether or not they were hunting for me, my path was already set.

I asked Curt if he could give me ten minutes alone so I could write my last journal entry. He hesitated briefly and then told me okay, but that I had to leave his house after that since his parents were going to be home soon.

I'll give this journal to Curt and ask him to read it. Maybe he'll believe what's in it. Maybe he can explain to Wesley why I needed to steal his dad's comic book. I'll also ask him to send a copy to Detective Thomase. Maybe Thomase will also believe what's in it. Maybe he'll find a way to get it out to the public. If that happens, who knows, people might actually be suspicious if dogs start disappearing in their neighborhoods, or even consider the possibility that one of their neighbors might be a demon if they see dogs desperate to do anything to get away from that person. At least I hope that something like that happens.

I'm going to have to find a way to fix up my hand. And I'm going to need to get a hold of some money. But if I can elude the police, I'll go somewhere else where I can hunt demons. Maybe to Europe where one or more of those other four points to the five-pointed star must be. Maybe I'll even start another journal.

Acknowledgments

I'D LIKE TO THANK CURT TUCKER FOR GETTING HENRY Dudlow's journal to me, and of course Henry for everything he went through to write this and to save us from the Demons.

Thanks also to my editors, Mark Krotov and Dan Crissman for all their work in getting this book in its best possible shape. A big thanks also to Kait Heacock for all her energy, enthusiasm and terrific ideas in promoting Demons. I'd also like to thank Peter Mayer and everyone else at Overlook Press for their continued support and faith in me by publishing my fourth book with them, even though for legal reasons Henry's journal had to be categorized as "fiction".

I'd also like to thank all my fellow students (even the Ralph Malphi-like ones) and teachers I knew back in Newton North high school some 38 years ago—those memories and experiences made working on this book both cathartic and highly enjoyable.

Most of all I'd like to thank my wonderful wife Judy for all her support through the years.